MW00979116

AIRBORNE

R.A.Watson-Wood

Disclaimer

This is a work of fiction. Names, characters, businesses, places, events, locales, and incidents are either the products of the author's imagination, or used in a fictitious manner. Any resemblance to actual persons, living or dead, or actual events is purely coincidental.

Unless, that is, I was completely and utterly inspired by a certain person, place, or thing. In which case any similarity may be considered a great honour.

Any resemblance to any person, place or thing described in this book in a bad light should be referred back to the first paragraph of this disclaimer, obviously.

R.A.Watson-Wood

Copyright © 2020 R.A.Watson-Wood

All rights reserved.

ISBN: 9781980654247
Imprint: Independently published

For

Grace Elizabeth Dixon

Julie Warren

Dedicated to the memory of

Patricia "Patsy" Rawlings

Captain Dave Harris

Captain Janet Alexander

Thanks…

Patsy; Julie; Laura; Richie; Janet

R.A.Watson-Wood

-1-

Leigh's eyes flickered open. She instantly squeezed them shut again, in some kind of vain attempt to wake them up more.

When she opened them again and glanced around, trying not to move her head, she took in the dark blue wallpaper; the black bedspread she was lying on, the sparse furnishings; and surmised this was definitely a bachelor pad.

She tentatively rolled onto her back and peeked sideways, checking to see if anyone was there.

Still there, she corrected herself.

He was. *Thank God.*

His back was turned to her, facing away, towards the wall. His body moved up and down, his slow and steady breathing telling her he was in a deep sleep. She did *not* fancy having to exchange pleasantries over a quick instant coffee in the kitchen.

Leigh got up as softly as she could and quickly dressed, making use of the stealth she had learned over a few years of getting herself out of certain predicaments quickly.

She looked back over her should to see if she could catch a glimpse of his face while he slept. No such luck. He was mostly covered by the duvet. Just the top of his head, a mop of dirty-blonde hair was all she could see. Leigh shrugged to herself and sighed.

She might have left it there had her curiosity not got the better of her.

Since she was satisfied that he was still asleep, she dared herself to lift the duvet a little, and try to catch a glimpse of his manhood – wouldn't like to leave without some idea of what she'd been entertaining last night. She was pretty sure she'd have stiff thighs for at least the next two days; it would be nice to know it was warranted.

She wasn't disappointed with what she saw. If she'd had any inclination to be involved with anyone, he might have been on her radar.

But she didn't; so he wasn't.

She turned and stepped over used condoms littering the floor on her way out of the room. At least they had enough wits about them for that, then. She counted four before she left the room.

As she sneaked down the stairs towards the front door, a bang from the back door startled her.

Leigh flinched, and froze on a middle stair.

A housemate? A girlfriend? *God, please no..!*

Would the noise wake him before she left?

She looked back upstairs and listened for noises – either of him waking up; or more noises from the kitchen.

After what seemed to her like an age, she heard nothing further; and braved creeping down.

Reaching the bottom of the stairs, she looked around as much as she could without physically moving from her spot; noting that there were no Christmas decorations up.

Definitely lives alone then, she thought to herself.

No other person appeared. She tiptoed closer to the front door, and managed to stifle a scream when she felt something brush against her leg.

Looking down, she saw a large, ginger cat as it continued to rub itself against her. She turned back, and through the kitchen could see the back door, with a cat flap in it.

Leigh heaved a sigh of relief. *That must have been the source of the noise*!

She shooed the cat away as quietly as she could, and deftly let herself out.

Once through the door, making a noise didn't worry her so much. She let the door slam behind her and took off in a hurried walk, as fast as she could in her heels from last night, towards the nearest bus stop.

Thankfully, it was the middle of December, so even dressed up for a night out, she'd taken her only warm coat; a long pale blue trench coat; for which she was now grateful, as in the cold grey winter morning she would have looked extremely questionable tottering along to the bus stop at … *God what time was it*? 8am on a Sunday morning, dressed in a sequined halter top and black leather mini skirt.

Sunday. The battered and vandalised timetable on the wall of the bus shelter, she could barely make out, told her that the Sunday service from this unfamiliar part of town was about to make the start to her day even more miserable. There was at least another hour to wait.

Dejectedly, Leigh perched on the bench at the back of the shelter and stared out blankly. The rain was the fine, drizzle type that gets into your clothes and seemingly under your skin.

She yawned.

Maybe she was getting too old for this? Staying out to the early hours of the morning dancing, and going home with total strangers for one-night-stands, purely because she knew that she had the next day off to recover (*sleep all day*), and remain single, with no pressure from anyone.

She vaguely had the notion that this guy wasn't quite a stranger. Hadn't she been introduced by Lucas in that gay club last night?

"Used to work with him at the fast food joint", she thought he'd said. They'd got chatting as they were the two 'token straight' companions… having gone to the club because their respective friends didn't want to go alone. Besides, it played a better music than most of the other places.

She hadn't fancied him.

At least, she didn't *recall* fancying him.

It was more of a case of 'right place, right time'.

And she was pretty adamant they'd not have to cross paths again.

The rain became heavier and pattered on the roof of the shelter, somewhat soothingly.

The sex hadn't been bad. Passable, she had to admit. It was all coming back to her, slowly. It always did.

But then she'd drunk far too much and probably hadn't put in as much of an effort as she might have. Not that it mattered. Leigh went ahead with hook-ups like that for her own benefit rather than to impress anyone.

Of course, it wasn't an impressive record for a woman to boast about, anyway, was it? She winced whenever she thought about 'how many'. Even when their break-time chats in the staff room turned raunchy, which it did quite often, it was never about how many, it was all about technique and experience.

Sometimes she felt a sting, and would quieten down a little, when someone in the office, like Anya, would speak up about how her husband was the only man she'd ever slept with, married since 18 and still happy thirty years later...

Leigh was reaching the 'mid-morning depression' part of her hangover a little early. Tears began to sting the corner of her eyes.

Images of Sasha and her fiancé, came to mind, against Leigh's best intentions.

Sasha was her best friend, and along with Col, worked at the airport with her, in different departments. They would be all over each other every chance they crossed paths. Leigh could only imagine what their home life must be like. A million miles from hers, she supposed.

Leigh shook her head in an attempt to clear it. Waiting here was doing her no good. She knew a walk home to her flat from here would be around an hour anyway, so decided to suck it up, and risk her £10 shoes.

She set off across the car park of the supermarket in front of her. It was closed and deserted at this time on a Sunday morning.

She might have walked around the ring road but didn't want to risk doubling back past his house, in case he was up now and looking through the window. The last thing she wanted was to be taken pity upon and offered an awkward lift.

And let him know where she lived.

The most direct route home from the other side of the supermarket was across the high-school field and round past the old mental hospital. Neither would likely be very populated with people on a Sunday morning, even if it hadn't been raining.

She finally reached home, and kept her head down as she climbed the stairs to her door, in order to avoid the glare of Mister Dennison, the old man who lived in the flat across the hall. He'd been out to collect his Sunday paper.

He was disapproving at the best of times, with jibes of "You'd look much better if you didn't plaster that gunk all over your face!", or *looked like a trollop* in as many words, whenever he had the chance.

He didn't seem to want to listen when she tried to explain that presentation and colour co-ordination was part of her job. So she just aimed to avoid him as much as possible; hoping that someday soon she could move out, or that his children would finally persuade him to go in to a retirement home.

'*Oh boy*', she thought to herself as she almost fell against her door as she unlocked it. That walk in the rain with the wind whipping her hair around her face had really done her some good.

Once she was inside, however, the hangover began manifesting itself again. Maybe it was just the stench of stale cigarettes that always lingered in the shared hallway of the dingy block of flats; but it was all she could do to get as far as the bathroom before throwing up.

There wasn't much to bring up, but the retching itself was enough.

One look in the mirror was enough to want to send herself to bed, but she made time for a large glass of orange juice, and washed her face with cold water first.

Leigh was pretty sure she wasn't going to see much of the rest of the day.

-2-

"God you look awful!" Sasha exclaimed as Leigh meandered through the office door; forgetting to stoop, so getting her hair caught in the gaudy festive garland that had been hung up in the doorway as part of their 'Christmassing up' of the place. "Missed the train?"

Leigh felt a sudden longing for the days when she shared her commute with Sasha. They used to work together a lot more often. The morning moaning session, or gossip about the night before, over a mud-like coffee from the pokey train-station café was a good set-up for their shift.

These days, Sasha managed to co-ordinate a lot of her shifts to come in with Col, as he was in checking inbound luggage and cargo shipments arriving at the airport. The two were almost inseparable. As had Leigh and Sasha once been, as both friends and colleagues.

Leigh shook her head. "Nah, Clive was driving past as I left home and saw me, so he pulled over."

"Ooh, arriving in style eh?" Mina, the passenger services co-ordinator, their immediate supervisor, interjected as she stuck her head around the dividing wall that separated the rest-area from the operations desk.

Clive was a young pilot who had trained at the local flying club, at the other end of the runway, right behind Landing Lights, the airport's social hub – a greasy-spoon café-come-bar-come-nightclub.

Clive had been lucky enough to be taken on by a small, start-up executive flying service, offering chartered business flights from the general aviation part of the apron.

The Passenger Services agents fell over themselves to go and handle those flights. Few passengers, generally wealthy business types who were no trouble; and the whole operation was so small, used to flying in and out of smaller airfields or using the more relaxed private flight facilities at larger airports, that the flight and cabin crew seemed more approachable and had easily gelled with the ground handling team.

Clive himself was a personable young man. Portly, with mousy hair and thick glasses; that, if seen without his uniform and epaulettes, could easily be mistaken for a nerdy teen, who spent his Saturdays in front of a games console.

Which, to be fair, he had been; playing flight simulator games had been what got him interested in aviation to begin with; rather than the glamour and thirst for travel that usually attracted people to the industry.

When his grandmother died and left his parents a large inheritance; his mother, worried about him sat in front of the console all day, enrolled him in real flying lessons in an attempt to get him out of the house. He'd never looked back.

He had been a First Officer with ClassOne for over two years now and, being the only single, childless pilot working for them, was willing to spend every waking hour working; within the flight time limitations. He was easily counted as one of the more familiar faces around the office. With no ties & still living at home with his elderly mum, his wages were his own to do with as he wished. He'd recently forked out and treated himself to a brand new, bright red Ferrari.

So, had Leigh been in a better mood, she might have been thrilled to be seen being dropped outside the airport terminal by a pilot in a bright red sports car. As it was, she was simply grateful to not be exposed to the close proximity of strangers on the train, and the myriad of aromas that brought, for fear it would exasperate her still-fragile state.

God, what HAD she been drinking on Saturday night? Sleeping all day Sunday, getting up for a bath then heading straight back to bed hadn't seemed to do her any good at all.

"Speak of the devil...Morning!" Sasha beamed at Clive as he came in.

He tipped his cap with a gentlemanly air, just as Reuben, in his dispatch uniform, came in carrying a pile of paperwork.

"Just in time! Here ya go…" Reuben dug through the pile of paper on his clipboard and pulled out two stapled-together piles of A4 paper. He held the first one out to Clive.

"Weather and…" he held out the second after Clive took the first, "…flight plans for Leeds-Bradford".

"Uh…I'm not going to LBA today…" Clive frowned

"Aren't you?" Reuben looked confused.

He'd only been promoted to dispatcher a month before in preparation for the new handling contract they'd won.

With more flights to handle, they'd need more Load-Controllers calculating the weight and balance and loading instructions; and Dispatchers turning around aircraft from inbound flight arrivals to fully laden and ready to depart.

They'd also taken on a larger number of temporary summer staff that year, on fixed-term contracts to cover the holiday season rush.

Then, there were new flights, and busier winter and year-round schedules, the company had extended more of those temps onto permanent contracts after the summer season had ended. The whole place seemed to be growing into less of a close-knit family they'd once been and felt more like a 'real' airport. Sometimes.

Mina's head appeared around the divide again from the Ops office. "Nope, they've been rerouted to Aberdeen.

Here…" she said as she held out a different pile of paper. "I did these on my way in this morning. Watch out for snow…"

Clive smiled, took the new paperwork and tipped his hat to everyone again before sauntering out.

Sasha grinned as she watched him walk through the check-in hall. He was enjoying the air of authority his uniform gave him as admiring passengers watched him pass.

Then she turned back and looked at Leigh, eyebrow raised. "You OK?"

"Fuck knows what I drank on Saturday night..." Leigh groaned, collapsing back into the ancient sofa they'd adopted from somewhere; after having hung her coat up in the cloak room.

"Everything from what I saw!" Sasha chided, as she attempted to stifle a giggle.

"She was still going when we left…" added Reuben, as he sorted the rest of his flight plans into pigeon holes next to the door, ready for relevant crews to collect on their way up to their different airlines' crew rooms, spread all over the airport.

"Get off my case! I'm fit for work. I just might not enjoy it that much today…" Leigh groaned moodily, "And someone else can do the gate announcements."

Finally, a valid excuse, Leigh mused. Her least

favourite part of boarding duties was attempting to sound professional and authoritative over the gate tannoy system, pretending not to notice when people took no notice of the instructions she'd just read from the laminated card for them to have passports open and for only specific rows to come forward for boarding.

Mina appeared again, this time walking all the way around the partition and holding a piece of paper with some scribbles on it.

"I need someone to go round to the baggage office and look for…"

"I'll do it…!" Sasha jumped up.

"Reuben can do it on his way out to the ramp office." Mina interrupted her.

Reuben grabbed the note out of Mina's hand and winked at Sasha.

Sasha frowned. The baggage office, where any missing, delayed or damaged luggage and any lost or found property they were handed from aircraft, was all dealt with, was right next to the Her Majesty's Customs office, where Col was based.

She jumped at any chance to be stationed over there for any length of time. Besides which, Olga, the baggage services supervisor, made lovely cups of tea from her refreshments stash in the corner.

Mina was pleased for Sasha, of course she was, but she

wasn't about to let it affect the work of one of her best members of staff.

"You two can go to stand seven and meet the *YouKayAir* from Budapest." Mina suggested, "All the check-ins are covered for now."

Leigh seemed to perk up, if ever so slightly, at this suggestion.

"Has it called up yet?" She asked the supervisor.

Leigh had always thought there was very little point going out too early. If the flight crew hadn't given the office a courtesy call on the air to ground radio to their handling team, it usually meant they were too far out. It wasn't a necessity, and occasionally it was forgotten, but not often.

The departure station, where the flight was coming from, would send a departure message after take-off as a telex, containing the confirmed number of passengers on board and any service requests; like someone requesting a wheelchair service from the gate; so the crew calling ahead before their arrival, sometimes 20-30 minutes out, would give the ground staff a little prior warning of the expected arrival.

"Of course they have. It's Captain Bowen; everything by the book!" Mina laughed, almost to herself, and turned back to the operations office.

Leigh and Sasha were already in the process of putting their coats and their bright yellow high-viz waistcoats on by the time Mina had finished talking. When she turned to check they were going, they were out of sight.

"Which way we going?" Leigh asked as she rummaged through her pockets for her small silicone ear-plugs.

"Through baggage?" Sasha motioned in the direction of the out-of-gauge luggage reception door at the end of the row of check-in desks. Sasha watched her friend frantically searching for her ear protection and tapped hers; linked on a long twine, tied to her security pass. Far more organised.

"Like I couldn't have guessed!" Leigh said. Sasha rolled her eyes.

"Oh come on, you know security is going to be busy upstairs!" Sasha told her, matter-of-factly. Leigh knew she was right.

It was nearing Christmas. People were travelling for the nicest reasons, going home or away to visit family; or spend Christmas somewhere spectacular.

But there were more of them.

There were the inevitable few who were trying to take Christmas presents of bottles of wine, and boxes of crackers and party poppers through security in their hand luggage. Not the best laid plans, really, since the crackers couldn't be accepted in any luggage outside of specialist cargo. Most of the bottles were too big. New rules for carrying liquids on board a plane meant anything over 100ml had to be checked in, or dumped before security.

The faff of dealing with restricted items, and having to explain the ever-changing rules kind of made Leigh even more glad that she wasn't on check-in this morning.

Dealing with people begrudgingly checking in extra luggage to send their liquids to the hold, or asking for a bag to be brought back for the bottles to be put in. On top of that, the different airlines had differing rules on charging for extra weight or separate items.

She wasn't prepared for those arguments today.

On the other hand, much as Leigh loved Sasha and Colan, she wasn't sure she could face the smooching just now.

It had been over a year since Colan had started working at the airport as part of the airport's HM Customs contingent; after having met Sasha in a whirlwind holiday romance in Cornwall; and proposed to her on his first day.

Neither of them seemed in a hurry to get on with wedding planning, appearing just happy to be together.

Much to the disappointment of the girls in the office, and the boys too for that matter, since an airport wedding was, to them, the best kind of excuse to have a party.

The two girls started walking towards the ramp entrance to the security check-point behind the outsize luggage belt. Leigh continued to muse over the last major event they had celebrated together.

Last Christmas had been a subdued one; with them all worried about their futures.

After the downturn in global aviation that had happened after the September 11th attacks in the USA in 2001, a panic spread out across the industry, world-wide. Air travel was out for a lot of people.

Over the next couple of years, passenger numbers were down significantly, and smaller airlines with no safety net went out of business. Even the larger airlines streamlined their operations.

The main airline that had used *Air2Ground* handling's services here had announced they were pulling out of this airport. It was just one of 8 airports they were cutting completely from their network.

Within the year, another of their smaller carriers had gone out of business completely.

Although they had other work, it wasn't much. The second largest, and other prominent airlines, used the rival ground handling agency, *OptAir,* across the check-in hall. They were nice, pleasant in passing – everyone knew everyone around here; but there was a rivalry between the ground handling agencies.

Even though there were suggestions that if *Air2Ground* were to close their office, leaving *OptAir* as the only ground handlers, they'd have to take on the remaining small contracts that *Air2Ground* left behind, and would still need extra staff. But even if they chose to take on experienced staff from *Air2Ground*, there would still not be enough work for all of the combined staff numbers. Besides, certain specialised roles would be duplicated, and therefore one would not be required.

After the airline's announcement to cease operations, that's when the big meeting with *Air2Grounds* head office representatives had happened, last April, right at the start of the summer season. Men in suits who came to tell the family of workers that come March this year, they'd no longer be required.

As the two friends meandered through the baggage reclaim hall, Sasha veered away from Leigh and tapped lightly on the Customs office door. She was hastily dragged inside and the door closed behind her.

Leigh smiled meekly; remembering that meeting where the bigwigs gave them the news. It was that meeting, that threat, that had forced Sasha's hand to head back to Cornwall after a disastrous first week down there, and ultimately led to her and Colan falling for each other.

This had led to him transferring here, last November. Leigh recalled thinking at the time, that out of all of them, Sasha would be fine.

From the beginning of that year, however, rumours had been abound that a brand new airline was starting up. No-one could quite believe it at first; in a time when other airlines were going under or tightening their belts?

Despite that, they had come through.

In May, leaving it down to the wire, *YouKayAir*; with their tails, and puffer-jacket uniforms emblazoned with a weird, jazzed-up version of the union jack and the promise that it was 'an airline all about YOU, the British People', began advertising their low-cost flights, taking Brits to Benidorm and anywhere else that was a hotspot of ex-pats, *Day-Glo* nails, lobster-tans and Irish pubs; and signed a contract with *Air2Ground* for handling, all at once saving around 150 jobs. In the process, they created more; and a new life was breathed into the tight-knit family of workers.

Once the announcement was made, they'd even thrown a party for *Air2Ground* staff, as though it would endear them to their new handlers.

Not that it was required.

The staff were endeared enough by still being employed; despite a number of them having to be dressed in the garish *YouKayAir* uniforms as ground representatives for the brand.

The party was just the icing on the cake. But they all knew how to party and it went down well.

Leigh totted up in her head, that had been back in May, now it was December…they hadn't left it that long to have a good old party in years. One of the reasons she'd been so desperate to get out with the boys on Saturday night.

Once again it had been one of those *'pint watching the rugby at "the Lights"'* afternoons that turned in to a full session. Enough for Leigh to make the effort to go home and get changed in between leaving Landing Lights and catching the train in to town to crawl the pubs.

Leigh reached the side door that led out to the apron, not far from stand 7 where their flight was assigned to park. She checked back over her shoulder, looking for Sasha, who stumbled quickly out of the customs office straightening her uniform and looking a little flustered.

"Seriously?!" Leigh exclaimed, laughing at the same time. Her radio clipped to her waistband crackled into life as one of the ramp hands out on the apron called that the Budapest had landed.

Sasha overheard and smiled sheepishly at her as she scurried past. Leigh shook her head and followed her to the door. They stood inside the double doorway at the end of the corridor, watching through the window as their flight taxied to the stand, with Mike waving his batons to marshal Captain Bowen in.

"Sorry about that." Sasha said as she tidied away a few loose strands of hair.

"Bloody insatiable! You two are like rabbits." Leigh chided her.

"No we're not!" Sasha blushed. Leigh raised an eyebrow and looked at her questioningly.

"Well…make the most of a good thing, eh?" Sasha replied to Leigh's silent challenge, as she pushed her ear-plugs into her ears and made sure her coat and *hi-vis* waistcoat were done up, and pushed the door open onto the apron. Leigh did the same, and closed the door behind her.

The two women waited next to the wall as the aircraft came to a standstill. Up in the glass corridor on the pier, Leigh could see Carl and Anya at the gate, already preparing to call the outbound passengers for this flight, such was a quick turnaround. Carl was watching them through the window. It was too early to call any passengers just yet, and his spot at the top of the boarding gate gave an ideal view to gauge when to begin the boarding process.

Carl waved and motioned to them. He seemed to be pointing. Sasha frowned and put her hands out as though to let him know she didn't understand. Leigh turned and then tapped her on the shoulder.

Behind where they were standing, next to the end of the terminal building, was where the perimeter fence ran around the airfield.

This little corner of wasteland the other side of the fence, behind one of Cargo's storage sheds, had been used as a makeshift crew carpark while some landscaping was being done to build a new multi-storey car park opposite the terminal.

Standing behind the fence with her hands over her ears was a short, stout woman Sasha recognised as Captain Bowen's wife, Sandra. She'd accompanied him to a good few airport parties and seemed just as much as 'part of the gang' as if she'd worked there herself in some capacity. She actually spent her time administrating the small flying club that operated out the back of Landing Lights.

Sasha made her way over to her. As the engines began to shut down it was almost possible to make out a shouted conversation. Mrs Bowen held out her hand through the high, chicken-wire style fence. Sasha reached out for what she was holding. She looked down at her hand and saw a small set of house-keys. She looked at Sandra questioningly.

"I have to go out!" Sandra explained, shouting. "Paul didn't take his house keys this morning, so I left him a message saying I'd drop them here for him. Can you get them to him?"

Sasha nodded animatedly and waved as she moved away from the fence and back to her waiting spot by Leigh at the door.

Sandra jumped back in her car and left.

Leigh looked questioningly at Sasha. Sasha held up the keys and shrugged. This seemed like enough of an explanation to Leigh.

The two walked over towards the aircraft as Mike and a couple of the other ramp lads put heavy rubber chocks behind each wheel of the aircraft to stop them from accidentally shifting as the engines shut down.

Sasha waved up at the flight deck crew as she passed,

and held up the keys. Captain Bowen looked up from checking his phone he'd just turned on and gave her a salute to acknowledge he knew what she was holding.

"I'm going to open the doors. Hand these to the Captain, will you?" Sasha said as she handed the keys to Leigh.

Sasha scurried over and opened the nearest door that led into the inbound passport control corridor, while Leigh waited at the bottom of the aircraft steps that were being positioned up to the front door at the aircraft side.

Leigh felt the life seeping slowly back into her. The bitter temperatures and the steady breeze whipped around her head and she breathed deeply as it seemed to gradually calm her fuzzy head. She gazed up at the gargantuan vehicle above her.

At her first opportunity, she bounded up the steps and knocked on the door to let the cabin crew know she was ready. Her heart skipped a beat as she touched the side of the aircraft. She glanced back over her shoulder at Sasha, waiting patiently at the bottom of the steps now to lead the first passengers in to Kevin and his Immigration staff at the passport control point.

Leigh realised she was going to have to let Sasha in on her little secret soon. She tapped her pocket as she turned to greet Ricky, the purser, as he opened the door.

He grinned at her, pushing a lock of his floppy black hair back from his face, brown eyes twinkling at her.

"These are for the captain." Leigh held up the keys to him.

"Did it come?" He asked her in a thick Spanish accent, taking the keys with barely an acknowledgement.

"Yup!" She nodded excitedly, "I'll be at *YouKayAir* HQ next Monday!"

-3-

Later that day, Leigh made her excuses to not accompany Sasha and Anya to meet Col in the staff canteen for a coffee break.

She gambolled up to the *YouKayAir* staffroom on the top floor and knocked, before sticking her head around the door.

Captain Paul Bowen noticed her and winked. He had been based from this airport for years, with one airline or another. He'd joined *YouKayAir* from the get-go as a senior Captain, as soon as it became clear that his previous employer was thinking of basing everyone elsewhere and retraining most on different aircraft-types.

He was too old for that, he told them, and wanted his seniority and years of RAF by-the-book experience to be put to good use rather than starting at the bottom again. It had been a pleasant surprise for all at *Air2Ground* to find out they already knew the new Base Captain well; since they'd all be working together so closely.

Leigh smiled back at him just as Ricky noticed her and waved frantically. He air-kissed the girls who had been flying with him today and waved goodbye to them, before rushing over to whisk Leigh out through the door.

He linked arms with her and the pair half-skipped over to the abandoned seating area looking out through the large picture-windows across the airfield.

"So, what did it say? Spill..." he gushed at her as they sat down.

"Just that I passed the second round interview...nothing special" She sighed.

"Of course it's special! Do you know how many applications they got?" Ricky laughed excitedly. "Aren't you excited?"

"Trying not to be." Leigh shrugged.

"Why? They'll love you! You're perfect for this life." Ricky nodded at her as though to confirm what he said. Leigh looked up at him.

"I'm still not sure how to tell the guys downstairs..."

"Nothing to tell them yet. Why is it an issue though?"

"Dunno. Sasha seems to look down on hosties." Leigh sighed.

"Well tell her not to. It's an important job" he replied.

"You're not in it for the glamour?"

"Well, there is that too" he laughed and tossed his head back into a pouty pose. Leigh laughed at him and punched him playfully in the shoulder.

"Guess you need a drink tonight to loosen you up, eh?" He winked. She smiled and nodded, then checked her watch.

"I need to get back. Good to see you." She told him.

Ricky watched her go, contentedly.

Leigh almost floated down the two main staircases back to the office in the check-in hall.

As she entered she bumped straight into a manly chest in a customs uniform.

"Woah!" Col laughed as he held her upper arms either side to steady her.

"Oops!" she blushed, "Sorry!"

"Seems like all the women round here can't keep their hands off me." He winked at her and stood aside to let her pass, before shaking his head in amusement and heading back in the direction of his office.

Leigh was still a little red in the face as she went in to check the duty roster. Sasha, around the corner donning her coat, noticed her.

"What's up?"

"Nothing," Leigh replied, unnecessarily defensively. She wasn't sure why, it just didn't seem worth mentioning bumping in to Col. It confused her as to why she would have felt so flustered over a split second. Leigh did wonder if it was more to do with hiding her cabin crew aspirations and being more flustered over Ricky…

"So, how was Ricky?" Sasha almost seemed to be reading her thoughts…

"Um…" Leigh was gathering up the courage to mention her application.

"Hold that thought," Sasha muttered as she grabbed a walkie-talkie from the charging point beside where Leigh was standing, as she listened out and heard the radio in the ops office next door crackle in to life as the First Officer called down.

Reuben was at the ops desk covering for a while as he organised his load-control paperwork from that morning of dispatching flights ready for filing. He answered and listened to the F/O telling him the passenger number and confirming that one wheelchair was required, and there was a pushchair in the hold for gate delivery. Reuben scribbled down the info and replied that the message was copied, and held out the piece of paper for Sasha to whip out of his hand.

"I'm off out to meet the Tenerife with Megan and Carl." Sasha told Leigh.

"Ok." Leigh smiled. She ran her finger down the page to find her name. There she was, assigned to the Aberdeen check in with Lucas. Oh, that'll be a laugh, she smiled to herself. Amazing how he'd managed to make friends with just about everyone, and knew everyone's ins and outs by now – it would probably be a quiet flight today so at least she'd be entertained in between.

She grabbed some blank boarding cards and baggage labels and headed down to load the check-in desk printers.

It wasn't long before he joined her, leaping down the metal steps to the side-by-side check-in desks and removing his coat at the same time.

"Been outside?" she asked him.

"Applied for cabin crew?" He surprised her with the response.

"What?" Leigh asked, eyebrows raised.

"Me too! Ricky says we're over *Lights* for celebratory drinks tonight?"

"Bloody hell that was quick!" Leigh whispered, "He only just suggested that upstairs 10 minutes ago!"

"Nah. We chatted in the baggage hall earlier after they'd handed over" Lucas told her.

After Captain Bowen and Ricky and the rest of the crew had checked the cabin, following Leigh and Sasha taking their inbound Budapest passengers into the terminal; they quickly handed over to the fresh crew who came out, ready to turn the aircraft around and take it on to its next destination. They had all disembarked and headed through the crew entrance into the baggage hall as a quick route back to the terminal and their crew room.

Lucas had been in the baggage hall following up with Olga on a lost property call he'd answered, and had collared Ricky on the way out and walked in with him.

"He told me about your recall letter. Told me not to tell you he told me but hey…" Lucas shrugged cheekily.

It was no secret that all Lucas wanted to do was fly. At only 19 he was one of the younger Passenger Services Agents they'd taken on last year, and he'd quickly proven to be adept at pretty much every aspect of the job.

He enjoyed it of course and got on well with everyone; but he never made any secret of his dream to fly. He told everyone in his first week that he'd been applying to all the different airlines with locally-based crew since he was 16 and hadn't even been deterred with letters they sent back asking him to re-apply in a couple of years when he was above the minimum age and had more aviation experience. So that's what he was doing. Getting experience. Of more than one kind as far as Leigh could tell, and smiled to herself.

Sasha mused that Leigh seemed to have cheered up by the second half of their shift, as she took over from Lucas on his desk when he was due to finish.

"What's up?" Sasha asked, without looking at her friend, signing in with her user-ID to the check-in computer.

"Huh?" Leigh hadn't noticed her arrival, "Oh hi." She recovered herself slightly. "Nothing's up."

"I mean you seemed miserable this morning. Perked up a bit. Ricky cheered you up?" Sasha winked.

Sasha's year of being un-single felt like it had flown so fast. She still felt...and acted...like they'd just met.

She wished sometimes Leigh would see the light, as it were; and Sasha wanted her so much to find someone so they could compare notes and double date and anything else that would mean she could spend time with her fiancé, and her best friend at the same time.

It was hard to believe there was a time when she couldn't have cared less about men, and was quite happy being single.

She'd noticed Ricky and Leigh getting friendly right from when *YouKayAir* opened their base. He looked just like Sasha would imagine a typical Spaniard would, like a young Javier Bardem, with a neat goatee and twinkling dark eyes.

Given how she herself had fallen for a dark-haired man with a beard; Sasha'd almost say he was her 'type'...if she'd ever thought she had one. She was pretty sure Leigh didn't have a specific type at all; but if tall, dark, handsome, exotic, foreign, and someone who flew for a living didn't do it for her, Sasha didn't know what would.

Leigh looked back at her knowingly. "Nothing gets past you these days does it? Thought you'd still be too distracted..." Leigh winked at her.

Sasha slapped her in the shoulder playfully and continued signing in to her computer.

"We're going to Landing lights after work. You coming?" Leigh asked.

"We?"

"Lucas is coming too. A couple of the other hosties I think." Leigh shrugged, trying to play down how much she was looking forward to going out.

A passenger approached Sasha's desk before she had a chance to answer. A tall, bespectacled gent carrying a satchel. She recognised him almost immediately and smiled.

"Hello Mister Collings. Edinburgh?"

The man smiled at her and nodded, passing his booking reference over the counter to her, and placed his bag on the scales next to her, giving her just enough time to note the weight, before picking it up again. Well practised at commuting. Check-ins like this were a doddle most days.

Leigh looked over to the *YouKayAir* check-in desks at the end of the hall.

A hotchpotch of holiday-makers, city-breakers, stag dos, the odd student and business travellers queued up in front of the two check-in desk for that afternoon's flights to Majorca, La Rochelle, Prague and Glasgow.

YouKayAir was one of those 'no-frills' airlines that had

sprung up over recent years.

People still wanted and needed to travel; but where finances were a problem, everyone was fighting for the cheapest seats. So, why not fill a whole plane with the cheapest seats and do away with optional extras like business class, and food…and as rumour would have it, toilets were under threat, too…

YouKay marketed themselves with a snazzy, jazzed up logo based on the Union Jack; claiming they were British through and through and how they were run by and for British travellers. They certainly cornered the market in patriotism and sentimental national loyalty.

Their cabin crew, instead of pencil skirts, neckties and blazers, wore unisex cargo pants and puffer jackets in red, white and blue.

Leigh had to admit, she rolled her eyes at the twee marketing campaigns they ran and the annoying animated characters; but she was excited by the chance to work from her home base and with people she knew and liked. And those passengers in that queue were the ones she'd be working for.

Mister Collings accepted his boarding card, and asked Sasha if the Executive lounge access code was still the same. She scribbled the new one on the back of his boarding card for him and waved as he headed for the main staircase.

"Yeah, we'll come along." Sasha continued, as though their conversation hadn't taken a break at all. Leigh was amused that Sasha never seemed to refer to herself as 'I' any more.

"Wish I could be like you." Leigh mused, half to herself. Sasha frowned.

"Jealous?" She smiled slyly.

"Not really. I'm glad you're happy...but... I dunno, I just don't think I'm a relationship type of person. Not at the moment. Remember when you wanted dream-man to not be there in the morning?"

"To be fair, that was before I discovered morning sex..."

"Woah!" Leigh exclaimed, in a vain attempt to keep the conversation clean on check-in.

Sasha giggled.

"It's OK. Hooking up is not the be all and end all. Have fun. If it happens, it happens. If not, at least you're enjoying yourself." Sasha seemed to be sounding far more philosophical than necessary.

"Pirates and smugglers and exploding boats not necessary?" Leigh raised her eyebrows; remembering the explosive way Sasha and Col's relationship began while he was working undercover trying to stop a smuggling ring.

Sasha winked at her. "Well, not everyone gets that lucky!"

Leigh was about to pluck up the courage once again to

let on to Sasha about her cabin crew application, but as she looked up at the passenger who had approached Sasha's desk, she saw another three heading towards her own desk. The afternoon rush was beginning. After those passengers were swiftly dispatched up to security, the queue had former behind them. Sasha and Leigh both realised that their down-time was over. After closing this check-in, they'd be swiftly on their way up to gate 12 to turn-around the inbound Cork to the Edinburgh outbound.

As she took the ticket paperwork from the next man in front of her, out of the corner of her eye, Leigh saw Ricky and the girls he'd been flying with heading through the concourse towards the main entrance. He waved flamboyantly at her and made a 'Call me' sign with a huge smile. She smiled back and returned a more reserved wave. Her passenger, a jovial lady in her 50s, wearing a twin-set & pearls, turned to see who she was waving at. She turned back to Leigh and gave her an exaggerated wink and an approving nod. Leigh smiled and proceeded to check her in to the Brussels flight.

him.   To be perfectly fair, she had nipped home to
change and had had a sneaky glass of wine while she
was doing her hair; pulling it out of the tight chignon
she'd had it up in at work. Maybe it was the wine; but
she doubted it; she tended to feel that way if she just
walked past him at work.   She hoped that since she still
felt like this after a year that the feeling would hang
around a lot longer.

Sasha made her way over to the gang at the bar after
taking her leave of Paul and Terry.   She was surprised
that Leigh hadn't beaten her back here.   She was pretty
sure she'd taken longer to get ready than Leigh would
have.   Granted, she'd been a bit over zealous about
preening, shaving her legs quickly and a bit of extra
grooming – since both she and Col had the next day off,
they'd be making the most of not having to get up for
work in the morning.

Sasha, seeing that Col had left his jacket, tie and epaulets
in the car; had driven home and got a taxi back up the
hill from the cottage she and Col had recently moved
into together.   She'd brought Col a pair of jeans to
change from his work trousers; knowing he'd just keep
his shirt on with a few top buttons casually open.

Leigh lived less than a mile from Landing Lights, along
the airport perimeter road; and given that she was so
practiced in being ready to go out, Sasha had expected to
at least meet her in the car park.

Col caught Sasha around the waist as she reached him
and drew her in for a long lingering kiss.   In the past she

might have been shy about this kind of public affection but given their slightly brazen history, and the reputation that had grown up around them; most of those around them didn't bat an eyelid. Kevin practically swooned; and Philippa watched longingly, before staring back into her beer in front of her.

To look at Philippa, most would think she was quite reserved, but although being a Customs Officer was her 'real job', she'd gone into after her father had a long career in the service and opened a few doors for her out of college; her passion at school had always been English, she would sneak the romance novels her mum had discarded and spend her time reading, and always dreamed of writing similar stuff.

She had been excited to get a position at the airport; Heathrow at first, but had moved out here when her husband, who worked with Terry in Air Traffic Control, had taken a transfer after the extra stress of the busier airport had gotten to him. The glamour of the aviation industry seemed less in the back rooms than it appeared on the surface, but the camaraderie had hooked her; and occasionally, just occasionally, something would happen that she felt she would one day write about. Watching her boss and the world's friendliest CSA right now, she knew they were one of those things.

Col whispered something to Sasha, his fingers running through her hair, she giggled. Philippa sighed and Gary gave her a shove and slung a friendly arm around her shoulder.

"Why not?" She challenged him, standing up.

Ricky was taken a little by surprise. He could have taken the opportunity to tell her about his training promotion and remind her she was about to start working under him but he was lost for words at the flashes of defiance in her eyes. Their work situation clearly hadn't crossed her mind. And something told Ricky, it wouldn't matter to her if it had.

He saw a younger Valentina in her for a split-second – no remorse, no sentimentality. Sex was sex, work was work. Instead of standing his ground he felt like he was being worn down, to do pretty much whatever Leigh would have him do. Ricky pursed his lips and grunted out of frustration, and headed back into the kitchen while Leigh finished her cigarette.

As he entered, Jason handed him a mojito with a jolly pat on the back.

"You look troubled my man?" Jason asked him, concerned.

"Nah…nothing a drop more rum won't handle!" Ricky removed the sprig of mint from the top of the glass and downed the cocktail. Jason laughed at him.

"One more mojito it is then!" Jason grabbed the glass from Ricky's hand and set about preparing a fresh drink. Ricky turned round and saw Lucas sat on the sofa in the corner while Jenny, May and Ayisha, three of his *YouKayAir* hostie colleagues were oblivious to any drama; making the most of their impending 'hangover days', dancing around the kitchen with Kevin, who was about as oblivious as they were.

Jason handed him the next mojito and Ricky wandered over to sit by Lucas.

"You ok?" Ricky asked him, concerned.

"Yeah. You and Leigh, eh?" Lucas, he could tell, was trying to sound indifferent about what he'd seen, and possibly heard, outside the bathroom. Ricky was about to answer when Leigh walked in and started chatting flirtily with Jason, teaching him how to make some cocktail she must have asked for that he didn't know. Which was unusual. Lucas watched too.

"She's pretty attractive, I guess." Lucas said to Ricky, as though he had to give his blessing.

Ricky looked at him. "Not your type, though?" He asked, knowing full well she wasn't.

"I wouldn't have thought she was yours either." Lucas was starting to let his disappointment show through now. Ricky laughed lightly, amused.

"Oh I have a very wide range of what constitutes my type." Ricky told Lucas, patting his knee. Lucas turned to stare at him, and before he knew it, Ricky was fondling the younger man's crotch. Lucas did nothing to stop him, but repositioned himself slightly so that Ricky's hand could have more access between his thighs. Two mojitos downed straight were taking effect.

A shadow fell over them and neither noticed Leigh standing over them. She didn't particularly want them to, either.

She was sipping a Dark'n'Stormy through a straw, marvelling that Jason had managed to make it perfectly just from her vague description.

Ricky moved in and started kissing Lucas on the lips. Lucas reciprocated, not a nervous young novice they may have expected from looking at him; but perfectly confident in what he was doing. Lucas's hand had made its way across to Ricky's lap and was mirroring what Ricky's hand was doing to him. Lucas reached a bulge and squeezed hard, catching Ricky by surprise, making him break away from the kiss and stare at Lucas; before looking up and realising that Leigh was standing there, and looking lustfully at *both* of them.

Leigh's lips raised into a one sided smile, she looked between them and cocked her head towards the door into the hallway. Ricky shook his head briefly, and then looked at Lucas, whose eyes were wide with anticipation.

Leigh downed the rest of her drink and reached over to put it on the breakfast bar. She waved at Jason, over the music, and motioned to him they were leaving. Jason waved back enthusiastically.

Leigh grabbed Lucas by the hand and led him down the hallway and out through the front door. Ricky, against his better judgement but already too far gone to miss out on what might happen next, followed.

Out in the street, Ricky found Leigh phoning a taxi.

"Ok, no probs. Thanks." She flipped her phone shut, "Ten minutes." She told them.

"Should we wait inside?" Ricky frowned.

"Oh, I can think of ways to stay warm" Leigh said, flirting, and she turned to look lustfully at Lucas. She pushed the boy against the front wall of Kevin's house and started kissing him. Lucas at first wasn't too sure. Ricky wasn't sure he'd ever really touched a girl before; and raised his eyebrows in anticipation of what Lucas might do.

After a second or two, Lucas just fell in to sync with Leigh and started kissing her back. Ricky was even more surprised to see Lucas's hand start to roam around her waist, down to her backside, before he broke off the kiss and leaned sideways, moving his hand around to her inner thigh, and up her leg, pushing her skirt up, enough to place his hand on her crotch. Ricky could have laughed out loud from shock, but just grinned and crossed his arms in front of himself to aid keeping a bit of body heat in; enjoying the spectacle and Lucas's face as he became acquainted with the female anatomy for what Ricky was pretty sure, now, was the first time.

Ricky knew now he was in too deep to walk away; even though now would have been the perfect opportunity. He was freezing, so needed bodily contact to help keep him going before the taxi got here, so he moved forward, thrusting his crotch part way between the two and creating a strange, triangle kissing session; neither of the other two flinched at his touch, accepting him as part of the one entity they were becoming.

When the taxi pulled up and beeped, they were somewhat grateful that he had come from the direction of town, meaning they were mostly hidden behind a large bush in the front garden. They broke apart, exchange lustful, excited grins, and clambered into the car.

Leigh gave the driver her address.

They couldn't go to Lucas's – he still lived with his parents; and Ricky had a good house-share going with two of the girls from the duty-free shop and a guy from security. They kind of had a house-rule about certain behaviours and keeping stuff relatively clean. Leigh, on the other hand, couldn't care less if they were about to give her snooty old neighbour the thrill of his life.

Maybe it'll give him a heart-attack, she told herself, somewhat spitefully. But she was too distracted with the lust and anticipation of what the next few hours would bring.

The three of them tumbled into Leigh's little flat. Leigh made no effort to be quiet; although Lucas and Ricky appeared to have more inherent manners. They seemed to be trying, failing drunkenly, to appear courteous to anyone in earshot.

After showing Ricky where the bathroom was, 'to

freshen up', he'd told her, Leigh went into the kitchenette to pour herself a shot of whisky – for courage, she told herself. Lucas followed, but turned down a drink when she offered.

"I don't need courage, hun, I got plenty. I need a smoke though…"

Leigh motioned to the glass bi-fold door at the end of the long kitchen-diner-living space; that opened up to a tiny juliette balcony. Enough for him to hang over and let the smoke billow out across the street. Of course the smell still infiltrated her flat but Lucas stemmed it a little by pulling the curtain across behind him. At least she could take it down and wash it before the landlord next inspected.

Leigh tottered, in her inebriated but still surprisingly compos-mentis state, over to stand next to him and breathe in the fresh night air.

It was crisp and wintry. She made the most of the second hand smoke that washed her way; and marvelled how acute her senses were considering the amount they'd been drinking.

"It's probably the cold that's kept us so alert" Lucas told her when she commented on it. "I recon we've been using the alcohol to keep us warm rather than get us drunk!"

"Chemist now, are we?" She asked him sarcastically.

"Not sure…is that chemistry or biology?" he asked.

Leigh shrugged. "Not sure I actually care." She told him, licking her lips.

Sucking up any remaining reservations she had, she slid towards him, took the cigarette from his fingers and drew the remaining puffs from it as seductively as she could.

The way he looked at her amused her. It wasn't lust; or at least, not in the way she had experienced it before from men she'd been with.

He looked at her with a simple curiosity. His eyes dropped to her groin, and around her waist. He gently lifted her skirt with his hand and raised his gaze to her face again. Leigh finished the cigarette, extinguished the butt on the edge of the metal balustrade and tossed it out onto the grass verge below.

She returned her gaze to his, as his hand explored between her legs. She was amused, the corners of her mouth raised slightly, at the astounded look on his face as he explored between her legs with his hand. She was amused to think, was it possible, that he'd never felt a woman before?

She hadn't fancied him at all; his youthful looks, his stature more slight than the more full-bodied men she'd usually been in to; but the soft, careful and sensuous motions of his hand were such that she couldn't help but get very wet. Her mouth watered slightly in response to the rest of her body, so she licked her lips to dampen them, swallowed hard, then leaned forward and kissed

Lucas passionately.

At that point, they both knew it was time to move to the bedroom. She took him by the hand and gently led him away from the door, sliding it shut with her other hand, before leading him to her room.

When Ricky came in from the bathroom, they were both writhing on the bed. Lucas was removing Leigh's panties slowly, marvelling at the sight that as so new to him.

Ricky stood and watched them for a few minutes. It was as though he was trying to dissuade himself from getting involved. He, and Leigh, already knew that it was too late, he already was involved. They shared a glance, confirming their intentions, while Lucas was busy with his fingers between Leigh's legs. She was enjoying the sensations – not some fumbling of an inexperienced guy trying to impress her, thinking he knew what to do; but purely interest, being explored, and treated with respect for allowing him to do so.

Lucas looked up and saw Ricky, looked at the older man, wide eyed, as though waiting for him to teach him.

Ricky groaned under his breath and rolled his eyes, before Lucas sat back on his haunches and left an inviting space for Ricky to come over and show him how it was done. Ricky crossed the room in almost a single bound and removed his shirt as he went. He collapsed at the end of the bed, next to Lucas, and dived in head first, finally reciprocating Leigh's actions from

Kevin and Jason's bathroom. Lucas, meanwhile, remained next to him, watching and learning, but all the while with Ricky's balls in his hand, his other hand moving up and down Ricky's spine, as high as his hair line and as low as his buttocks.

Leigh, making the most of the sensations Ricky was sending shooting through her, watched the two of them at first, amused at the teacher-and-student look they had about them; until she was driven to one of the most memorable climaxes by Ricky's tongue...and she knew this whole night was going to be just as memorable.

-6-

Leigh opened her eyes. It took her a moment to come around and realise there were extra bodies in her bed, warmth emanating from them; a hand on her breast from one side and a strong hairy arm under her head from the other direction.

She smiled to herself and glanced sideways in each direction. She felt absolutely fabulous! It had been an age since she'd woken up in a happy mood; but after all that partying and drinking last night? The music? The intoxication and then... She should have the mother of all hangovers.

But she didn't. What had they done to her?

Well, she told herself, she knew very well what they had done to her. She recalled every position and combination of any two and all three they had experimented with last night. She smiled contentedly again.

Her mobile phone vibrated on the bedside cabinet. She looked over at it, and then looked between Ricky and Lucas again.

They both looked so peaceful; she didn't want to disturb

them. She bit her lip, hoping the phone wouldn't keep going. She listened out carefully…it didn't vibrate again. Not a call, just a text, she told herself. They can wait. She stayed where she was, shifted her neck a little to stretch it, and then closed her eyes for a while, breathing deeply and meditatively.

She could hear birds tweeting their dawn chorus outside the bedroom window as the winter sun, low in the clear sky, shone through the gaps around and between the curtains; and felt a contentment that made her wish she could be here forever.

She lost track of time a little and didn't know how long she lay there before Ricky stirred, shifted his weight slightly and opened his eyes. He looked at her, and then his gaze shifted downwards, not looking at anything in particular.

Leigh thought she saw uneasiness in his expression. Given that she'd woken in such a great mood, she was a little unnerved; wondering what might cause it. She pushed the thought right to the back of her mind, in an effort to keep her own mood bright; and consciously made an effort to improve his.

"Morning!" she half-whispered.

Ricky smiled sadly at her. Leigh lifted her head slightly so he could move his arm out from under her neck. Once free he turned over and sat up on the edge of the bed.

From the back she could see he had already put on his

underwear at some point during the night. Climbing out of bed, he picked up his shirt from the floor, slung it on and headed out of the bedroom.

Leigh frowned a little. She could hear him rattling around in the bathroom, then head into the kitchen. She heard the radio spring in to life and the kettle begin to boil; and she suddenly felt very hungry for breakfast of some kind.

She gently lifted Lucas's hand from her chest and shifted herself sideways, placing his hand down on the warm empty space on the mattress. For some reason, she felt more exposed, standing there naked in the morning light, than she had the night before. Just the alcohol, probably; she told herself. With a sudden agitated rush, she searched around the room for some clothes she could put on without opening the squeaky cupboard door and risking disturbing Lucas.

Leigh looked at him as she thought that; he was sleeping still, and looked so peaceful. And young, it struck her. He looked younger than she generally pictured him day to day, in work, with his wayward mouth and cheeky attitude. Leigh shook her head, willing herself to get into gear. She pulled out a baggy t-shirt from under the bed; and a pair of leggings that she'd slung over the chair in the corner the other day after she'd been swimming.

She chided herself a little for not keeping her place a little neater, putting her clothes away or in the laundry bin; but at the same time, felt a little relieved that she had something to hand to cover herself up.

Leigh tiptoed out of the room, pulling the door closed quietly behind her.

She padded into the kitchen.

Ricky had obviously been waiting for her. He had a steaming mug of tea ready, and placed it down in front of her almost as soon as she perched on the stool in front of the kitchen counter that separated the kitchen area from the small living area of her tiny flat.

She smiled a thank-you at him and took a sip. Ricky nodded and turned away. A second later, he turned back with a plate of toast; thick-cut bread dripping with butter and Marmite.

Leigh's spirits instantly lifted.

"How did you know I like Marmite?" She asked.

"It's your kitchen…" he reminded her and shrugged.

Leigh blushed. Of course it was. Her head really wasn't straightening itself out this morning. Her groin and thighs were aching - she knew why…

"About last night…" Ricky began. Leigh snapped her head up to look at him, the first slice of toast half-way through being bitten. It was as though he was reading her mind. Or so she thought… "It really should not have happened." He continued.

"I thought we all enjoyed ourselves?" Leigh felt a little dejected as she spoke. She tried not to let her voice sound like it was breaking from the disappointment. It was too late, Ricky had already sensed it. His face softened into a sympathetic smile.

"Of course we did, it was amazing; but Leigh, you're about to start your dream job! So is Lucas…" Ricky made his way around the counter and sat on the next stool.

"Exactly! We'll all be working together…" Leigh reminded him. "Think of all the night-stops…"

Ricky held a finger up to her mouth in an attempt to shush her. She was silenced. She looked into his face, searching for some explanation. Ricky didn't break the gaze, just looked back, his face deadly serious.

"Leigh, it won't happen, darling." He told her, with finality in his voice. "I will be….I AM…your senior. Downtime, Night stops, Training courses away, even when we're socialising. Nothing will change that." The realisation hit Leigh as he was speaking.

"Is it against the rules?" Leigh suddenly felt like she may have ruined her career before it had even begun. Ricky saw her trepidation and smiled. He reached out and rubbed her shoulder, reassuringly.

"Not yet, don't worry…You haven't started yet, remember? But we need to clear this up now. Because once you, and Lucas, start…the past is behind us, do you understand?" Ricky looked into her eyes as though searching for her answer.

Leigh looked down for a moment, in thought. Then

nodded, before looking back at him, a little sheepishly.

"Don't feel guilty!" Ricky soothed. "It was wonderful. But we're not in love, right?"

Leigh had to admit, he was right. She'd been admiring his physique for a long time; and, well, when it came to Lucas, she'd always just thought of him as cute; but she didn't really fancy him either. And hadn't she been trying to explain the same thing to Sasha for years? Relationships weren't really her thing. At least, not at the moment. Sex, on the other hand she was pretty sure was something she did have a need for.

"I guess I just thought..." Leigh began, "You know. A regular partner..." she thought for a second before correcting herself, "well, partners, maybe...would be a more stable...than..."

"Than your life so far?" Ricky winked at her knowingly, trying to lighten the mood; as he grabbed her empty cup and took it over to the sink with his own.

"Kind of, yeh." She confirmed.

"Listen honey," He continued, his accent drawling through the words lightening the mood intensely without even trying, "You, as I fully imagined you would be, are fantastic at sex...many, many, forms of it as you have proved last night...and I, for one, am honoured to have been entertained in such a way. But let's leave it at that, shall we?"

Leigh nodded and smiled. She looked at him with a

flirty raised eyebrow. "That good huh?"

"I would thoroughly recommend you. Were it not quite unseemly to do so." He raised his eyebrows at her.

"Likewise." Leigh took a bite out of her toast, still looking at him.

"Oh. Em. Gee. You guys!" Lucas bounced in, fully dressed and acting as though he'd just had the best sleep ever.

They both looked at him, although he was oblivious and grabbed the second slice of toast from Sasha's plate. He was half way through it when he looked up and realised they were looking at him.

"What?" He queried.

"Lucas," Ricky began with a deep breath. Lucas cut him off.

"OK, OK, I get it, right? What happens in Vegas stays in Vegas. Except that we'd have a bigger suite if we were in Vegas, right?"

Leigh and Ricky both burst out laughing at the same time. Any hint of uneasiness had suddenly been diffused.

"What?" Lucas was taken aback by their response. "Hey, I might be young but that does NOT mean I'm inexperienced. Although..." he added a pregnant pause, possibly for effect, Leigh thought, as she noticed Lucas looking at her lustfully, and pointing at her with a long and terribly camp finger, "You, have completely changed my mind about girls…"

"What?" Leigh's eyes opened wide. She looked from Lucas to Ricky and back again. Ricky just shrugged at her, just as surprised.

"Just kidding Hun," he winked at her. "But thanks for letting me experiment! I shall make sure I'm far more adventurous from here on in."; and with that, Lucas grabbed his satchel he'd carried around with him all night, from the sofa in the corner where he'd tossed it when they got in the night before, and sauntered towards the door.

As he let himself out through the front door, Mister Dennison was on his doorstep wrapped in a scarf and heavy coat, with a newspaper under his arm. A creature of habit, he walked to the corner shop every morning to get his paper whatever the weather.

He turned and stared disapprovingly at Lucas.

Lucas turned back to Leigh and Ricky and blew them a kiss. Mister Dennison's eyes widened as he spied the two of them in the kitchen; comparing the 'morning after' look that the three of them shared; and when Lucas got the measure of the man from a simple glance, he decided to really wind him up. Lucas straightened up and looked Mister Dennison directly in the eye; before blowing the old man a kiss and camping up his walk, swinging his hips as he made his way to the dowdy staircase and down the stairs. Just before he disappeared out of view, he threw his hand in the air, and blew them a kiss and shouted "Bye bye darlings!".

Leigh got up gingerly from her stool, shaking her head and trying to avoid Mister Dennison's glare, she pushed her front door closed on him.

She went back into the kitchen and looked at Ricky. They both burst into fits of giggles and couldn't stop for some time after; not even enough to make another cup of tea.

-7-

Leigh spent her Christmas day the same way she had for the past 7 years; at work, checking in the ski flight to Chambery, heating up a pre-cooked roast dinner in a Tupperware container from her aunt Sophie, opening the office doors for the armed police officers who patrolled the airport since 9/11, the ones who had drawn the short straw to also be working on Christmas day, to come in and rest their feet on the table and use the coffee machine.

It might be the worst tasting coffee in the airport, but it was also the cheapest. Some deal had been done to get the vending machine installed and prices capped at 11 pence per drink. Invariably it was the destination for everyone's loose change. For the one who forgot, and tried to put in a pound coin for one cup of sludge, they'd be stuck with 89 pence change in 1 and 2 pence coins.

This usually meant the coins would be left in a paper cup next to the machine as a free-for-all with the understanding that the next person to make the mistake would do the same. And so it went on, that the ground handlers survived through delays and night shifts on a combination of unidentifiable, lime-green cordial, and something that claimed to be coffee but tasted undeniably of sour milk mixed with chicory.

The only unusual thing about this particular Christmas day was the absence of Sasha. Even though Leigh didn't exactly feel like she would burst into tears, there was a distinctive melancholy mood following her around all day.

For 7 years they'd both volunteered to work the Christmas Day shift. They had both been single and childless, preferring to avoid their respective extended families over Christmas festivities; and allowing colleagues with partners and families to have the day off. It had actually worked out well for both Sasha and Leigh – they probably would have been each other's first choice of who to spend Christmas day with anyway; plus they had the perk of Christmas Day overtime bonus on top of their shift pay.

Of course, Sasha was distracted this year. Leigh's last Christmas as ground staff. Had she been a more emotional person she might well be shedding a tear right now. It seemed that Sasha had all but forgotten about her.

No, that was a little mean. Leigh was happy for her. Something niggled at her, but she knew it was just that they'd been a double-act for so long, the two unattached girls – pretty much everyone else had someone – married for years; partner; long-term girl/boyfriend…or simply a string of regular girl-or-boy-friends.

Sasha and Leigh had leaned on each other as being the ones that everyone else seemed to want to 'set up' with their friends, pair them up with somebody, anybody... Sasha had always talked of wanting to be in a relationship but Leigh had been mildly thankful when Sasha had once stated that she felt quite relieved that her 'dream man' was just in her dreams...not real...not having to deal with 'the morning after'...which Leigh had spent years drumming in to her was the thing to avoid – make an agreement outright to enjoy the night and leave scot-free.

And then, Sasha had met someone, and Leigh knew right from the first time Sasha had told her about him, the way she spoke, the faraway look in her eyes...Sasha had never thought of him as a one-night stand.

And when she'd finally met Colan herself, Leigh could hardly blame her. She had, actually, admitted to herself, a tinge of jealousy.

Right now, Leigh sat alone on the top floor viewing terrace, watching the evening lights come on in the town across the airfield, and the runway inspection truck driving along runway 12 checking for debris and anything that could compromise a landing. She missed having her friend there, dancing to a bit of *Kylie* and singing '*Islands in the Stream*' at the top of their voices, as they raided the odd selection of lost-property CDs using the old boom-box in the corner of the office to pass the time, and make-believe they were enjoying a Christmas party all of their own.

Not that there was much make-believe; today's shift was pretty much one of the easiest.

One ski-family arrived off their flight from their winter-ski resort complaining that their precious ski-boots had been lost in transit somewhere. And of course, Leigh rolled her eyes, they couldn't possibly last the rest of the winter season without them.

Sometimes she didn't mind covering the baggage hall for Olga. Especially on quiet days.

Olga had been an unwavering feature of the airport from the mid 1970's. She had been self-teaching herself the baggage tracing computer system since it had been introduced, and became the go-to person to ask about luggage enquiries. Eventually, as they got busier, she took over as baggage supervisor; spending most, if not all, of her shift in the baggage tracing office.

Olga, of course, couldn't be there twenty-four-seven; and a few of the passenger services, Sasha, Leigh, Carl and Lucas mainly, had taken it upon themselves to spend some of their downtime with the base's matriarch, learning her organisational system she'd set out for keeping track of lost and found property; which made her feel better about leaving it in other hands occasionally.

Leigh could do customer service. Of course she could, it was what made her good at her job; and had shone through in her cabin-crew group interviews.

Admittedly, she didn't *always* enjoy it…but in certain

instances where she felt like screaming that 'the customer wasn't always right'; she had learned to bite her tongue, smile as sympathetically as she could in the circumstances, and take it out in a moan in the baggage-handlers' "smoke-hole" afterwards.

Leigh suddenly realised, at the thought of the smoke-hole, that she was alone. She looked around the deserted floor. This was unusual. Inevitably, people always wanted a view of the runway. From the die-hard plane spotters, to grandparents entertaining the grandchildren, who'd never been on a plane yet, for a few hours.

Not on Christmas day; when the skeleton staff were holding the fort, and no-one wanted to use the airport, but those who'd decided to forego their Christmas lunch; or delay it; or celebrate a few days early, in return for being able to book a cheaper than usual flight ticket on an aircraft that would otherwise have still had to position out empty on a day when no crew wanted to operate so would have to be paid extra anyway. So, the airlines involved had worked out that they could still make a bit of money back selling tickets and operating the flight on Christmas day rather than a positioning flight heading out ready to operate flights back the next morning.

Leigh checked her watch. She still had a good couple of hours until the flight from Stuttgart came in.

She'd barely seen anyone else all day from *Air2Ground*.

Lucas had been in to check in the winter-sun flight to Fuerteventura with her. A flight operated so that

AirMidlantic could get their aircraft and crew back to their home base in time for Christmas day…

"Morning fag-hag…" Lucas had bounced in at 5am, grinning and winking at her, arms wide ready for a hug and air-kissing his way towards her.

Leigh had been overjoyed to find he had no hang-ups or qualms about their drunken night with Ricky.

Not that she had really been bothered about it; but she'd had workplace hook-ups before over the years; right from her first work-experience placements at 16, and even though most had been fully eyes-wide-open and the unspoken understanding that it was all casual and experimentation; there had been a few hiccup occasions when one party or another had become too infatuated. Leigh had only made the mistake once of falling for a guy who was not in the least bit interested in her; and she had vowed never to repeat it.

She had been the subject of someone else's continued affection and advances following a one-night-stand a number of times. At first, Leigh had tried to sit down and explain to the other party that there was no relationship; after a while, she'd just taken to hiding, actively avoiding them as much as possible; gradually learning her lesson – either choose someone you DON'T work with; or else make very clear the position from the start. Preferably before the experimenting with positions begins…

She wasn't sure from memory if it had been made clear

that night at Kevin's; but she was pretty confident that both Ricky and Lucas had been fully aware of her, and their own, intentions.

She'd not seen Ricky since he'd left hers that morning but they seemed to have parted ways on the right foot. She'd done a few shifts with Lucas – it seemed Mina had tried to make the most of their notice periods when she'd altered the Christmas period roster to cover all the leave that everyone else had requested.

Lucas had come in, quiet and reserved, the first time they'd worked together after their erotic three-way. He'd waited for their chance to be alone together and he'd broached the subject; sat on the outbound pier near gate six as they waited for the regular Amsterdam flight on the Friday afternoon after it had happened. In his usual bull-in-a-china-shop way, while rolling himself back and forth along the abandoned corridor in one of the airport's wheelchairs.

"So, you're still walking like a sumo-wrestler I see…" He nudged her with his elbow. Leigh spat out her water she'd been sipping, in surprise.

"LUCAS! Oh my God!" She burst out laughing. He grinned and slung his arm around her shoulders casually.

"I mean, good job you had me behind you…imagine if you'd had Ricky up your arse…you'd be asking us to push you round in a wheelchair with one of those special cushions on it…"

Leigh was speechless, laughing harder and threw her

hand out to whack him on the chest; just as Lizzie and Roger from *Seccombe*, the aviation security contractors who ran the security around the airport, from manning the access gates around the airport to checking anyone going airside, staff, crew and passengers alike, let themselves in through the double doors at the end of the long pier, doing a regular spot-check around the terminal.

They'd do this at seemingly random times, to check that doors had been closed and there was no access to restricted areas. They patrolled past Leigh and Lucas, eyeing them slightly suspiciously; Leigh surmised she and Lucas must have had guilty, sheepish looks on their faces as a result of being interrupted.

"Awright, you two?" Roger had asked in his estuary English accent, raising his eyebrows questioningly.

He stopped in front of them while Lizzie nipped down the stairs to the inbound area of gate five to double check the door; which had a habit of closing but not locking properly on the magnetic door catch. It regularly got overlooked and left unlocked by the less careful ground staff following the last passengers in up to immigration.

"Hi Rog. All ready for Christmas?" Leigh asked quickly, covering and changing the subject completely from her and Lucas's previous chat.

"Course, Julie's a master wiv Christmas, isn't she? She'd come in and do this place if they let her!"

"Kids excited?"

"What kids don't get excited for Christmas?" He shrugged happily. "You two working?"

"As usual!" Lucas answered with a light-hearted shrug. "You?"

"First Christmas off in two years!" Roger answered. "Can't wait! Lizzie too." He added, as Lizzie appeared at the top of the stairs as though on cue.

The security officers had wandered off and as soon as they were out of earshot, Leigh and Lucas had looked at each other and burst out laughing again.

From then on, Leigh knew their friendship had resumed at its normal pace. Their shared experience was every now and again touched upon when they were alone; and never discussed with others. That was the way she preferred it.

On this Christmas morning they had not mentioned it at all. They'd enjoyed the jolly, festive mood gleaned from pretty much everyone else around. Those who had to work were resigned to that fact and were making the most of it.

They'd been round to the Immigration offices to wish Kevin...once again having drawn the short straw, a Merry Christmas, and been given a very small glass of what Kevin reassured them was non-alcoholic mulled wine that Jason had sent in with him in a thermal flask...although they all felt a tad merrier after toasting each other with it; and opened check-in desks adorned with mini-Christmas trees with garlands hanging down over their heads, causing great merriment when taller passengers tried to haul their luggage onto the weighing scales at the end of the luggage belts to the side of each desk, and got their heads caught in the garlands; amusing everyone else in the queue.

For once, nobody even seemed to mind queueing that much. Even holidaymakers for the rest of the year, heading off for exotic climes and a break from work, still managed to get a little less relaxed when they saw the queues at Check-in.

Christmas day just seemed different.

Lucas had only been working for the morning. A short 5-10 shift to see that flight off. Between the two of them and Max, the Polish dispatcher who'd started as a passenger services agent, they managed the single flight check-in, prep, boarding and departure. Max had gone back to the airside 'ramp' office to send the departure message to the destination station, then joined the other ramp agents who were in that day to do a deep clean on a 737 that was parked out on the general aviation apron.

At least it was a casual job on a day like this; they could take their time and not rush. Lucas had given Leigh a huge hug, and a Christmas present…which he'd made her promise to not open until after he was gone; 'in case of temptation' he told her, cryptically, with an Ann-Robinson-Style wink. She'd smiled and given him a box of chocolates she'd got him.

"You need fattening up you beanpole!" she grinned.

He'd opened them there and then and they'd shared them, over bad machine coffee; and then he'd headed off to his parents' house for a traditional family Christmas dinner and the overindulgent afternoon that came with it.

Leigh had met the Chambery ski flight herself, Max coming in to follow the last passengers in through the arrivals corridor and close the doors. She'd cleared the arrivals hall herself, dealt with the family with the missing skis; and shared a tearful goodbye with Kevin as he was about to finish his shift and go home to Jason. Kara, he said, would be in later for an hour or so just to see the last flight in.

And here she was, sat on the top floor, alone, contemplating the next stage of her life. Out on her own once again, although she was suddenly hit with a huge wave of gratitude that Lucas and Ricky were the two who would be with her every step of the way. Or so she hoped.

Leigh made her way down to the smoke-hole. As with the rest of the airport, it seemed that the airside baggage sort area and the ramp in general, were operating on skeleton crew.

There were no check-ins open so the belts were off.

Any night-stopped aircraft had already been checked, doors sealed with security seal stickers – used to show the next crew opening up if the doors had been tampered with or opened at any point; and chocked with heavy rubber stoppers behind all the wheels to prevent accidental movement of the aircraft.

There was little for the ramp agents on duty to do but sit around the small enclosed dedicated smoking area playing cards, waiting for their one inbound flight, and be there in case of diversions.

This place stank. But it made sense to have it there.

There had been countless times over the years when they'd all experienced having to tell the odd passenger who got off a flight that wasn't attached to an air bridge, at the bottom of the steps, right in front of the engine and fuel tank, to not even think about lighting that cigarette, as they were poised with a lighter or matches.

More often than not it also happened just as the fuel tanker truck trundled past them ready to refuel the plane for its next flight on a quick turnaround.

Of course the ramp agents had all had aviation training and regular refreshers, but even as regular smokers, most of them, it seemed like it should be obvious to not light up in the vicinity of aviation fuel.

The smoke hole was a small, walled area around the back of the terminal building, its doorway-sized entrance guarded from direct access onto the apron by a large courtyard area, across on the other side of which the baggage belts exited the security scanner behind the check-in area; and brought the luggage out to be lifted, their labels scanned and loaded on to relevant trailers to be taken out to the destination aircraft.

There was no roof, although the overhanging edge of the terminal building two floors above was enough in conjunction with the high walls, to keep out the worst of any bad weather whilst also allowing for the smoke, and the worst of the tobacco smells, to escape and a little fresh air to come in and replace it. Technically, therefore, it met all the requirements of not smoking indoors; but allowing a safe designated place for smokers to go away from their work area. Over the years, it had become a surrogate common-room, where pretty much anyone, whether a smoker or not, as long as they didn't mind the second-hand smoke or the lingering stale smells, to hang out at. As it became less and less commonplace to smoke, and more staff were giving up, non-smokers outnumbered the smokers, yet the smoke-hole remained just as busy.

With it's hotchpotch collection of old plastic chairs interspersed with the odd tatty & torn office chair, and a leftover row of gate-chairs from when the old pier was refurbished a few years ago, it was the most comfortable place for the ramp agents in their grimy workwear to chill out in between the hard manual labour of baggage on-and-offloads; attaching aircraft to pushback bars, 'dropping' toilets in between flights; and the myriad of other things that passengers waiting in the departure lounge took for granted.

Leigh smoothed her hand over her backside, making sure her dark navy uniform-issue trench-coat was covering her skirt as she perched on the cleanest looking chair. She maybe shouldn't have bothered coming down. There was no one here either, and it had started tipping it down outside.

At least the sound of the rain hammering on the corrugated shelter roof of the baggage sort area outside was matching her mood. Until Frenchy came in and tapped her on the shoulder.

"Merry Christmas love," he said as he loafed down next to her and dug around in his pocket for a crushed cigarette packet and lighter.

"Merry Christmas French!" She answered. "Thought you'd be busy today?"

"Nah, 'Lise is alright there, anyone who's not here is all at home having family Christmases aren't they? Besides, Jason was there for a bit until Kev finished and wants paying double time, so my shift here'll cover that, I recon!"

"Isn't that robbing Peter to pay Paul?"

"Nah, excuse to get away from the mother-in-law over Christmas dinner!" Frenchy grinned at Leigh and she giggled.

He took a deep puff on his cigarette. Leigh inhaled deeply, too. She was strange, she knew.

They'd had this discussion in the passenger services office before. Most of the ex-smokers in there were die-hard haters – they avoided the smoke-hole mostly; and admitted to screwing up their faces when confronted with a smoker in public, being able to smell it a mile away and hating the smell they'd once got so much pleasure out of.

Leigh on the other hand, was surviving as an ex-smoker, barely, apart from the odd puff on a night out, but only by getting the odd fix of passive smoking; and that, at least, was one thing the smoke hole was good for. She settled back in her seat and picked up an old magazine section from last week's Sunday newspaper that someone had left there. She idly flicked through articles she had little interest in to pass the time.

"You off soon then?" Frenchy murmured after a while.

"Last day, today" She answered.

"Leaving without a fanfare, aren't you?" he blinked at her. "Pegged you as one who'd be having a big leaving do…"

"Not like I'm leaving, really….I'll still be based here; just not hanging around on the ground like the rest of you"

"Ah… like that is it?" Frenchy raised his eyebrows. Leigh realised how snobby she must have sounded, and made an attempt to backtrack.

"No…not like that; I mean…well, most of my work will be in-flight…so I'll see everyone, just more in passing. And I'll still come to Landing lights…the other YouKay lot do!" she said, speaking quickly. Frenchy grinned.

"Winding you up, I am!" He winked. "I know we won't be able to get rid of you that quickly!"

Leigh felt a wave of relief.

She suddenly realised something she'd subconsciously known for a long time – it was the people around here that made her job so much fun.

Until this afternoon, she'd thought simply changing jobs would be a doddle. Now, she wondered if her new job would be just as much fun – seeing them all so much less; and spending more time with the crew she had up until now, only passed brief amounts of time with on turnarounds.

Only time will tell... she told herself.

-8-

The imposing structure emblazoned with the grotesque colours of the airline logo loomed over them as they drove up to *YouKayAir* HQ.

It was the middle of a grey, wet January.

They were on a drab, but busy, industrial estate on the outskirts of Slough.

Leigh had opted to drive her old beat-up Fiesta and Lucas was happy to bring the snacks.

"Oh. Em. Gee." Lucas stared up at the logo, just as one of *YouKayAir*'s 737s flew overhead having taken off from Heathrow airport. "It's HUGE!"

"That's what she said…" Leigh joked.

Lucas elbowed her, causing to swerve the car, narrowly missing a crew minibus, also covered with the gaudy red, white and blue logos. She corrected her course immediately and pulled into an empty spot before turning to deride him. "LUCAS! Come on…we're supposed to be responsible adults now."

"Well, you maybe honey, you know they only hired me to be the on board entertainment!" He crossed his eyes and put on a funny smile making her laugh and shake her head.

"Come on, idiot. I bet we're the last ones!" she said getting out of the car and fetching her satchel from the back seat.

Lucas followed suit, and swung his jacket over his shoulders as he closed the passenger door.

"Yeah, well, you're never popular if you come first, right?" Lucas quipped, without waiting for a response, stalked forward towards the main entrance.

Leigh shook her head again in disbelief at his coarse and suggestive language. She knew she should be used to it by now; and wondered if he thought he could get away with it more with her, now, given their past.

Leigh followed him in. A sudden wave of nervousness overcame her. She hadn't been the new girl in a long time, and looking up at the building and overwhelming branding reminded her of the high regard in which she'd held the position of cabin-crew. It didn't help that May had been on airport standby a week before Christmas and had been revising for a refresher exam; and shown Leigh just part of the airline manuals they were expected to know – a thick volume clipped inside one of the thicker style of ring-binders; amendments interspersed all the way through in different coloured paper, depending on when the amendment was added. Just the thought of keeping on top of that much information purely 'just in case' they were needed to recall it to save passengers lives was almost enough to make her turn on her heel right there and then. Until Lucas stuck his head back out through the main entrance door he'd disappeared through to check where she was.

"Come on slowcoach…I'm not doing this alone!" he waved her in. Leigh grinned a little.

They entered the large conference room that the receptionist had directed them to after signing them in and handing them security IDs. She was cabin crew herself but on grounded duties due to her obviously pregnant state.

Leigh was relieved to see that pretty much everyone else who made up their training class looked far more nervous than she did, as she remained touchingly close to Lucas.

At least they had each other; she surmised most of these others knew no-one and had travelled far from home chasing a dream job. She'd chatted to enough current hosties to have heard their advice and their experiences of starting out.

Lucas led the way to two empty seats on the end of a row half way back in the block. The chairs had been set out in a sort of audience layout, in rows with an aisle through the middle. They were facing a whiteboard with an overhead projector setup on a table in front of it connected to a laptop.

There didn't seem to be much loud chatter, but a few around them had braved up enough to break the ice and started to chat to the one next to them.

Lucas looked around them and nudged Leigh. She looked at him questioningly and he nodded his head in the direction of the other end of their row of seats.

"Oh my god…" Leigh whispered to him. "Is that Carl?"

Lucas nodded excitedly and whispered back, "Yeah!"

Carl had never seemed like the type to be hankering after a flying job. He had been at *Air2Ground* for a few years and seemed a steady type; wife and two small children at home and quite happy in his job. He generally didn't socialise outside work but then not everybody did. It didn't make them outcast from the social circle.

He'd taken a generous redundancy package from a previous long-term job, something to do with oil in the middle-East. Because of that, his mortgage was paid off and he appeared to be working mainly for the fun of it.

He was the last person they would have expected to see here.

"I didn't see him at the group interviews" Leigh muttered.

"Me neither; but I think they did others before us."

Carl must have realised they were talking about him, he turned and waved happily. He must have seen them come in.

Leigh wondered why he hadn't made himself known when he saw them. And surely he'd have heard before now, on the airport grapevine, that they were going flying? How come he hadn't said anything?

Carl stood up and shuffled along the row as soon as he'd acknowledged them. He took a seat behind them, and leaned forward, leaning on the back of their chairs, so they could have a three-way conversation.

"Morning! Heard you two might be here…" he said, smiling excitedly.

"Wish I could say the same," Leigh told him, "had no idea you were even interested in flying?"

"Well, caught the bug I suppose…" he shrugged.

They would have carried on talking but the chatter in the room died down to a murmur as a frenzy of activity at the front began to catch everyone's attention.

People, presumably their instructors, entered the room. A well-poised, older lady, maybe mid-fifties, Leigh surmised. She was accompanied by a middle-aged gentleman, complete with middle-aged spread; bursting through his supermarket shirt but at least making an effort in a well-pressed suit and seemed to have combed what little hair he had efficiently. Lucas wondered if he could see very many of them through his thick glasses, but felt it would be inappropriate to make Leigh laugh this early on in the proceedings, so he decided to keep his thoughts to himself.

"Good morning, ladies and gentlemen!" The older lady began as the room settled. She had lifted her hands slightly, almost like a pastor attempting to settle his congregation. It had worked. The recruits became quiet, everyone seemingly mirroring the lady's poise, hands clasped in laps and shoulders back.

"My name is Gloria Masters. I am the head of Cabin services here at *YouKayAir*. I know I've met some of you at various stages of the interview process. I'll hopefully get around the rest of you at some point over the next few days. Congratulations everyone! You've made it here. Now the hard work begins!"

There was a murmur through the crowd as some people started whispering to their neighbour as to whether they'd met her or not.

Gloria raised her hands half way again, holding them out in front of her; and the murmurs suddenly stopped. Leigh was impressed…this lady knew how to command a crowd.

"Now, while we're waiting for the instructor who'll be taking you through your induction training; let me introduce Connor McCarthy, The CEO of YouKayAir."

Gloria led a polite round of applause that everyone joined in with, as the portly gent behind her stood up and timidly took a half bow.

He was the least commanding CEO imaginable. He spoke quietly, Leigh even though she caught a hint of a stutter as he began to speak.

Connor launched in to an introduction, why he'd started *YouKayAir* and his ethos...but by this time, Leigh had lost focus on him; as their instructor entered the room quietly as Connor was speaking.

Leigh had glanced behind her at the door just stretching her neck and glancing around the room, just in time to catch sight of Ricky.

Before she knew it, her heart skipped a beat. She frowned slightly at herself.

He was an old friend. Admittedly, with benefits...in the past. And she didn't get like this; but after the skip, she felt a funny sensation as her eyes stayed on him and followed him as he made his way to stand next to Gloria.

Ricky wasn't wearing his uniform, or casual jeans as she'd seen him in before. He was wearing a well-cut suit. His hair was slicked back and his goatee well groomed. She'd never thought of him as particularly effeminate despite his wide-ranging taste in partners; but today his aura radiated masculinity.

She hadn't realised she was staring until Ricky caught her eye. An expressionless glare that simply made her aware that he knew she was there; a silent acknowledgement of her presence and her location in the room.

Leigh smiled very briefly and dropped her gaze, a kind of silent hello and acknowledgement of his authority. She let out a small breath, unaware until them that she had been holding her breath a little.

She avoided looking up towards the front to watch Connor and Gloria as they took turns speaking, each describing their past careers and explaining how the training would go for the new recruits; for fear that if she looked at them, her gaze would fall back on Ricky again.

Lucas tapped her on the knee, so she looked at him. He winked at her. Of course he'd noticed Ricky as well but in Lucas's case, he hadn't seemed to have been attacked by the same emotional response as had overcome Leigh.

She offered him a weak smile and a small nod of acknowledgement, then in an effort to avoid his eyes too; she glanced around at their new classmates.

Ricky's entrance had clearly had an effect on a number of them – both male and female.

Leigh was somewhat amused to see the response he'd generated. Dreamy-eyed stares. A few shifted in their seats as though some physical response had been generated by his presence. It certainly had in her own case, but she was pretty sure that she, aside from Lucas, was the only one to have had any previous experience of Ricky to be causing the stirring between her thighs.

"…Ricardo Da Silva." Gloria announced at the end of an introduction to a rapturous applause; which Leigh wasn't sure anyone else had noticed was a darn sight more enthusiastic than the polite applause Gloria had received earlier.

Ricky stood up from the seat he'd taken behind her, and used the same hand-raising motion to settle the clapping.

In his case, however, one hand was enough. An air of confidence and authority surrounded him.

"Thanks everyone. Don't get too excited, though, I'm going to make you work hard!" A snigger, and a couple of '*Whoop*'s stifled around the room. Gloria snapped her head up and searched the audience accusingly with her eyes but settled on no-one.

Ricky continued. "Now that you're here; you're going to realise that passing the interview stages was the easy part. You think you know what you need to learn? Think again. You think we're going to be easier on you than some well-established international airline with business class and impressing millionaires in first? No. They have nothing to prove. They've been doing it for years. My job is to make you BETTER than them; we are the pioneers of this airline and WE are the ones who need to make *YouKayAir*'s name in the industry!"

His conviction had riled up everyone, including Connor who nodded all the way through Ricky's rousing speech and rose to his feet to lead more applause as Ricky reached the end of the speech.

Leigh was even more impressed, and a little sadness washed over her. Ricky clearly meant business. She wondered if his conviction was over-played in order to drive the point he had tried to make to her – that the business of their jobs and any previous pleasure would definitely not mix.

Then she chastised herself. *Building up your part again,*

girl? She warned herself. *Don't make everything about you.*

She had a habit of doing this. She had been held back from feeling as pleased for Sasha and Col over the past year since she had met Col on his first day. Her being pleased for them had been overshadowed by tinges of jealousy. She missed having her closest singleton friend to go out with, to moan about men with, and to discuss intimate sexual desires and details with… Of course, they still could, but not as much as before as Sasha seemed to always be at Col's beck and call. And it might not have been so bad if Leigh hadn't been just a little bit enamoured with how good looking Col was…

Then, she'd met Ricky. It wasn't as though she had fallen head over heels for him; but he had an infectious appetite for life that matched her own and they had similar tastes…in music, in people, in humour…which led to her spending a little more time in his company than as a hanger on to Sasha and Col.

And here she was, once again making it all about her; as though she should be the centre of his thoughts.

Lucas nudged her as he passed a pile of notebooks and pens to her. She had been daydreaming and missed the instructions but gathered, since everyone before Lucas appeared to be holding a pen and a notebook that she was to take one and pass it on. She handed the pile back to Carl behind her and scribbled her name on the front of the book she'd kept for herself.

Leigh forced herself to concentrate for the rest of the session. Overcoming the unexpected emotions of seeing Ricky walk in was a must if she was to stand any hope of at least getting through the first day.

She figured that if she didn't do at least that, it was going to be a struggle getting through the induction period of classroom based work; and she knew it was going to get tougher after that.

Already lagging behind, she noticed a few of those around her, Lucas included, had already started noting down a few facts and figures that Gloria and Connor had been giving them in passing about the airline's history and current corporate make-up. Leigh had been preoccupied with her own thoughts...verging on the erotic...and had been only vaguely aware of them droning on in the background.

"Didn't they say this would all be in the training manual?" she whispered to Lucas.

Carl leaned forward and whispered back, "Still worth showing a bit of willing."

It suddenly struck Leigh that Carl may turn out to be a bit of a teacher's pet during the training.

She'd not spent that much time with him in the past; and worried he was going to turn in to a bit of a hanger on.

Lucas leaned in. "I'm not sure how much of the manuals they'll bog down with this stuff. You know we're already going to have a hell of a lot to learn, right?"

He was right.

The airline had started out with a fleet made up of two aircraft types; to save costs on running two full compliments of cabin crew each trained on a separate aircraft type; *YouKayAir* were pioneering having all cabin crew trained and signed off on both aircraft types and being interchangeable. Which meant aside from basic training, aviation security, aviation medicine, the safety and emergency procedures that were general to all aspects of the job; they had to be familiar with two different aircraft types; knowing off-by-heart the locations of all the safety and emergency equipment on each and every aircraft they might get assigned to; which may not happen until the morning of their assigned flight.

Leigh nodded at him, suddenly worried. How could she have let herself get so distracted as to lose sight of the goal?

For the rest of the morning, Leigh hankered down. Gloria and Connor eventually left the room, and Ricky had them all up, moving their chairs into first a large circle for personal introductions – not so much that they'd all remember each other straight away, more of an ice-breaker; then into smaller groups with instructions that they would learn something from a particular section of a manual he gave them; with a view to presenting it to the rest of the trainees afterwards.

He told them not to worry too much if it didn't sink in straight away – it was a technique he was showing them that working together to study might be easier for some than simply sitting in their room, alone, trying to read hundreds of pages and hoping it would sink in.

By the time lunch break had rolled around, Leigh had almost set aside any previous thoughts and feelings towards Ricky, and was seeing him as simply their trainer.

She had become quite chatty to the girls who had been grouped with her – it seemed even without making a point of it, Ricky had figured out a way of splitting her from Lucas and Carl and making sure they were all with people they didn't know.

Emmeline, slightly older than Leigh was, mid-30s maybe, from Bournemouth; who'd been a nursery school teacher purely because her mum ran a nursery but had wanted something more for herself; and saw this as a way to see the world. Leigh liked her, a little reserved, sheltered life so far, positive and eager. Leigh couldn't help but worry about her and feel like she needed looking after.

Brandon was a heavy set, totally camp and utterly loud and hilarious 40-year-old with sandy hair, freckles and a thick Lancashire accent. Within minutes, their small group had been in fits of giggles at him promoting himself and it had been unanimously agreed that he would be the one to make their presentation. He told them he'd once wanted to be a drag queen, could handle the heels and make-up but couldn't find tights and stockings to fit him as everything chafed around his crotch then ended up around his ankles. And not always on purpose either…

Lunchtime came and they were given directions to the canteen where a special complimentary buffet had been laid on for them.

Ricky joked with them about it "Don't get too used to it, ladies and gents…from here on in, it's going to be leftover airline food that passengers didn't want…" he winked at them.

Everyone sniggered, and heaved a collective sigh of relief that their first morning was over.

Aside from a small tea-break that morning which had doubled as a rush for the toilets and a smoke break for those that wanted to; this was their first chance to let their hair down a little.

Some broke off to explore the building a little. A couple gathered in the corridor outside the conference room where glass case displayed large scale-models of *YouKayAir*'s aircraft; with cut-out cross-sections along them showing the seating configurations and holds and everything else inside the aircraft; they began studying them and trying to be fastidious, but eventually wandered off in search of food.

Leigh had intended to join Lucas and Carl in the canteen and told Emmeline and Brandon and the others she'd meet them down there.

As they left, heading to the door to file out slowly,

mingling with others as they left, Leigh stayed where she was. She wanted a moment or two to herself. She went back over the notes she'd taken, making sure she could read them, and then started flicking through the manual they'd been handed as a group. A large lever arch file filled with hundreds of pages about the 737s. They'd been tasked with explaining a small section of the manual, about the emergency exit door release functions; but there was so much more information in here.

Far from feeling overwhelmed from the information, she was feeling a determination to really make the most of the next 6 weeks. She'd dropped her guard a little this morning; excitement and anticipation at the start of the day, and the false sense of security at having the moral support of someone she knew next to her; followed the shock of her physical reaction to Ricky arriving, had thrown her concentration off; and she didn't want that.

She'd wanted to be here and it would be stupid to throw away the opportunity because of silly emotions and feelings.

She glanced quickly at her watch. Five minutes alone in here wouldn't hurt. She glanced back and saw the tea table set up in the corner; and went to get herself a cup. As she stood by the table, she felt a hand on her shoulder.

"Hey," Ricky said behind her.

Leigh jumped a little. She'd honestly thought she was alone in here. "I thought everyone was gone…"

"You not going to say hello?" He grinned at her.

Leigh relaxed a little. His smile was so warm and welcoming, any animosity she'd felt from his stare that morning must have been imagined, she told herself.

"Hi!" she smiled back.

There was an awkward pause as they stared into each other's eyes.

Then there was the inevitable break in the stare and the stifled giggle to mask the discomfort, and Ricky moved forward to give her a huge bear hug as though they were the world's oldest friends who'd been separated for ages.

Leigh suppressed a sudden surge in her lower abdomen as she recognised how good he smelled. They separated from the hug and Leigh turned back to dunking the teabag into the hot water in her cup.

"So you got here ok?"

"Yeah! I came with Lucas."

"Don't we always…?" Ricky said, suddenly camp and full of innuendo again. He winked at her.

"Behave!" She said, checking around the room again just in case, even though she knew they were alone.

"I know," Ricky said. "I'm sorry."

Leigh looked up at him. The look on his face told her his apology was sincere.

"I think it's going to be a long six weeks" Leigh told him, matter-of-factly.

"Hey, it's a good group I think. I was sitting in on some of the other group interviews. I think you'll all work well together."

"I wasn't talking about the group." Leigh looked at him. She wondered if her point would get across.

"Oh." He said and pursed his lips.

He dropped his gaze again and sat back, leaning against the edge of the table.

Leigh squeezed the tea bag and fished it out with a spoon, and put it in the little bowl that had been left on the table to collect rubbish. She added a drop of milk. Ricky watched, thoughtfully, as she sipped.

"You following it along okay so far? "

"I dropped concentration a little at the beginning, but it won't happen again." She said, determinedly. As an afterthought, she added "You look good in a suit".

"Thanks!" Ricky said, "I don't wear it much but want to make a good impression, you know? I'll probably be in a t-shirt tomorrow…" he looked up at her, and realised the compliment implied more about her attraction to him and her reason for being distracted, than praising his choice of outfit.

"Ah." He acknowledged.

Leigh sipped more of her tea, looking into her cup, or at the blank wall in front of her the other side of the table, anywhere but at Ricky.

"If this is going to be difficult, maybe we can..." he began.

"Why would it be difficult?" Leigh cut him off. "Don't worry, I can control myself."

Ricky raised his eyebrows, "Can you?" He asked her.

Leigh made a sarcastic face at him. "I've wanted this job longer than I've known you. You're not THAT special!" she snorted and playfully slapped at his shoulder.

Tension – broken, they both realised. Ricky grinned at her. He checked his watch.

"Listen, we should go get food. I don't wanna be a failed trainer on my first day for not keeping to the schedule"

"That WOULD be naughty of you!" Leigh looked at him and winked.

"Are we just gonna talk in innuendo for 6 weeks?" He asked, preparing to lead the way out of the conference room.

Leigh put down her cup and headed for the door beside him.

"Why not? Might make the whole course a little more

memorable…" she said as she led the way down the corridor.

"You'd better hope you remember it all…otherwise we'll both be in trouble" Ricky told her.

"I just can't wait for it to be over and done with so I can get flying!" Leigh said, suddenly beginning to get excited again at the prospect.

"Make the most of it, Leigh, it's going to go by so fast we'll be back at the airport before you know it…"

"We?" she asked him.

"Hell yeh…you don't think I'd take this job if it meant I'd be stuck here in a suit permanently, do you?!"

"You DO look good in a suit." Leigh winked at him.

"I'll remember that for the future then." He said, winking back.

Leigh smiled and pressed the button, calling the lift to take them to the next floor down. She breathed deeply in, and out, and felt a little relieved that the deadlock had seemingly been broken somewhat; she could get on with what she really came here for.

-9-

The next 6 weeks, as promised, flew by.

By the second afternoon, the new recruits had been introduced to some currently-serving cabin crew, and been taken down to the purpose-built simulator in a hangar attached to the back of the HQ building.

They couldn't believe the size of the thing. But, as Ricky explained, it was built to the size and specifications to be an exact replica of the aircraft they'd be operating on.

They had been treated as passengers in a role-play, while the current cabin crew did their jobs, welcoming them on board, showed them to seats, gave them the cabin safety briefing that they had all been familiar with from traveling abroad; and after a presumably pre-recorded announcement from the 'captain' of 'cabin crew doors for departure', a take-off was simulated. To the recruits' surprise, the whole cabin moved and shook; as though they were in a real aircraft.

After the initial movement subsided, they settled in their seats to enjoy their 'flight', fully expecting to just be watching the cabin crew do a full service, so they could take mental notes to refer back to later.

This was not to be, as just as they became accustomed to their situation, there was a loud bang. The cabin suddenly began to fill with smoke; and the serving cabin crew sprung in to action, evacuating the recruits and showing them exactly how it was done.

At the bottom of the inflated escape slide, in fits of adrenaline-fuelled laughter, the recruits found Ricky standing, as he had promised Leigh, in jeans and t-shirt having ditched the first day good-impression, with a baseball cap and a whistle, around his neck, like some jobsworth sports coach, a stopwatch in his hand.

"Well done everyone! We all out?" He called to them over the laughter.

"Just me!" called Brandon from the top of the slide. He jumped and barrelled himself down the slide, causing the rest of them to shuffle out of his way before getting cannonballed. They all burst out laughing again. "Sorry…my bad….didn't realise it wasn't a real toilet, see…"

"I think we've just identified beyond doubt the class clown, don't you, everyone?" Ricky announced; resulting in a group cheer and a few pats on the back for Brandon.

And so the training continued.

Carl had struggled a little with the Aviation Medicine

and First Aid section that they had moved on to at the beginning of the second week.

That's when the impromptu pajama-party had occurred. A few of them, including Leigh, Lucas, Brandon, Emmeline, along with Sue from Luton who'd been working as an administrator for another airline's crewing department, had descended on his room with pizza and a couple of 'resus-Annie' dolls and they'd all stayed up all night practising and revising. They fell in to building up their bonding on the fledgling friendships that had been building since they met.

They'd all been put up in a chain hotel across the motorway from the HQ; which helped with the bonding process.

Even though they were all to be based out of different airports, there were sometimes crossovers, covering other bases and meeting each other at other stations swapping aircraft and so on; so getting to know each other better was going to be in their interest.

It wasn't long that evening before the conversation turned to their main trainer.

The studying had fallen by the wayside, as their concentration turned to eating a hotchpotch of different takeaways and per-packed supermarket snacks.

It was all quiet for a moment as they all sat cross-legged in a circle on the floor. It reminded Lucas of being in primary school.

"So, what brought us all here then?" Emmeline asked, between mouthfuls.

"Pepperoni..." mumbled Leigh through a mouthful, making Lucas spit out half of his through a laugh.

"No!" Emmeline scolded. "I mean, to training, applying for the job and stuff..."

"Divorce." Sue stated, matter-of-factly.

"Oh," stated Emmeline dejectedly.

"There's no 'Oh' about it. Couldn't have come soon enough, to be honest!" Sue laughed. "Kids are grown and I'm free and single and thought it's about time I came out in to the world and did what *I* wanted."

"Seeing how the other half live, eh?" Brandon interjected.

"I tell you what," Sue continued, holding up her energy-drink can, "The lot I used to work with over there...some of the most promiscuous people I've ever met. You wouldn't BELIEVE some of the stories they came back with..."

"Really?" Emmeline looked a little shocked, partly worried. "Is that, like, part of the job...?"

Lucas patted her on the back, smiling, as Brandon winked at her, but told her reassuringly, "It's not a requirement, darling!"

Carl laughed, "Hope not, my wife would ground me

straight away!"

"Still, opportunity's there if you want it, I recon." Sue stated.

"You sound like you do then Mrs?" Brandon winked at her.

"Why the hell not? I've decided they're right. Life begins at 40. And I wouldn't mind starting with our lovely trainer..." She raised her eyebrows and took a determined gulp from her can, before picking up another slice of pizza.

Leigh and Lucas exchanged a knowing glance; then Leigh looked around, hoping no-one else had picked up on it. It didn't seem so; Brandon let out a loud belly laugh and patted Sue consolingly on the back.

"Sorry, Darling, something tells me he's not really after your type..."

"Oi! Nothing wrong with an older woman..." She retorted, a little offended.

Carl blinked disbelievingly that she hadn't understood Brandon's meaning, and exchanged a glance with Emmeline, who despite being possibly the least worldly of the group had cottoned on straight away.

"I mean," Brandon began slowly, "I don't think he's batting for your side..."

Sue suddenly realised, and stared at him.

"No! Ricardo?" She asked. Brandon nodded slowly.

"I wouldn't have said so either, Sue," Emmeline supported her, "But isn't it one of those things that it takes one to know one?" she asked innocently, directing her question to Brandon.

"If you say so, darling." Brandon reassured, patting her hand.

Carl interjected "I'm more of the mind that it just takes a bit of experience to tell. I mean we know of quite a few different orientations at our base, right Leigh?"

Leigh was a little shocked to be brought in to the conversation; having so far preferred to stay on the outskirts, looking in and nibbling quietly.

"Uh…yeh…" She offered, shoving another slice of pizza into her mouth.

Lucas laughed to himself quietly, watching her discomfort.

Emmeline piped up again with a realisation. "Wait a minute; isn't Ricky based at the same place as you?"

Sue, thinking she was talking to her, answered, "Luton? Really?"

"No not you, Lucas and Leigh and Carl…"

Lucas spoke quite innocently and nonchalantly. "Yeah. He was one of the first intakes of crew when they opened our base."

Carl furrowed his brow, remembering. "Hold on, yeh! You're quite friendly with him, aren't you, Leigh? I mean, Sally never likes me going to these airport parties…crazy some of them, right?" he rambled as he took centre stage of the conversation, "but I hear some stories from the others. I thought you were quite close with him?" He looked directly at Leigh.

Oh God, she thought, how much does he know? She looked at Lucas, as though searching for backup. Lucas shrugged but remained tight lipped.

"Well, we chatted a bit, that's all. Group dancing after a few drinks most of the time!" she shrugged it off; and it seemed to have worked. "We usually crossed paths at work because we were ground handling…" she motioned to include Lucas in the 'we', forcing him into the discussion "…and we'd meet and board flights Ricky was on"

"Really?" Emmeline seemed puzzled. "Oh, you never seemed to know him very well in class"

"Yeah, no better than the rest of us…" Sue added.

Leigh shrugged. "Well, we told him before we Christmas we'd both been accepted and he said he was on the training team so we had a chat and just made sure that we'd get the same treatment as everyone else; you know, no favouritism." She spoke quickly, attempting to get the conversation to move on.

"Fair enough," Brandon said. "To be fair, glad it wasn't me…if I'd been working with him already I'd definitely have jumped his bones…"

"BRANDON!" Emmeline was shocked at his language.

"Get used to it, honey, you might not have to partake in what some of us get up to, but you'll definitely be privy to all the gory details the next morning." Lucas told her.

"Really?" Emmeline asked, wide-eyed.

"Seriously…I dated this guy for a few months who was based out of Glasgow for *Prestair*. Some of the tales he told me of their night stops…phwar!"

"Nah, you're making it up…" Sue interjected, "I mean not saying it doesn't happen. I mean, in my case I'm fully hoping it does…but surely it can't be that bad?"

"Not always with colleagues, obviously…that would be like, workplace incest eventually!" Brandon chortled loudly again, making himself laugh, "But, you know, that saying what happens in Vegas stays in Vegas? It's kind of like that but it don't stay in Vegas…"

"Bloody hell!" Emmeline gasped. Leigh sniggered.

"Honestly, Ems, it's not that bad. It's just the few…er…more active and adventurous ones REALLY love to tell their tales. Sometimes it sounds worse than it is." Leigh told her, reassuringly. "I'm sure it happens in other workplaces…" she trailed off.

"Are you one?" Emmeline asked.

"One what?" Leigh said.

"Are *you* active and adventurous, Leigh?" Lucas clarified, knowing eyebrows raised at her. Leigh sneered at him. Of course he already knew the response. She was going to keep it under her hat.

"Me? I'm a lady. I keep my mouth shut." She answered.

Lucas snorted, "Only while you swallow!"

Leigh threw a cushion from behind her on the sofa she was leaning against and the rest of them fell about laughing.

"So," Sue started again, as the laughter died down, "We're thinking Ricky's batting for the other side then?"

"Pretty confident." Brandon confirmed "Eh, Lucas?"

Lucas pretended to choke on the can he was drinking from.

Catching Leigh's eye contact, he nodded. "Oh yeh, definitely not available to you, I'm afraid, Susannah."

"Bloody hell it's 3am!" Leigh exclaimed.

Emmeline and Carl looked shocked at the time, Brandon and Sue appeared to have already been aware of the time but not caring.

"Sorry gang, but that's me done for the night. Beauty sleep needed!" Leigh leapt up, gathered the notes she'd brought with her and stumbled over the pizza boxes and 'resus Annies' on the floor, trying not to step on anyone.

"Sorry!" she mumbled with a giggle as she almost fell on the Brandon's lap.

"Steady on girl!" he grinned.

"More tired than I thought!" she apologised.

He grabbed her hand to help steady her. As she headed towards the door, Lucas got up and brushed himself down too.

"Hang on love, I'll walk you back on my way."

After passing around more 'goodnights' and 'goodbyes' and 'see you in the mornings', Lucas and Leigh finally made their way out to the corridor and the door was closed behind them.

They walked in silence a little further away from the room before talking.

They knew Emmeline and Sue and Brandon had been starting to think about leaving too; and neither wanted to risk being overheard discussing Ricky.

"So…" Lucas broached, as they went through a heavy fire door that partitioned the corridor.

"So…what?" Leigh asked him.

"Oh, come on. First day, I saw you and him come in to lunch at the same time chatting, so you've definitely touched base with him without telling me."

Leigh stopped and turned to face Lucas, leaning back

against the wall.

"Nothing has happened." She told him. "I was hanging back to sort out some of my notes – I told you that. He came over to say hi and just checked that we were OK, and that everything was…ok…and we agreed that everything was…fine…and then he said, fine, let's go and join everyone for lunch. And we've been fine ever since."

"That's all?"

"That's all. He hasn't even said hello to you?" Leigh queried.

Lucas was silent. He opened his mouth as though about to speak, then looked away, as though searching for the right words.

"Lucas?"

"OK, yes. We spoke. And then…" he trailed off.

Leigh became aware of a sinking feeling developing in the pit of her stomach. "And then what, Lucas?"

Lucas was looking down at the floor; seemingly gathering the courage to continue; when they were interrupted by Brandon, Sue and Emmeline. The three were giggling, muttering quietly, trying but failing to make their way back to their rooms quietly for the benefit of any other guests in the corridor.

"You two still here?" Sue asked as they burst through the fire door.

"SH SH SH!" Brandon over-exaggerated in a failed attempt to keep the noise down.

"On our way, just comparing notes about our base." Leigh offered as though it was explanation enough.

Emmeline yawned and shook her head. "Too late for me...night everyone..." she wandered off, fishing her room key from her pocket and disappearing into her room a few doors down. Sue and Brandon shrugged and offered silent goodbyes to Leigh and Lucas by patting them on the shoulder and each disappeared into their own rooms.

After they were out of sight, Leigh grabbed Lucas's hand and guided him to her room. She opened her own door, and pushed him in first, following and closing the door behind her.

Lucas slumped down on the small blue sofa that ran along one wall parallel to the bed. The rooms were all pretty identical. The sofa-beds were used to double as single put-me-up beds if a family or twin room was booked. As each of the recruits had a room to themselves, for privacy and to aid study periods they had been told, and they were there for 6 weeks all in all, the sofas were a welcome alternative to a sitting room.

Leigh perched on the edge of the bed, facing him.

Neither of them said anything for what seemed like an age. Leigh had a feeling she didn't really want to know what he was about to tell her, Lucas was struggling to put into words what he had known was supposed to be secret.

Leigh was first to break the silence. "You slept with him?"

Lucas looked at her, held her gaze for a moment, then shook his head. "Nah, hardly call it that. We just…"

"OK, but something happened?"

Lucas nodded sheepishly.

"Oh Lucas!" Leigh felt so let down and betrayed, by both of them.

It wasn't even that she felt jealous.

They had shared him once, it wasn't as though one had been chosen over the other.

She was disappointed in them both, for giving in when they both knew it wasn't to happen. They'd all agreed, the three of them, and she'd fought so hard to make it OK over a cup of tea on the first morning. And Ricky had seemed so confident that everything was ok between them…and that's when it struck her.

She WAS jealous. At least a little bit. Ricky had managed to abstain when it came to her. But had given in to do…whatever…with Lucas?

Leigh couldn't think of anything else to say. She wasn't sure she really wanted to know what the 'something' was that had happened.

"It wasn't anything much…"

"I don't want to know." Leigh confirmed, as much to herself as to Lucas.

But it seemed to Lucas that he needed to get it out. "After our swimming tests, on Friday…"

Of course…Leigh cottoned on. There were more women than men on their course. The men's dressing room would have been a hell of a lot quieter than the women's…easy to overhear each other's conversations.

"Brandon had been ribbing Carl into discussing blow jobs, so the conversation fell into that; Brandon dragged me into it. Pretty soon the room had cleared out and it was only me and Ricky left in the whole dressing room. Ricky decided to carry on the conversation…"

Leigh could understand. Ricky had been last out of the pool and back to the dressing room. She knew, she'd been watching him, lifting diving aids and equipment out of the pool and clearing away rescue dummies they'd been practising pulling from the pool.

She'd been convinced at one point they'd briefly caught each other's eye; but he'd glanced away so quickly she had told herself she'd imagined it. She had sucked up the courage to turn away, and ducked into the ladies changing room to get change. She had headed straight for one of the private shower cubicles and closed the door, removed her swimsuit and responded alone to her body's sudden need to be touched. She'd masturbated herself to an orgasm with the image of Ricky, damp, in his swimming shorts, lifting the heavy equipment fresh in her mind. She had been so glad he'd not noticed her; scared of what might have happened.

And now she found out that at the same time, next door, he was doing...goodness knows what...with Lucas.

What she couldn't have known was that Ricky HAD seen her watching him. And it had irritated him, to the point of distraction, the thought of her in her swimsuit, thin scraps of material covering her body.

When he'd entered the male changing room and walked in on bolshie Brandon's chat about blow-jobs; and hearing comparisons of Carl suggesting girls he'd known (making it clear he'd never talk about his wife that way so these were girls he'd known before getting married); and Brandon telling him boys were better given their intricate knowledge of the penis...Ricky had tried his best to not get turned on.

He'd shrugged off their attempts to drag him in to the conversation; holding an air of authority over them as his reasons for separating and heading for the showers with his towel strategically held at his waist to avoid them noticing the growing bulge in his shorts.

Out of view, he'd still been within earshot and took in every morsel of their conversation; especially when Lucas joined in. Lucas had been in a changing cubicle when Ricky had walked through; up until hearing his voice joining in, Ricky had thought it was only Brandon and Carl in there.

Ricky was attempting to cool his ardour with a cold shower as he listened to them. And their subject matter was not helping. He turned the hot tap off completely so the water turned icy.

It was working until Lucas had taken over the narrative, describing the first time he'd been presented with a male penis to practice with, at 17, and he'd not seen anything bigger since.

Lucas had picked up his description of events to Leigh at the point where he was telling them of his exploits.

He had been getting in to so much detail that Carl had been increasingly uncomfortable, and being pretty much dressed had grabbed his belongings and bowed out politely, cutting Lucas off mid-description and leaving Brandon laughing. Brandon had announced that he, too, was pretty much done, and wasn't waiting around in here.

"So Brandon and Carl left, said they'd see me in the breakout room after. I had this hard-on and just wanted to, you know…quickly…before I went out…so I went into the shower. I honestly didn't know Ricky was in there…"

Leigh felt her breathing shallow. She couldn't believe she was letting herself get excited by listening to Lucas's story. She felt her labia begin to contract a little, moving on from twinges she'd felt earlier. The more Lucas talked, describing his experience, the less she felt like she wanted to stop him.

"He didn't see me at first. Pretty sure he didn't know I was there – his shorts were off."

Leigh's eyes widened. Lucas looked at her, as though waiting for permission to continue. She barely moved; he took her lack of response, lack of protest as a sign to continue.

"He was there, pumping himself with his hand…and I just…well…I watched. 'Course I was getting turned on, I should have left quickly, I know. But…oh God, Leigh, you should have seen him. The water was cold…I could tell coz his nipples were, like, out here…" Lucas made a motion with his hands against his own chest, "Rock hard. Dunno why he was feeling he needed a cold shower but it clearly wasn't working. I dropped my shampoo and he turned around."

"And?" Leigh was egging him on to finish, now.

Lucas shrugged. "And…look, Leigh, I was convinced he was going to get angry, tell me to get out of there, but he didn't say anything. I dunno…with all the talk of blowjobs and, well, he was certainly…*ready*. I just…" Lucas's voice trailed off.

"Oh my god Lucas! You gave him a BJ at the pool?"

Lucas nodded sheepishly.

"And then what?" Leigh needed to know how it was left. For something they were all supposed to forget about, their hook-up encounter after Kevin's house-party seemed to be causing all sorts of subliminal difficulties now that the three of them were working in a totally different dynamic to where they had been at the time.

"Nothing."

"Nothing?"

"I finished. He finished...I mean...when it was over, I got up, washed under the other shower; he turned around and finished his shower and then he went to get changed." Lucas shrugged.

"You didn't talk about it? Didn't agree to 'not let it happen again'? Nothing?"

"Look, Leigh...we did all that at your place. This isn't a thing. It's not a relationship. It was just something that happened. I'm OK with that. That's how he treats me, how I see him. You, on the other hand..."

Leigh felt like she'd been prodded with an electric shock. "What about me?"

Lucas shook his head and looked her straight in the eye.

"Look, every time he enters a room, you take notice. Every time he's mentioned your eyes go into this faraway look... I'm quite happy to use him and be used for sexual pleasure. You are in love with him."

"I am not!" Leigh snapped. Feeling the need to change the subject quickly, she challenged him. "You want sexual pleasure? Fine... I can do that too..."

Leigh stood up and sat next to him on the sofa and

kissed him softly but firmly.

Lucas shuffled back away from her and sniggered at her. "You don't mean it."

"Wanna bet?" Leigh challenged him, indignantly.

How dare he suggest he knew anything about her feelings? She was determined to show him. She moved towards him again and kissed him harder.

Lucas kissed her back. He was out of his comfort zone a little, without another man there to be his main point of concentration. His only experience of girls was Leigh...as a side-show to Ricky.

And here she was...clearly turned on by his description of his shower encounter; and challenging him to take back his analysis of her feelings. He'd seen her rocking her pelvis subconsciously on the bed opposite him as he'd spoken, as she attempted to deal with the wetness that was building.

He wasn't sure what to do. He'd gone down on her, of course, and during their threesome, and Ricky had guided him to her anus while Ricky had been rocking in and out of her vagina. Sod it, he thought, just go with it. Leigh was exploring his mouth with hers, kneeling on the sofa, over him, now. He closed his eyes and raised his hand slowly and brushed it across her breast, to which she responded with a moan into his mouth, and her nipple sprang to attention under the thin fabric.

She didn't break the kiss for a moment but her hands

began to fumble with his pajama bottoms, he instinctively raised his behind so she could pull them down enough to expose his erect penis.

Leigh stopped kissing him and started directly into his eyes, without a hint of emotion, but full of determination and purpose. She removed her own pajama shorts, and straddled him. She was soaking wet and slid down onto him with ease, not dropping eye contact for a second.

Lucas's mouth opened with an involuntary gasp as he felt the warm softness of her surrounding him. She wasn't as tight as what he was used to, this seemed a much easier fit, a different experience for him entirely. She removed her top as she began to move up and down on him. Her small, pert breasts were directly in front of him when she rose. She closed her eyes.

He knew full well she was totally fantasising about anyone else but him – most likely Ricky – but that didn't stop Lucas immersing himself in this experience that for all he knew, he wouldn't experience again. He leaned forward and took one of her nipples in his mouth and sucked hard.

Leigh raised her arms and stretched above her head, before steadying herself again with one hand on the back of the sofa; she took her other hand and placed it on the back of his head, using it to guide his head between one breast and the other, as he took it in turns to suck and nibble each one.

The more he concentrated, the harder he sucked and

nibbled the more frantic her movements up and down his penis became. Within minutes, she began to shudder, move faster still and then, held his head closer to her chest as she reached her climax and sank down one final time around him.

Lucas leant back a little to watch her.

The state of complete release and ecstasy showed on her flushed face, he was fascinated. He had the sudden urge to come himself, and so from nowhere built the motivation to stand, lifting her with him deftly, and some acrobatic move whereby he lay her down on the floor in front of the sofa with himself on top without once separating their groins enough to remove his penis from inside her.

Leigh opened her eyes and looked at him in shock at his sudden masculine authority. He placed a hand either side of her head and began pumping himself up and down, in and out of her as though he'd known what to do his whole life.

Leigh lay there, watching him, in awe of his natural ability, and after a couple of minutes, decided to join in and help him along a little.

She took her right hand down to her clitoris, still soaking wet from her juices having flowed and been spread everywhere. She rubbed for a few seconds, bringing her back to a peak ready for another orgasm.

Then, using the wetness on her fingers, she reached round his taught midriff and found his buttocks. As his thrusts became more and more powerful and determined, she waited for the exact moment, and inserted her wet index finger into his anus. Lucas groaned in ecstasy as almost in direct response he ejaculated deeply inside her. Leigh responded by contracting her abdomen muscles and those inside her vagina tightly around him and releasing her own orgasm at the same time.

They froze in that position of release for seemingly endless moments, the only movements were the twitching of his penis inside her. When the initial shock wore off, he collapsed on top of her and she wrapped her arms around him in a hug, seemingly of congratulations, or simple comfort. A little more time went by as they lay there before he rolled off and lay next to her on the floor. They both stared up at the celling.

"Oh my god" Leigh finally said.

"Wow!" Lucas responded.

They both rolled onto their sides to look at each other. Leighs expression was defiant, challenging, waiting for him to say something else first.

Lucas felt equally defiant, however. He simply got up and made his way to the bathroom, bending down to pick up his pajama bottoms first.

Leigh watched him go, a little in shock.

She got up, dressed herself, went over to flick the small hotel-room kettle on, and reached for two cups.

She dug around in the little pot of single-serve beverages and found two instant hot-chocolate sachets. She heard the shower briefly, and by the time the kettle had finished boiling and she poured the water, Lucas came out of the bathroom drying his hair with a towel. She was sat on the desk chair, and Lucas planted himself in the small bucket arm-chair that was at the end of the desk-come-table. Leigh passed him one of the mugs and they sat in a comfortable silence, sipping, and making eye contact over the rims.

"You know that's not going to happen again, right?" Lucas asked her quietly.

"I know. I wouldn't expect it to." Leigh answered matter-of-factly.

"Don't think I don't know you weren't thinking of him the whole time." Lucas smirked, sounding, all of a sudden, more camp than he had all evening.

Leigh looked at him, cocking her head to one side sassily. "Like you weren't?"

"Nah. His cock feels bigger in my ass!" Lucas winked at her. Leigh was speechless and just widened her eyes, half amused, half shocked.

Leigh drained her hot chocolate and put the mug down. She stretched her arms above her head again and without another word, stood up, wandered over to the bed and climbed between the crisp white sheets and pulled the duvet over her. Lucas watched her settle down, and she looked back at him, sweetly.

There seemed to be some unspoken bond now, telling them both that their friendship was still intact; and that this experience would be another one that would never be shared with anyone else.

Leigh closed her eyes and settled down, she could feel sleep creeping up on her.

Lucas watched as he drank the rest of his hot chocolate. After a moment's thought, he went around the other side of the bed, climbed in under the duvet next to her and put a protective arm over her. Leigh, drifting off to sleep snuggled into him, and within minutes they were both in the deepest sleep either of them had enjoyed for a long time.

-10-

"Why didn't they tell me in advance there was going to be a photographer here?" Emmeline exclaimed as she straightened her neck-tie scarf in the mirror of the ladies bathroom at the training centre.

"Longest six bloody weeks of my life." Chimed the disembodied voice of Miriam, in her broad Glaswegian accent, from the cubicle behind them.

Emmeline, Leigh and Sue were touching up their make-up in the ladies' room before their graduation ceremony.

In full uniform, there was a renewed sense of excitement, and impending sadness.

Leigh looked back at the girls next to her in the mirror. Six weeks ago she didn't know them.

And this time next week she would be in work without them. They'd be heading back to their respective bases, only to pass each other briefly in Alicante or Prague on an aircraft changeover; or seeing each other's names scribbled in the cabin logbook.

"And no more sexy instructor to gaze at…!" shouted Sue

with frustration. Emmeline and Miriam laughed along with her.

Leigh smiled, more to cover any subliminal desires she may betray if she didn't.

"Oh come on, ladies, one word….flight deck…" Miriam offered an over-exaggerated wink.

"That's two words…" Emmeline corrected her, seriously.

Sue snorted with laughter in a very unladylike fashion.

"Yeah? Well, Man in uniform is three. Still means the same thing…" stated Miriam, before putting on a deep, Austin-Powers-esque accent, "…Sexy!"

"Seriously…you haven't seen half the flight deck crew at my place…you're in for a wakeup call!" Leigh laughed at her.

"Hey, I don't need half of them, darlin', just the one'll do me…." Miriam said.

"…at a time…!" Sue added and everyone laughed again as they all headed for the door.

They strolled down the hall to the conference room where they'd first started their classroom training.

Gloria and Connor were back, along with 7 other members of the *YouKayAir* board of directors; and a few other notable members of staff, who had all been introduced at some point but remembering their names at this point hadn't seemed a priority.

"Well, speaking of men in uniform, don't we brush up nicely, boys?" Sue stated in almost honest surprise at quite how smart the rest of their group looked.

Lucas had calmed his floppy curls a little; his hair controlled just enough to stay in place over to one side without being gelled to within an inch of its life.

Carl seemed extremely comfortable in his uniform, carrying himself well and exhibiting an air of confidence they hadn't really noticed in him before.

Leigh had seen him in work as the laid back, fatherly type who just smiled along with the office gossip, but rarely interacted with any sticky situation, always preferring to be the backup.

But this Carl was oozing customer service approachability from every pore. Even Sue was impressed.

"Ooh if he weren't so…married…" she whispered to Leigh, causing her to laugh out loud, attracting the attention of some of the suits in the corner. Leigh bit her lip and looked down, embarrassed.

Within seconds she felt comforted by a familiar arm draped around her shoulder. Lucas whispered in her ear. "We did it! Can you believe it?" He asked her, wide eyed.

Leigh felt a rush of relief that she'd had Lucas there to

lean on for the tough weeks they'd experienced.

After the two of them had woken in her room, the morning after the conversation about Ricky in the changing rooms, everything between them had miraculously returned to normal, once again. Lucas had jumped up, realising the time, and comically run around the room looking for his clothes, making Leigh laugh as she came to.

"Idiot!" she'd told him, "You came in your PJs"

He'd stopped and looked at her with a sarcastic grin. "I think we both did, didn't we?" and he'd followed it with a genuine smile.

Leigh instantly felt like this was something they had taken in their stride; and had felt a wave of gratitude to have a friend like him. He'd rushed over, kissed her affectionately on the top of her head and ruffled her hair as though she were a child, and rushed for the door, grabbing his room key and pile of books from the shelf next to the door where he'd dumped them on the way in the night before.

As he left, he shouted "See you in class, hun." And she'd shaken her head as she climbed out of bed, in a vain attempt to clear it somewhat from the late night they'd had. She'd opened the thick blackout curtains and found a beautiful, sunny, early spring day.

The weather remained like that for their remaining time; which had helped on days where they were taken to the airfield to practice on some of *YouKayAir*'s real aircraft, that had been grounded for maintenance or were otherwise not being used on that particular day.

There were certain hours that Ricky had set aside for them all to study for their written exams, and they took advantage of the grassy area to the side of the HQ building and sat in the sun testing each other on questions.

Ricky had seemingly been true to the silent promise between himself and Lucas. He'd acted between them, and in front of everyone, like there was nothing amiss.

By Wednesday last week, after they'd all sat their exams that day, the remaining two days were to be filled with completing paperwork and administrative bits and pieces to sign for their uniforms and apply for their airside passes at various airports; Ricky had even joined them for drinks at the hotel bar.

Lucas and Ricky had a quick chat about good bars to visit in Barcelona when Lucas and Brandon went on a city-break visit they had agreed upon during some leave they planned to coincide in a few months for Brandon's birthday; and Leigh had noted how the two of them spoke like the old friends they were before she and Lucas had started their training here.

When the music had started playing a little louder, following a request to the bar manager, Ricky had grabbed Leigh by the hand and dragged her to the dancefloor.

Not one of their companions batted an eyelid. After all,

it had become common knowledge by now that they were old friends from their base, and it had been proven from experience that Ricky had no favouritism in class, Lucas, Carl and Leigh had not benefitted from any special treatment during training at all.

During a slow-dance, Ricky had looked into Leigh's eyes and double checked, simply with, "We're OK, right?" and she'd nodded.

"Of course! Can't wait to get back to work!" she smiled at him, as they continued moving around the floor until the end of the song. Immediately after that, Ricky had said goodnight, telling them this was their time as new recruits to celebrate and he needed his beauty sleep.

Despite numerous protestations about him definitely not needing any more beauty sleep than he was already getting, he took his leave and the rest of them had enjoyed their night.

Many had suffered for it the next morning; but rather than being a tyrant, Ricky was amused; he had, after all, pretty much given them permission; since Thursday was mostly paperwork.

And here they were, on Friday, ready to be awarded their wings.

Captain Anders Monroe, the fleet captain; and his deputy Captain Sarah Morris, were the ones tasked with handing out the small pewter lapel pins to each of the new cabin crew members who had passed their final exams. They did so with an air of authority and gravitas, letting each new hostie know over their handshake that they were from now on tasked with the safety and security of the passengers on board every flight. They needed to remember that beyond the smiles and the answering questions and helping put a bag in the overhead locker; it was their knowledge and experience that could someday save lives, and that, at the end of the day, was what they were on board for.

Each and every one of them accepted the advice, and the pin, with pride.

They smiled proudly for their individual photograph with the Captains, followed by a group photo with Ricky on one side and Gloria on the other to commemorate their training group.

There was a great sense of excitement when Ricky pointed out that their group photograph would go up on display alongside all the other previous years' graduating classes photographs in the foyer; and that this being his first year as training officer, would be the first photograph with him in it.

He also reminded them to behave themselves and not make any mistakes; otherwise they'd make him look bad. "And you all love me so you wouldn't want that, right?" he had asked them, with a wink; to which they'd all replied "No!" almost simultaneously. Leigh felt a wave of self-conscious heat rise in her cheeks, recalling Lucas's suggestion that she was in love with Ricky. Glancing around and realising no one had the slightest notion of her discomfort, she took a couple of deep breaths and pushed the thoughts aside; just in time to beam brightly for the photos.

And so, they had ended their final day. Most of them were leaving straight away. Heading back to their home bases that evening to make the most of a well-deserved weekend off, before getting their first rosters on Monday morning. Leigh and Lucas were two who were. They had offered Carl a ride back up the M4 with them, but he'd declined. Sally and the kids, he said, were coming down to join him and they were going to make it a weekend in London.

"See you Monday!" Lucas shouted to Carl through the wound down window as Leigh started the car and slowly nudged her way out of her parking space and headed for the car park exit. Lucas reclined his passenger seat a little and put on his sunglasses against the setting sun they'd be heading towards on their two hour drive up the motorway.

Ricky came out of the HQ building just as their car left. He stood next to Carl who was checking his watch.

"Hey, Carl. You not heading back?"

"Nah, family coming down for a weekend in the city. Should be here in about half an hour"

"Ah, making the most of it, eh?"

"Yup. Hey, thanks mate, you're a really good teacher, by the way!" Carl offered his hand and was surprised at how strong Ricky's grip actually was, considering he'd had him down as batting for the other side, after the study group conversation.

"Well, let's hope it shows through in everyone's work, eh? Listen, I'll see you on Monday, I'll have some rosters to hand out in the crew room but pretty sure you three will have an easy week to begin with."

"Sounds good to me! You heading home yourself?" Carl queried.

"Yeah."

"Shame, you just missed those two, could have jumped in with them."

"Nah," Ricky told him, attempting not to give away his real reasoning, "Can you imagine being stuck in a car with those two all the way back?"

Carl laughed and nodded, knowingly.

"Listen, I'll see you Monday?" Ricky said.

"Yeah, take care buddy."

Ricky jumped into his car and slid on his shades. He pulled out of the car park leaving Carl stood alone, checking his mobile phone. He glanced up and watched as Ricky disappeared out of view.

-11-

A clear Monday morning in mid-April seemed to be promising to be a sunny day. If anything like the past week they'd had, then a very hot one too.

Sasha was alone.

She was perched on a stool in the Customs office, head resting on a hand that was supported by her elbow leaning on the windowsill. The morning cargo flight trundled past and she checked her watch, taxying at 5.30am, right on time. She sipped her coffee and concentrated on the hum of machinery from outside, in an attempt to focus her thoughts.

Col had entered as the plane had blocked out the noise of the door opening. When his arm snaked around her waist from behind she was a little startled bringing her back to the present.

"Hey," he whispered. "You OK?" Sasha turned her head to him and nodded. He picked up her coffee and took a long gulp. He grimaced at the taste.

"There's no sugar in it." She reminded him.

"Hmm." He acknowledged, handing the cup back to her. He kissed her on the cheek. "You're here early."

"Missed you." she admitted, looking into his eyes. Col smiled at her and put his other arm around her, hugging her from behind as they both watched through the window.

"You're gonna be tired," He said.

Col had been on a night shift; Sasha was about to start training the new Summer-season ground staff recruits.

In a month's time, the airlines' summer schedules would kick in, including far more 'holiday' flights; charter flights to holiday hot-spots, carrying mainly package-holiday-makers to resorts across Europe and short-haul destinations.

The summer season's bloated schedule meant the ground-staff numbers were boosted by at least 20 new members of staff. Some returned year upon year; some were youngsters on their way to university; others started and shone and were offered permanent contracts at the end of the summer season.

"I couldn't sleep." She told him. This was true. She wasn't sure if it was that he wasn't there; or whether she was just nervous about taking on the new trainees on her own. In the past she'd had Leigh there for banter and as a back-up. This year would be different. And to be honest, most of this year had been a little strange without Leigh.

Col kissed her on the head and left her, walked over to his desk to sort out the paperwork he'd brought in with him. Sasha watched him.

She couldn't help wonder if it was her fault. She wondered if her spending so much time with Col since they had met had somehow driven Leigh away to look for a new job – she'd never mentioned cabin crew aspirations before.

Sasha wondered what else she didn't know about her friend.

Now she was worrying that she was having second thoughts about her relationship. Was the fact that she was no longer very interested in their girls' nights out; that they weren't the twosome they had once been anymore because of Sasha spending more and more of her time with Col?

Sasha shook her head a little, trying to clear it. She was having trouble understanding the overly-emotional state that seemed to have taken over her these days.

"I'm going to head over the office and get the paperwork sorted." Sasha told him, heading over and kissing him on the cheek from behind and headed towards the door.

"Hey!" he stopped her. Sasha turned to find him right in front of her, having covered the distance between them in a couple of strides. "That wasn't much of a parting kiss, was it?" He didn't wait for a response and bent down and kissed her.

Sasha closed her eyes. When the kiss ended she rested her head against his chest as he hugged her tightly, and she breathed his scent deeply.

"I really missed you last night." She told him.

"I'm gonna miss you today" he said in response. "If you're lucky I might cook for when you get home…"

"I'd rather you didn't…" Sasha raised her eyebrows and shot him a sarcastic look. Col laughed.

"Hey, there's nothing wrong with my cooking!" He showed mock offence.

"If you say so!" She smiled, "I'd rather you concentrated on getting more sleep though."

"I'll try. Won't be easy without you there."

"Soppy git" Sasha murmured and kissed him briefly again before purposefully heading for the door to avoid getting interrupted again.

She wandered out of his office with a wave in his direction. She walked through the baggage office just as Olga shuffled in, taking off her overcoat and hanging it on the coat stand in the corner.

"Morning Olga." Sasha smiled at her.

"Morning! You're early aren't you?" Olga quizzed, "Not been up to anything in there?" Olga cocked her head towards the office door and winked. Sasha laughed.

"Not this morning! Just came in early to get myself organised for the newbies."

"Ah, that time of year again!" Olga flicked on the switch of the kettle in the corner. "Col on night shifts, isn't he?"

"Yeah, Won't see much of each other this week really."

"Aw shame. You getting on ok?" Olga seemed genuinely interested, possibly, Sasha thought as she looked at the older woman, a hint of concern?

"Getting on?" Sasha asked

"Well, you know, you've been together a while now…"

"Over a year…" Sasha trailed off and suddenly came to the realisation that this was by far her longest ever relationship. No wonder she was feeling a little apprehensive…

"You know, I was married to the same man for 47 years before Noel died." Olga stated; as though, in a way it was a standalone statement. Until after a beat, she turned and gave Sasha a knowing glance. "Don't worry if you feel like things are changing occasionally. Relationships evolve." Olga shrugged. She looked at Sasha and cocked her head at Sasha's slightly furrowed brow. "Oh love I didn't mean to scare you! Changes for the good I mean. Don't worry; you've got a good one there." Olga reached out and rubbed Sasha's shoulder.

Sasha smiled, then took her leave and made her way back to the Passenger Services office.

By the time she got there, it was six o'clock and Mina was already in, fiddling with the display system and putting the flight numbers, destinations and airline logos on the screens above each check-in desk ready for the morning's check-ins to open.

Pilar had been in since 5, manning the bag-drop desk at the end of the row, for the cluster of morning commuter flights, usually full of their regular business travellers on small turbo-prop Jetstream41s or Embraer jets, heading off to Paris or Brussels, Belfast or Aberdeen.

Within an hour, between 7 and 8, they'd all take off, along with flights to Newcastle and London City airport.

Sasha was absentmindedly inspecting the check-in planner on the wall that roughly laid out the duties of everyone rostered that day when Mina called to her without lifting her head from the ops desk.

"Can you dispatch the Paris this morning? Reuben's going over to do that football flight so he'll be too far away."

"Hmm?" Sasha snapped back into a lucid state. "Eh? What football flight?"

"It's on your Mayfly." Mina by this time had stood up and was looking at her, eyebrows raised, through the doorway between the ops office and the passenger services connecting office. "You do have a mayfly, don't you? You've been in 5 minutes and you haven't memorised it? You're slipping." Mina rolled her eyes and turned back to her desk, without awaiting an answer.

Sasha dug around in her pocket for the folded paper she'd stuffed in there earlier. "I've been here an hour, and *I'm* the one who printed them off this morning, if you don't mind!" she stated as she found it.

The list of flights they handled that were scheduled to depart that day along with all the scheduled departure times, in both local time and UTC, or universal time coordinated.

Sasha hated the part of the training course where she had to try and explain the use of GMT, or 'Zulu' time, to the newbies; almost as much as they hated using it. But was a necessary evil when it came to dealing with flights that crossed time zones and communicating arrivals and departures with other airports around the world. At least they were only ever 1 hour off GMT for half of the year. She dreaded to think how aviation staff in faraway countries with time differences of hours managed to cope using to simultaneous times when dealing with passengers on one side, and computer systems and other airports on the other.

"It's not like Stephen to not put them out for this morning." Mina mused.

"I don't think the reges came through 'till late though." Sasha told her. "The *Midlantic* ones were still on the printer when I came in so I had to put them in myself."

Sasha was referring to the registrations, or tail number, of the aircraft that would be operating each flight.

The airlines' operations department assigned the aircraft

to the routes the night before, usually; after taking stock of certain things like which vehicle had enough hours left to fly on it before it was due a maintenance line-check or other scheduled down-time.

The registrations were then included on the mayflys for ground staff so they knew which aircraft to go to if they were sent to deal with a particular flight.

Mina tried to hide the fact that she was a little impressed. "That might explain it then. Thanks Sasha." Mina turned back to her desk and busied herself paperwork.

As they had been speaking, the rest of the morning's check-in staff had been filtering in, signing in, collecting mayflies, opening check-ins.

By the time Sasha looked out across the check-in hall again it was infinitely busier than it had been earlier. At the other end of the hall, the other ground handling company were busy checking in another of the season's early charter holiday flights. It looked mildly comical in their UK climate at 6.30 in the morning to see people shivering in shorts and t-shirts and flip-flops queueing in a less than warm check-in queue.

A thought occurred to Sasha. "What shall I do about the flight paperwork? For the Paris I mean?"

"Steve's back in at 7.30. Probably why he didn't stay late last night."

"Another double shift? He's pushing it, isn't he?"

"After Duty Manager job I think," Mina mused. "Anyway, he'll be up in time to do the Aberdeen and the Brussels so he should be able to do your load sheet. If not, gimme a shout and I'll do it down here and send it to the printer at Gate 5, he can check it and sign it for you."

"Is it on time?" Sasha asked, glancing at the pile of induction manuals she'd been preparing for the new staff; who'd all been under strict instructions to arrive ready for their first day by 9am.

Mina caught on. "There'll be plenty in by then to come and relieve you if it has a slot." she told Sasha, referring to Air traffic restrictions that staggered take offs to fit in with the flow of traffic on the main flight paths.

Sasha sighed deeply and grabbed her hi-viz tabard and ear-defenders, and took the passenger list and load-plan paperwork that Mina was holding out to her.

She wandered out of the office, past Pilar at the end check in. "Any Specials?" Sasha asked her colleague.

"Nope. There was an *UM* but they haven't turned up yet; check in closes in five minutes."

"Jordan?" Sasha asked. He was the most regular Unaccompanied Minor they saw on the flights to and from Paris. He attended a prestigious boarding school out in the countryside and flew to his parents for the holidays.

Pilar nodded. "Yeah."

"Well, they should know better, they're always here for check-in early to make sure he gets escorted to the gate. Nothing else?" Pilar shook her head, Sasha shrugged in return and waved her hand absent-mindedly, before turning and heading for the security access to airside.

She removed her shoes, and placed them with her walkie-talkie and everything else from her pockets into a tray to go through the x-ray.

John and Lizzie were deep in conversation about some big storyline on last night's soaps, and so barely missing a beat in their discussion as they went through the motions of John pressing the button to begin the belt through the x-ray and looking at the screen, knowing full well he'd see nothing he didn't see twenty times a day already as staff he had known for years passed through this access. Lizzie looked at Sasha's work ID, held up for her from the lanyard around Sasha's neck, with a sarcastic grin.

"Nice mugshot!" Lizzie joked, knowing full well Sasha hated her photograph and had done for years. The passes doubled as access cards to swipe through doors throughout the terminal building and the cost of replacing them negated anyone applying for a new one for frivolous reasons like a new photo. Sasha had at one point considered dying her hair just to get a new photo; but she'd never looked good as a brunette; and pink, blue and purple and pretty much anything else 'un-natural' were frowned upon in the uniform regulations. As she put her shoes back on, waved at them while walking away, she mused as to whether Col would appreciate some unconventional hair colour.

Sasha headed through the baggage sort area, now bustling with baggage handlers loading the baggage from the check-ins onto various large trailers and peeling a sticker section off each bag as they loaded it, then sticking it onto a card to log what had been loaded on that trailer. She poked her head around the door of the baggage supervisor's office. Frenchy was in there, resting his head on the desk.

"Late night?" She surprised him and he jolted up.

He shook his head. "I wasn't sleeping!"

"Nah, course you weren't. Load plan for the Paris." She told him, holding out one of the pieces of paper Mina had given her.

Frenchy took it and frowned as he scanned it. "You sure? Looks a bit tail heavy this way round."

Sasha shrugged. "Dunno, I didn't plan it. Speak to Mina."

Frenchy nodded to her.

Sasha smiled and headed off towards the pier, the long corridor protruding from the terminal building where most of the boarding gates were located.

By the time Sasha got to Gate 7, via gate 5 to ensure the printer was loaded with paper and turned on to receive the paperwork, the aircraft on Stand 7 adjacent to her gate had already been opened up. She turned on the computer at the gate, and headed out to see who was there. She had glanced at the load sheet and hadn't recognised the name Mina had put under the section that named the captain.

She climbed on board and glanced down the deserted cabin, dark as it had been all night. *No life at all*, she told herself with a frown. Suddenly she heard a noise from the flight deck and the door opened to reveal Tom Klein.

In his late fifties, Tom had been chief engineer for the *YouKay Air* base since they started up here and based three of their 737s at the airport. He'd been with *Air Midlantic* for years before that and, like many others around the airport, seemed like part of the furniture, regardless of which uniform he was wearing. In this morning's case, a blue boiler suit, covered in oil and goodness knows what else. Sasha smiled at him brightly.

"Morning Tom!" She said.

As was his way, Tom looked at her gruffly and nodded, with little more than a grunted "mornin'". Sasha stepped back into the galley opposite the door and let him pass.

He barely watched his footing, sure of his way around the aircraft and the attached steps, as he scribbled away on his report on the checklist on the clipboard in his hand.

Sasha watched him go. As he headed into the engineering office under the pier, door wide open to keep an eye on the aircraft that was in his charge until the arrival of the captain, something caught Sasha's eye. Flashes of blue and red in a bustle of movement heading across the tarmac towards her. At last, she thought, checking her watch. She should be calling the passengers within 5 minutes before they start complaining to the information desk...

As the crew got closer, Sasha's mood soared. There, amongst the familiar faces, sporting her new uniform like she'd been wearing it her whole life, was Leigh, deep in conversation with her fellow crew members.

Leigh glanced up and initially wasn't sure how Sasha was going to react. Of course, they'd been in touch for the whole time she'd been away with the odd text message promising to meet up as soon as her course had finished and she was back.

This hadn't happened, not through any fault on either side.

She'd only had a couple of days before her first rostered flight; and Sasha had already said she'd be preparing for the new course. But still it seemed like there was some rift; some effort that might be needed to be as friendly as they had been. Or so Leigh thought...

Almost as soon as her mind had been made up to raise her hand and wave at Sasha, Sasha had started bounding down the steps and trotting across the apron as fast as she could in her court shoe heels; launching herself at her friend in a bear hug.

"Finally! I've been itching to see you in your uniform!" gushed Sasha, throwing her arms around her. Leigh heaved a sigh of relief and grinned at her.

"Feels weird!" Leigh confided. "Almost walked in to the passenger services office this morning!" She laughed, and Sasha joined in.

The rest of the crew had started making their way up the steps apart from the Captain, who had removed her hat and left it on her briefcase at the bottom of the steps and began wandering around the aircraft, checking doors and seals.

Sasha frowned as she watched her. "Who's that?" she asked.

"Roberta Harris!" Leigh said, her tone suggesting Sasha should have recognised her.

"Really?" Sasha asked, eyes widening.

"Well, Roberta Murphy now. She got married."

Sasha looked again, crouching down to look under the aircraft. "Has she cut her hair?" She couldn't believe she had been so out-of-touch recently.

"Yeah. That was before the wedding..." Leigh frowned. Sasha stood up and looked at her. Leigh realised Sasha looked different. She couldn't put her finger on it, but something had changed.

Then again, Leigh thought to herself, a lot had changed within her own life too, while she'd been away.

Sasha's walkie-talkie crackled in to life.

"*Megan to Sasha*"

Sasha raised the radio to her face and pressed the button. "Go ahead" she answered, rolling her eyes at Leigh, who mouthed 'see you later' at her as she scurried into the cabin.

"*Shall I call the passengers?*" said the voice on the radio, and Sasha looked up towards the gate on the glass-walled pier. She could see Megan looking at her questioningly.

Sasha checked over her shoulder to see how far Captain Murphy had reached with her checks; and taking note of the progress the cabin crew were making; she turned and gave Megan a *thumbs-up* signal, before scurrying down the steps and back to the gate to start prepping the paperwork.

There was an extra spring in her step, having her friend back. Evan just crossing paths briefly like this, it felt like things were getting back to normal.

-12-

Here we go, Leigh thought to herself.

She looked at herself in the small scratched mirror above the hand basin in the cramped toilet. There was a tap on the door.

"Get a move on!" called Gaynor, the purser on the flight.

Leigh liked her. She was a straight talker, but fair. Rumour had it she was assigned as many newbies as possible on their first flights, to 'break them in' and give them a good start. She played by the rules, didn't cut any corners and set a good example.

"Coming!" Leigh called back cheerfully, before one last check in the mirror.

All of a sudden she was overcome with a wave of nausea. She wobbled slightly, both glad of the small space giving her less room to fall down; and simultaneously worried that it was her claustrophobic tendency causing the dizziness.

She gripped the side of the sink and closed her eyes, taking a couple of deep breaths to steady herself.

Making the most of what might be a temporary recovery, she flicked the lock on the door and extricated herself from the small room.

Gaynor, in the galley opposite, glanced at her, a look of concern flicked briefly across her face before she continued preparing coffees without missing a beat. "You OK?"

Leigh nodded enthusiastically, and answered immediately "Yeah, of course!"

Gaynor looked up again. "Good. Can you double check the headrests?" she asked, picking up the two steaming cups and heading to the flight deck to hand them over to the flight crew.

Leigh nodded; although Gaynor had already turned away, so she set off down the cabin, checking each seat had a fresh paper headrest cover attached to it, emblazoned with the *YouKayAir* logo.

She reached the back of the cabin, and noticed a small plastic bag partially hidden under one of the back seats.

Confused as to how the cleaners had missed it, she bent down to pick it up.

There was nothing identifiable on it. It was a small parcel it would seem, tin foil, wrapped in a plastic shopping bag from the supermarket down the road, and taped shut. Leigh shrugged.

Not a suspicious parcel she thought. Sandwiches,

maybe? The aircraft had been checked and sealed last night after shut down; not to mention Sam opening up, the cleaning crew double checking this morning and Gaynor must have done her initial walk through the cabin, hadn't she?

Leigh had a history of feeling this conflict. She herself had left bags places before, totally innocently.

But since starting work here, being subjected to annual refresher security training; watching cringingly badly over-acted training videos of a bunch of Scottish 'terrorists' plotting to blow up Glasgow airport, they were taught to never take a chance.

She'd almost pulled a case left behind on an arrival belt once, before Olga stopped her and pointed out it was making a low whirring noise and appeared to be shaking.

Had there not been a noise Leigh would have just dragged it to the lost & found office like anything else but the movement inside made them stop in their tracks.

Leigh had called security and within minutes the arrivals hall was shut down.

Inbound passengers were held at the immigration check-point and plans began forming on whether to evacuate them backwards out on to the apron and away from the building. People waiting in the landside section of the arrivals hall had been moved outside. Airport security and law enforcement had the bag checked out.

Leigh had been racking her brains, considering the

possibilities as she waited outside at the assembly point. What would have happened had Olga not noticed the movement and noise?

Shane from security had then appeared at the door apparently having trouble keeping a straight face. He'd led Leigh and Olga back in.

Inside the now opened case, nestled amongst bikinis and saris and sandals and a toiletries bag; was one of the largest sex toys Olga had ever seen.

Shane explained that the item must have somehow been activated and started vibrating during the bags being moved around in the hold, or else stacked on the baggage cart or tossed a little too roughly onto the baggage belt.

Leigh shrugged when they re-told the story later on, she'd seen worse...or better...depending on the point of view; but Olga maintained in all her years she'd not really had much involvement with such items.

Megan had questioned her on it, but with an exaggerated wink, Olga had insisted she'd never had much need for 'outside help' as she'd managed to find adequate satisfaction elsewhere; which had left everyone in the office in fits of giggles.

What had made the incident even more memorable was the look on the lady's face when she came back to collect her bag. She'd been surprised to receive a call from the local police regarding her case shutting down the airport.

They had been traveling as a group on a girly holiday to Fuerteventura. Some of their group had been left in charge of collecting the luggage while others went to retrieve their cars; and in the rush her case had been overlooked.

That she looked sheepish and embarrassed were understatements when she arrived at the check-in desk later that afternoon to be chastised by the police for being so careless; by customs for not collecting her own luggage and by aviation security for not remembering to remove the batteries before packing.

Leigh's mouth involuntarily twitched at the corners into a smile, remembering the outcome; but looking now at the package in her hands, she recalled the feelings running through her during the shutdown. What if something happened, and she hadn't reported it?

Taking a deep breath, she began back up the aisle with the package in hand to show it to Gaynor.

Just as she did so, however, Carl appeared behind her in the galley, a little out of breath having run up the back set of airstairs onto the plane.

"That's mine!" he gasped at her, quite pointedly.

Leigh frowned as she heard him. His sharpness shocked her. Mild-mannered Carl seemed quite uptight about his parcel, secretly obscured under the seat towards the back of the aircraft…

"Oh…" Leigh exclaimed, "Sorry. Wondered where it

could have come from."

Carl seemed to correct himself, as though he realised he was coming across a little intense. He straightened up and, having caught his breath, sighed a little; looking relieved.

"Yeah...sorry...it's...uh...a packed lunch Sally has me on... special diet of sorts." He mumbled, not meeting her eye.

"Really?" Leigh asked.

"Yeah...well, she wasn't sure what kind of food will be on crew-food... so... " he trailed off.

Another thought struck Leigh. "Hey, where were you? You came out with us earlier..." she asked.

"Yeah..."

"But you were running?" she pointed out, referring to his arrival just in time to catch her finding his lunch.

"Yeah, forgot this..." he grinned, holding up his airside pass. "left it in the crew room." And with that he smiled again and turned away, taking his package towards the crew locker, presumably to store it with his crew bag.

Leigh shrugged.

Their crew-room had recently been relocated and was now in an airside part of the airport; meaning they had to clear through security before reaching it.

Two of them were so new and Gaynor had wanted to make thorough introductions, so they'd had a longer than usual crew briefing that morning; and then she took them to one side to check they were up to speed with the modifications on this particular aircraft; and aware of certain ways she liked things done. It was a warm day and many had removed their outer layers of uniform. Carl must have taken his pass off at the same time.

Leigh shrugged off the niggling feelings, just as Sasha appeared at the front door of that aircraft.

Gaynor had come out of the flight deck by this point. Sasha passed her a passenger list as they crossed paths. Sasha knocked, then disappeared in to the flight deck with the paperwork for the flight crew as Leigh made her way up to the front galley to join Gaynor.

"Ready then?" Gaynor asked her. Leigh nodded and smiled. She looked out through the aircraft door and up at the glass walls of the pier. Hundreds of expectant happy faces looked back at her from the boarding gate.

"I'll go and warn them to give you a hard time, shall I?" Sasha teased from behind her. She'd come back out of the flight deck and found Leigh was blocking her exit.

Leigh turned and smiled, standing aside to let her past. "I'm excited, actually!" she confirmed, more to convince herself than her friend.

Sasha smiled and started down the steps. She turned and gave a questioning thumbs up to Gaynor who gulped down the last dregs of her own cup of tea, thumbed up to

Sasha with her mouth full and disposed of her cup.

Sasha looked at Leigh. "Catch up when you're back?"

Leigh smiled and nodded enthusiastically, then watched Sasha head into the building on the ground floor, and up the steps through the window.

Leigh glanced down to the back of the cabin and saw Neil and Carl manning the back door, ready to welcome passengers who had seats assigned in the rear half of the aircraft; reassured in a way, glad that she wasn't with either Lucas or Ricky.

She didn't think she could deal with being close to them on her first flight.

She told herself over and over that it wasn't anything to do with emotions, or feelings; simply that they were distractions. And she wouldn't want to distract them.

Given their histories, any time they saw each other turned into either a friendly banter session at the expense of all other duties at hand, or else descended into debauchery of some kind...

Leigh shook her head to clear her thoughts. Already distracted by them and they're not even here? She mused. She made a conscious effort to get her head back in the game.

They were heading to Paris Orly airport this morning and the return flight, followed by a slightly shorter hop to Glasgow and back; before another crew took over to operate a similar pattern in the afternoon.

Leigh could tell even from a distance that the majority of the people lining up at the gate seemed like relaxed, nonchalant, regular travellers, hopping over to Paris for work or a meeting; the odd couple maybe on a city-break.

A relatively quiet first attempt, she hoped.

Gaynor took a welcoming position by the front entrance to greet their passengers and help direct any to their seats; although Leigh suspected most would already have an idea where they were headed.

Leigh stood near Gaynor in the galley, allowing room for passengers to pass. She could see them begin to make their way across the tarmac from this position, guided by Megan who stood mid-way between the gate door and the aircraft on the apron.

Cheryl, one of the other PSAs, had joined the gate staff from check-in, and was stood idly under the end of the wing, by a traffic cone, occasionally guiding passengers who had been directed to the back door to walk around and not under the wing; which was slowly being filled with fuel by a bowser around the other side of the aircraft.

Leigh noticed Mister Collings heading their way as the first passenger through the gate. He hadn't noticed her yet. A regular passenger of some years; tall, distinguished; greying hair and a kind smile; he was a nice breath of fresh air that made it a joy to do their jobs;

always thanking them for every little thing; even as an extremely regular commuter, never throwing his weight around or trying to tell them their jobs.

He reached the top of the steps and was momentarily stunned then raised his mouth into an amused smile at the sight of Leigh.

"Switching allegiances young lady?" he asked her, noting the new uniform.

"Adding another string to my bow Mister Collings" she smiled.

"No wonder I haven't seen you around here for a few months. Well, make mine a G&T then…" he said with a wink as he headed off to his regular seat in row 5.

Gaynor looked at Leigh and raised an eyebrow. Leigh knew that in the past, Gaynor had for some reason held a little grudge against ground crew and seemed to look down on them becoming cabin crew; but there was a hint of a smile in her surprised look…maybe she was accepting of the fact that a familiar face transferring from ground to air might be reassuring to their passengers? Leigh hoped this was the case and smiled back.

Gaynor turned back to continue welcoming passengers.

Up on the departure pier, the long corridor leading from the departure lounge out to the boarding gates; Sasha busied herself counting the baggage barcode stickers on the sheets of card, as Anya entered boarding card numbers into the gate computer.

Megan strode up the stairs having seen the last of the current passengers across the apron. "Any more?" She asked.

Anya looked up at her from the computer after pressing a key entering the last of her boarding card numbers. "2 males, one bag" she murmured as she picked up the phone on the wall next to the gate, and dialled the extension number for the information desk. Sasha grimaced as soon as Anya mentioned a bag.

"Hi Suzanne! It's Anya; can I have a call for passengers Hayes and Jones on the Paris to gate 5 please? Yeah, last two."

Sasha looked over her shoulder at the computer screen, then reached over and tapped a key, bringing up the baggage tag number on the screen for the bag belonging to the missing passengers. She went back to her card and scanned it.

Anya watched with interest. She'd been fascinated with load control but had been too scared to back up her interest with an application for any of the new load control jobs that had come up. Lacking the confidence in her own abilities, she spent any second she could picking up on the tasks and skills needed.

The cards that Sasha held were a log of all the bags that had been loaded onto the trolleys from check-in, ready to load into the hold.

The Load controller would have to sign off that all the accounted for bags had been loaded, and no more, before the flight was allowed to depart. They'd have to remove the bag from the flight if a passenger was not traveling for any reason.

Checking through the card, Sasha found the number she was looking for, right in the centre of the second card. She rolled her eyes and shook her head. Checking her radio was turned on; she headed down the stairs, calling back to Anya and Megan as she went.

"Megan, can you go and check the departure lounge? Anya let me know if they turn up. I'll get the boys to start checking the hold."

Sasha headed out across the apron and flagged down the one ramp agent who'd been left to wait until departure. The rest of the loading team had closed up the front hold and moved on to loading another flight, a larger holiday flight around the corner which needed more hands. They always left one to wait for departure though in case of offloads. Besides, he'd need to drive the pushback truck.

Sasha got closer and was happy to see it was Frenchy. She wouldn't need to expect a groan or a prickly response to the potentially bad news.

"No shows then?" He said as he jumped down from his perch on the front of his tug.

"How'd you guess?" She asked

179

"Body language and experience!" He told her as she passed him the card with the number she'd circled. "You're kidding me?" He asked, looking up at her. Sasha shrugged. The number she'd circled was in the centre of the card – which most likely meant the bag itself was checked in somewhere in the middle of the check in and was therefore right in the middle of all the bags.

Frenchy shrugged and started to head to the rear hold as Sasha bounded up the front steps. Gaynor met her at the door with a head count.

"2 down?" Gaynor told her.

"Yeah" Sasha confirmed. "How long d'you think she'll wait?" she asked, cocking her head towards the flight deck door.

"Any bags?" came a voice from behind the flight deck door, as Sasha realised it was open a crack and Captain Murphy could hear their conversation anyway.

Sasha entered the flight deck. "One. Frenchy's looking for it now."

"OK well let's say they've got until he finds the bag. We've got a slot in fifteen minutes." Captain Murphy held up the loadsheet for Sasha.

"Do you want me to alter it?" Sasha asked, referring to the recalculations they'd need to have on there before it was signed off, to minus the two passengers and a bag. Captain Murphy shrugged.

"Up to you, I could, but shall we give them a couple of minutes first?"

"We do have a slot," the first officer reminder her, as though it would affect her decision.

Roberta shrugged. "Not for twenty minutes. We'll manage, eh Sasha?"

The controllers in the tower handed down specific take-off slots to some scheduled aircraft that had been passed to them from National Air Traffic Services.

On busy mornings the airways could become very busy in certain areas; and the best way to manage aircraft traffic was to slightly delay some take-offs to avoid the possibility of near-misses later on their route.

Quite often on a weekday morning when commuter flights were all vying for airspace; NATS would add a few minutes on the scheduled departure time.

This morning was no different; and the route from South Wales to Northern France was particularly difficult to police if filed flight plans passed over busy areas like London and Paris.

Sasha mused for a moment, and was about to answer when she spotted movement up on the pier. She tapped Roberta on the shoulder and cocked her head towards the glass-walled building to direct the captain's attention to the people rushing along the corridor.

"Won't bother then." The Captain said as she scribbled

her signature on the top of the sheet, took her carbon copy from underneath and handed the form back to Sasha.

"I'll get him to close up the hold then. See you later!" Sasha said as she added the loadsheet to her clipboard and backed out of the tiny flight deck. Megan crackled over the radio to her.

"Megan to Sasha, Got them…they're on their way out."

"Thanks Megan; Frenchy do you copy?"

"Copied" Frenchy chimed in, short and pointedly. Sasha hoped he'd not gone too far into the hold.

Sasha turned to scan the cabin for Leigh, who was busy helping a lady fit her hand-luggage into the overhead locker, and caught her eye for a quick wave.

Leigh, with her hands full, smiled back.

Sasha moved out to stand on top of the airstairs, and noticed Mike, the ramp supervisor, meandering towards them. He held his thumb up, questioningly.

She nodded and retuned the signal. He was covering ramp duties on a busy morning as he had little else to do in his office at that point.

The two late passengers scurried sheepishly up the steps past her and flashed their boarding cards at Gaynor, who through pursed lips told them they were lucky and where to find their seats.

Mike stood under the nose of the aircraft, far enough back for the captain to see him, and offered her a hand signal. She responded with a thumbs up, letting him know he could unplug and drive away the Ground power unit, or GPU, which the aircraft used for power on the ground without using up its fuel.

Sasha unlocked and slid back the side of the air stairs and helped Gaynor tug the heavy aircraft door towards her.

Behind Gaynor, Sasha saw Leigh securing all the catering trolleys in to position and give her an absentminded wave in between.

"See you later!" Sasha said.

Gaynor smiled back. "Bye!"

Gaynor closed the door mechanism from the inside and Sasha helped from the outside. She ran her hand over the door, checking the outside emergency handle was flush to the side of the aircraft, before activating her radio.

"Doors closed on the Paris" she advised into the mouthpiece.

"Copied" Mina replied from within the operations office.

As she trotted down the staircase, Mike was returning in his tug from having driven the ground power unit that had been plugged in powering the cabin until its engines started, away from the other side of the aircraft and parked it across the apron in the designated parking bay.

Mike waved her towards him as he stopped the tug next to the steps.

"Can you do headsets on this?" he asked.

Sasha checked her watch. "Supposed to be training today but could fit it in."

"I gotta take these over to stand 19 ready for the Malaga." Mike explained. Without waiting for a response, he reversed his tug into position ready to drive the front steps away.

Frenchy had started pushing away the back set of steps, having already closed up the hold.

From inside the aircraft, Leigh, making her way down through the cabin checking her passengers laps to see that all their seatbelts were fastened properly, caught the odd glimpse of Sasha through each windows as she made her way to the back; imagining her methodical procedure.

As she walked, Sasha checked she had the paperwork in order, and tucked her clipboard under her arm, freeing her hands to shove her earplugs into her ears.

She walked around the aircraft double checking the doors were flush to the aircraft side and the holds were properly closed.

By the time she'd walked all the way around back to the nose again, Mike had had removed the front steps and was driving away around the end of the pier. Frenchy was positioning the push-back tug ready to attach the tow-bar to the nose-wheel. Sasha trotted forward, opened the passenger side door of the tug and dumped her clipboard and pen on the seat, and her walkie-talkie on top of it, and grabbed the headset, thick earphones with a mouthpiece attached, connected to a long curled cable, that was on the dashboard.

"You supposed to be doing a pushback in those?" Frenchy asked her. He nodded towards her feet.

Of course, she'd come in to work dressed for a day in the terminal – pencil skirt and blouse and blazer; and her block-heeled court-shoes. Comfortable enough to be walking miles around the terminal in but not exactly health-and-safety adherent to be doing ramp work.

Sasha shrugged. "I'm supposed to be training today." She told him.

"Do as I say, not as I do, eh?" Frenchy offered.

"Same old, same old." Sasha smiled.

She closed the door of the tug, and walked to the other end of the long bar that was attached to the front of the tug, placing the headset over her ears as she went.

Sasha stepped over and straddled the bar, lifting out a small pin from a hole on the end. She gestured hand signals to Frenchy as he tentatively and very carefully nudged the bar forward towards the nose wheel of the aircraft.

When he was close enough she dropped the pin through both the end of the bar and the protruding metal attachment above the nose wheel, attaching the two vehicles together.

She gave a thumbs up to Frenchy and picked up the cable attached to her headset, that had been hanging down to her side.

Feeling along the concertina cable to find the end, she stepped back over the bar and headed to a small square flap on the side of the plane, below the captain's window.

It was no bigger than the flap on a petrol cap on a car; and opened the same way. She flipped the small flap open with her thumb and plugged her headset into the connection under the flap, securing it with a carabiner hook on the cable to a small loop alongside the plug. She stepped back from underneath the plane.

Leigh was sitting in the flight deck. She'd persuaded Captain Murphy to let her use the jump seat behind them during take-off.

She could see Sasha wave towards the flight deck, and heard the Captain's side of the conversation, telling her which runway the tower had told them to use

Sasha waved back at Frenchy and giving him a hand signal again; this time, holding up a series of finger signals to let him know which runway, and which way to turn the aircraft so it could taxy off in the right direction.

Leigh glanced over her shoulder and down the cabin behind her, before reaching back to close and lock the door. Carl looked a little nervous, strapped into the seat in the rear galley. He looked like he needed a hug, she thought. Neil sat next to him was oblivious to this and calmly looking out through the window.

She settled back as she heard the clunk of the tug being disconnected outside. She glanced out of the window again and found that they were facing the right way, the runway on her right. She could just see Sasha walking backwards with the thick metal pin that had been securing the push-bar to the nose-wheel, identifiable by the long red plastic tag attached to it, in her hand.

As she reached a good distance, Sasha held up the tag for the flight deck to see, showing the captain it was no longer attached, so it would be safe to raise the nose-wheel after take-off.

Once the captain acknowledged, Sasha waved and she moved out of Leigh's sight. Leigh imagined her friend walking across to the tug that had by now reversed away from the aircraft taking the push-bar with it; jumping in as they reversed a little further away, leaving the aircraft to taxy its way towards the runway under its own steam.

They reached the end of the runway and lined up, and Leigh could just about make out Sasha in her hi-viz waistcoat, sitting on the crash barrier at the end of the pier; and imagined her noting the take-off time on her dispatch paperwork.

Captain Murphy spoke with the tower and her co-pilot; but the business of the flight-deck blended into the background noise of the engines and the equipment in the flight deck as Leigh watched Sasha; then became enthralled with the increasing speed by which the lines on the runway in front of them sped past; followed by the sudden realisation that the ground was falling away. Leigh tore her eyes away from the disappearing ground and looked down towards the airport terminal on their right, as the aircraft started banking round over the top of it.

Leigh's memories of seemingly endless shifts hanging around on the apron; rushing around the pier and herding people to boarding gates; interspersed with goofing around in airport wheelchairs at empty gate areas, while waiting for inbound flights; arguing with passengers about how long it would take their missing bag to arrive, at the baggage services desk; all flashed through her mind as familiar landmarks on the ground became more and more unrecognisable from her new position.

Before long, Captain Murphy turned around and tapped her on the knee, with a wink; as she reached over and turned off the 'fasten-seatbelts' sign. Leigh took a deep breath. With the light off she knew it was her time to shine; or at least do her very best to not spill hot coffee over someone. She now had to leave the flight-deck and her privileged position and get to work.

Leigh stood, smoothed down her skirt, and patted Captain Murphy on the shoulder as a thank you. Murphy raised a hand in response barely turning to look at her. Leigh unlatched the lock on the inside of the flight deck door and the First Officer stood up ready to lock it again after she left.

Back out in the galley, Leigh could see Carl fussing far more than he usually seemed to – not his calm, laid-back self, but flustered and jumpy – at the other end of the aisle. She brushed off his behaviour once again as first day nerves; and turned to the coffee urn in the corner. Gaynor bustled back in. She'd been down the aisle talking to a passenger somewhere around row 14 or 15 from what Leigh could tell.

"Nervous flier." Gaynor shrugged, "Can you pass me some water?"

Leigh poured from a bottle of mineral water into a plastic cup and passed it to her. Gaynor's disapproving expression didn't pass her by.

"It's not their fault..." Leigh offered, misunderstanding.

"What?" Gaynor snapped.

"That they're nervous." Leigh offered.

Gaynor rolled her eyes. "I was about to say you need to get a move on with that. Don't make a habit of beginning every flight in the flight deck." Gaynor grabbed the water and turned, "and they can have their cuppa *after* everyone else." She stated, cocking her head towards the flight deck door, before taking the water down to the passenger.

Leigh bit her bottom lip. Chastisement on her first flight was a little hard to take. Another sudden wave of nausea overtook her, to her surprise; but she knew now wasn't the time for it. She took a deep breath and refocused her attention by looking through the window at nothing but clouds for a few moments; before rolling her shoulders back and getting on with the task in hand. She filled her coffee pot, checked the refreshments cart was fully stocked as she pulled it from its stowage under the counter, and started to make her way down the aisle, painting on a smile as she turned the corner to face the cabin full of passengers.

The rest of the flight passed in much of a haze. She worked diligently, provided morning snacks and beverages with a smile; and despite her earlier stresses, the flight passed without incident.

Leigh felt a little silly for somehow thinking it wouldn't; but kept her relief to herself until after their turnaround in Paris and they'd returned to their home base. They had a slightly longer turnaround before their shorter Glasgow-and-back flights.

She'd managed to hold on to her nausea long enough to see the passengers from Paris off the flight and then found herself needing to rush to Tom Klein's engineering office nearby and make use of their facilities while the ground crew were dropping the toilets of the aircraft; a brief service in between flights where they'd empty the waste tanks and refill the water.

Leigh managed to disguise her sickness from Gaynor.

She had no other symptoms so was pretty confident it was nerves and stress causing her upset tummy; she'd suffered from anxiety before and it seemed similar to her. She didn't want to be sent home sick from her first flight; going down in history for causing further delays on her first day.

She wasn't sure if there was anyone upstairs in the crew room in the terminal on airport standby – where they'd be called in to sit and wait, ready to go if another crew member either called in sick or was taken off duty; and calling someone in could be anything up to an hour. It was a pre-requisite to the job was to live within a certain distance of the airport to be able to arrive at work ready to go within a set amount of time.

No, Leigh was determined to complete her first day. Rushing back to the aircraft to a brief sideways glance from Gaynor as she took two more steaming cups into the flight deck, Leigh tried to ignore her stern glances, and took a seat a few rows back opposite Carl who had been flicking through one of the in-flight magazines. He spoke barely looking up.

"Unbelievable the amount of advertising they put in these things."

"Captive audience I suppose," Leigh mused. At the back of the cabin she heard suppressed laugh and turned to see Neil peering at something amusing him on a mobile phone screen.

Carl sighed in despair at the lack of interesting content

on the magazine and placed it back in the seat pocket, before looking up at Leigh.

"You ok?"

"Me? Yes, why?" Leigh answered quickly, taken aback slightly.

"Calm down! Just asking! First day and all that." He smiled at her.

"Oh. Yeah. You seemed a bit flustered earlier though."

"No...yes...just...I was running a bit late this morning so rushing around to get to work, you know how it is..." he let his words drift off, dropping eye contact and looking around the cabin.

"Got here in time though?" Leigh was a little puzzled.

"Yes, because I was rushing...not as organised as I like to be, like." He explained.

Leigh pursed her lips into a little understanding smile and nodded slightly. She looked up and half-waved at the ground crew who had given the cabin a once-over, as they left. She took that as a cue to stand up, brush herself down and took the initiative to head down the back of the aircraft and start checking the seats, walking back up the aisle.

She became aware of Gaynor noticing her initiative and nodding approvingly. Carl saw Gaynor do this and put in an attempt to busy himself checking the galley was ready.

Leigh glanced through the windows as she checked the seats were all tidy, logo-emblazoned headrest covers straightened, seatbelts crossed; checking the seat pockets had a magazine and sick bag and laminated emergency procedure card.

She was a little disheartened to see Reuben scurrying across the apron towards the aircraft, dispatcher clipboard, stuffed with paperwork, under his arm. Of course, she reminded herself; Sasha was supposed to be in the office today training new Passenger Services staff; and had only been covering this morning. Leigh straightened herself out to try and perk herself up a little;. Only Glasgow and back, she told herself, as Reuben reached the top of the steps and gave her a smile.

She hoped by the time they got back, she'd be in time to grab a quick coffee and a catch up with Sasha.

-13-

"Surely that's a good thing?" Sasha murmured, confused, as she sipped her coffee, "You know, everything going without a hitch?"

They were sat in the café overlooking the runway on the first floor. It had been a toss-up between this and the staff canteen; hidden away at the back of the check-in hall not far from the plant room that ran the mechanisms for the baggage belts.

The staff canteen would have been cheaper and quicker; with less requirement to stick to uniform regulations and keep their neck-ties done up neatly; but their idea of coffee was a sticky teaspoon on a grubby table with a catering can of instant coffee granules, and a jug of not-quite-boiling water. Barely a step up from the machine in the *Air2Ground* office.

Up here, with the chatter of the general public; from drop-offs and goodbyes, to plane-spotters moaning that the viewing deck was closed felt more like they were in the thick of it. Although the prices were significantly inflated – even with a staff discount - the beverages were at least a little more palatable.

Leigh shrugged. "Yeah, but it's kind of a let-down, you know? Is your coffee ok?"

"Yeah, why?"

"Dunno, mine tastes a little like the milks is a bit off…"

"Mine's ok…I think…" Sasha sipped hers again, as though savouring the taste to check. "What do you mean a let-down?"

"Well, I've just spent months learning and studying all this stuff you know, like the whole point of us being there is because we know exactly what to do in an emergency. So I'd sort of…prepped myself…you know?" Leigh paused and stared blankly out of the window. "I dunno, I suppose I was just waiting for something to happen. And it didn't." She shrugged, as though answering her own question.

"Do you think that anticipation is what made you feel sick?" Sasha asked, half-distracted by watching goings out on the apron outside.

An airport authority vehicle was racing along the runway checking it was clear. The airport fire service on the south side of the runway had their vehicles out, being washed down, making the most of the afternoon sun to dry them.

Leigh shrugged again. She glanced up at Sasha, trying to gauge whether her friend was suspicious of anything.

But it seemed to have been a rhetorical question that Sasha wasn't really expecting an answer to.

"So, how are the new lot?" Leigh asked, changing the subject, referring to the new trainees.

"Not too bad. Not sure about one girl. She was late. Seems a little flaky."

"Judgements, Judgements!" Leigh jibed.

"Yeah well, I said the same about you..."

"You did not!" Leigh answered in mock surprise. Sasha smiled.

"No. But then I never thought Carl was interested in flying either. How did he get on?"

Leigh shrugged again, and frowned slightly. "Not too sure to be honest. Actually, *HE* seemed a little flaky this morning."

"How so?" Sasha asked, a slightly confused look on her face.

"Not sure, really," Leigh replied. "He's just...different"

"Well, yeh, that's what I mean..."

"And he was like that all the way through training," Leigh cut straight back in. "He just seemed really antsy this morning"

Sasha sipped her coffee and thought for a moment. "Did

you ask him if he was ok?"

"Yeah. He just said he got up late so was rushing to get in to work and it threw him off. Anyway, he was down the back with Neil mostly."

"Yeah, well, see, he's a Virgo like me, see! Needs to be prepared at all times!" Sasha smiled and Leigh smiled back, brushing off any uneasy feeling.

"What time do you need to be back?" Leigh asked. Sasha shrugged.

"I let them go early today. First day and all that. Gave them a shedload of paperwork to fill in so told them to do it as homework!"

"Good thinking batman! So, plan for the rest of the day?"

"Don't go getting ideas. Just because you're a part-timer now…" Sasha joked.   Leigh raised her eyebrows, sarcastically. "I've got lesson-plans to sort and I have to dig out the ramp guys mandatory training records ready for next week too."

"Yay." Leigh stated monotonously, not even trying to hide her disappointment.

"Don't sound like that!" Sasha scorned her.

"I know. Just sounds so….normal…when you have your hot guy at home."

"Oooh! Speaking of hot guys…" Sasha began, changing

the subject quickly, then she stopped, looking expectantly at Leigh.

"What?"

"Well...I saw Lucas this morning..."

"Lucas isn't hot...When did you see him?"

"Maybe not to some of us. After you left... he was on the 10.30 Malaga..."

"See, I get a boring old Paris for my first flight, he gets bloody Spain...What about him?" Leigh's interest was getting piqued...along with an underlying hope that Lucas hadn't gone in to too much detail...

"Not much; just suggested that Ricky had attracted a lot of attention while you were all holed up in West Drayton..."

"Did he?" Leigh looked down into the dregs of her coffee cup; suddenly wishing there was more left in there to distract herself with.

"Apparently...he even found a little action himself..." Sasha probed further.

"Ricky?" Leigh exclaimed, looking up; and almost immediately hoping she hadn't seemed more concerned than she had wanted to let on.

"No, Lucas!"

"Oh." Leigh said quietly.

"So? Did you see him with any hot guys?" Sasha pushed, playfully.

"Ricky?" Leigh was losing track of the conversation as her own train of thought and the exerted effort not to let anything slip.

"No! Lucas!" Sasha repeated, choking a little as a drop of coffee went down the wrong way. Leigh was a tad relieved at that, distracting Sasha from noticing any hesitation in her reaction.

"Oh. No, not really. Most I saw of him was when we had study groups in our rooms. Took it in turns" Leigh said, and then added "the group of us" as an afterthought.

"Hm. Oh well; I'm sure he'll give me all the gossip when he gets back." Sasha sat back and checked her watch. "I should be getting back or I'll never have all the stuff ready for tomorrow." She said as she began to gather her things, placing her phone back into her handbag and picking up her empty cup to return it to the counter. Sasha smiled and waved nonchalantly as she scurried off to get back to her training paperwork.

Leigh felt a wave of relief suddenly that the conversation was over. She has missed Sasha, and had been looking forward to a catch up; but for some reason, this seemed neither the time nor the place to discuss the intimate details of what had happened during training.

Leigh did her coat up; partly because of a shiver she suddenly felt. The sun had gone behind a large bank of cloud that had appeared, and it suddenly wasn't so warm.

Despite the outgoing person she usually was, she felt a sudden desire to be alone, in her own place. That meant getting there without being bothered so keeping her head down and shoving her earphones into her ears seemed to be the best way to block out people. Any people, at this point.

Leigh sauntered downstairs and out to the bus stop. She hopped onto the shuttle bus that went around to the railway station. Waiting for the train on the exposed platform gave her an excuse to shrug her puffer jacket up around her neck and pull oversized hood up over her head as the drizzle that was rolling in along the coast greyed out her mood.

Reaching home, she tiptoed up the stairs to her flat quietly, let herself in with as little fuss as possible. She kicked off her shoes by the door, padded to the kitchen and grabbed a bottle of water from the fridge.

For a few minutes she leant on the breakfast bar counter that protruded across the room as a makeshift separation between the kitchen area and the cramped living area of her one bedroom flat. It wasn't big. Apart from this multi-use room, there was a bathroom, just big enough for a bath along one wall and a hand basin and toilet next to it; and her bedroom; which was sizeable enough with enough built-in cupboard space for most of her belongings; stuff that she didn't have stored in her grandparents attic for the one day, far off in the future, she figured; when she might live somewhere other than here.

For now, this was all she could afford; on her own, working as much as she could. And if she was honest with herself; it was pretty much all she wanted.

She was staring out through the French doors at the end of the room, facing west so with a good view of the coast. The sun was making the effort to break through the heavy grey clouds again, and slivers glistened in streaks over the water in the old dock area that the relatively recent development had been built on as part of a regeneration attempt.

Sometimes she got caught up in romantic ideas of long-term boyfriends and marriage; of houses with gardens and dogs and cats and children playing… but when it came right down to it, she mused, she was too independent. She didn't think she could face the thought of sharing her space, what there was of it, with someone else, twenty-four-seven.

And just like that, her contemplative mood was interrupted by another sudden nausea. It gave her enough notice to make it to the bathroom before she threw up again.

After cleaning herself up and brushing her teeth, she checked herself in the mirror. Leigh decided, once again, that she was not ill. Nerves from the excitement of the day, perhaps?

Maybe it was the milk in her coffee?

Leigh shrugged it off and reminded herself she didn't want to start off on the wrong foot.

She had to be up for another four legs in the morning and considering as ground crew she'd never missed a shift, through thick and thin, perfectly balancing her reputation for partying and work presence…and performance…in equal measure; she didn't want to lose that. Knowing full well she'd be under more of a microscope when it came to being alert, on time and having alcohol use under scrutiny, she downed another glass of water, quickly changed into comfy PJs and checked her bedside clock. The fact that it told her it was only 4pm gave her a strange buzz – going to bed in the middle of the afternoon because she didn't have to answer to anyone suddenly felt more exciting than coming home at 4am and collapsing in to bed for the very same reason.

Maybe she was getting old? In only a few minutes, Leigh fell into a deep sleep.

And surprisingly for the weirdly unsettling day she'd had, she had a smile on her face.

-14-

The first couple of weeks of flying seemed to go well. As well as could be expected. She didn't think she'd forgotten any of her training, and had, so far, completed all her duties effectively.

Leigh had flown with Carl, mostly.

He continued to be more concentrated & less jovial than he used to be. It concerned her slightly; but she figured he had put so much effort into application and training, and without question he always completed his duties perfectly when working.

His smiles to passengers appeared totally genuine. In a way, it made her feel safer. She was with someone who took his job and responsibility seriously. She began feeling a sense of security every time she saw him, and it was comforting.

He seemed like he was genuinely concentrating on knowing every procedure, for every eventuality. She had seen him checking the in-flight manuals along with his own copies, carefully on a few occasions.

She had flown with Lucas a couple of times, and their relationship was as just it had always been – thankfully, she told herself. Banter and sarcasm, and working together as a seamless team, were still there.

It was as though nothing untoward had ever happened between them; and Leigh was happy to leave it at that.

On this otherwise-standard Thursday morning, however, Leigh felt an anxiety as she stepped off the shuttle bus and strode into the terminal building; trying to ooze her outward confidence, that she didn't feel inside.

Up until now, she had always been rostered on with Gaynor as the Purser, or '*Number 1*', who was completing the training for the new recruits, and doing their line checks to ensure they were competent.

Today was different. She had worked, in turn, with pretty much every cabin crew member on their base at some point; except Ricky.

Some of the others had, of course. Ricky had signed off half of the trainees, and Gaynor the other half.

She tested herself on her way up in the lift to the top floor. She knew she had nothing to worry about in her performance.

She had so far aced all of her flights; she had managed to forget she was being watched and threw herself into her duties.

She knew her manuals, regulations and procedures

inside out. She was absolutely confident in that. Gaynor had, in her muted and uncomplicated way, told her straight that her line-check was flawless. Still, she somehow felt inadequate; convinced she was going to mess something up.

"Don't be so silly!" She chided herself under her breath, before realising she was lucky no-one else was present. She stared at herself in the mirrored wall at the back of the lift and took some deep breaths.

'In through the nose, out through the mouth…slowly' she thought to herself as she breathed.

She felt a little calmer. Not much, but enough to regain her confident posture as she stepped out of the lift and pulled her trolley-case along behind her.

The aging carpet hid any noise from the case, or clicking from her heels.

The emptiness of the vast room that had once been a land-side viewing lounge open to the public but now was being incorporated into the air-side of the terminal as the small airport expanded, was noticeable. The strange light of the early morning call-time encompassed her and seemed to put pressure on her; bringing her thoughts and worries to the forefront of her mind once again.

She slowed as she neared the door to the crew-room.

Glancing sideways, she saw the last of that morning's cargo-flights taking off along the runway and distracted herself, admiring the grace by which what was essentially a large chunk of metal could glide so smoothly up into the air by the marvel of engineering.

She allowed herself to be drawn to the large wall of glass that overlooked the concrete outside.

Without realising, she was accepting any excuse to not go into the crew room just yet.

She watched the first of many baggage carts being towed out towards the aircraft on the parking-stands, each neatly angled next to a boarding gate. Some were privileged to be attached to an air bridge, allowing their passengers to board without being exposed to the elements, or having to deal with stairs.

As she concentrated on the general bustling outside on the apron she was interrupted by a tuneful whistle from behind her. Not a wolf-whistle, more a friendly bird-chirp type tune. Leigh smiled to herself, she knew it was Lucas before she even turned around.

"Penny for your thoughts?" He cocked his head to one side.

Leigh winked at him. "You'd be broke…"

"How come you haven't gone in and got the coffee underway then Miz earlybird?" He sauntered over and linked his free arm in hers, his other dragging his own trolley case behind him. "I thought you were flying out of Bristol today?"

Leigh shrugged, and they began to head towards the

crew-room together. "They switched me and Carl a few days ago, something to do with his flight time limitations. You must be looking at an old copy of the rota. And I didn't really fancy any coffee this morning, to be honest." she added, nonchalantly.

Lucas was shocked. "Are you feeling ok?"

"Of course!" Leigh answered defensively, and maybe a little too quickly. "I had a cup of tea this morning. Before I left home. And still feel a little bloated from that to be honest."

"There's definitely something wrong with you…" Lucas chipped as he tapped in the security code on the key-pad to unlock the crew room door from the outside, pushed the door open, and took a position holding the door for Leigh to enter.

As he wandered in first he nodded to Captain Murphy as she passed him heading towards the flight planning computers in the corner, he then noticed Ricky in the corner, making the coffee he so desperately craved.

Lucas offered him a huge grin as Ricky turned to see who was coming in; which was reciprocated with a casual wave and a nod from Ricky as he brought his mug up to his lips.

Lucas turned back towards Leigh as she followed him in through the door; and he suddenly cottoned on to her seeming lack of enthusiasm in turning up for work this morning.

He looked at her and mouthed a silent, knowing "Oh!" with a small nod of his head as she entered and he closed the door behind her. Leigh shot him a sarcastic smile and adopted her confident walk again as she entered.

Today was the first flight she was rostered on to work with Ricky.

Lucas instinctively knew that it was down to him to try to break the ice, although by the time he and Leigh approached the briefing table in the corner of the otherwise open room, Ricky was engrossed in checking the flight plans with Captain Murphy.

"Why is he checking those?" whispered Lucas.

Leigh shrugged in response. She knew the answer, of course; she just didn't feel like talking.

Ricky had a keen interest in every aspect of the flights, and took any opportunity to learn about other aspects of flying other than being in the cabin. She knew a lot about him, of course. His likes, his dislikes, his ambitions...

Leigh took the opportunity to watch Ricky. Selfish glances for no other reason than she wanted to look at him.

Lucas had picked up the aircraft manual on the desk for a bit of last minute revising before Ricky, as cabin manager, would shoot them some questions randomly to ensure they were up to date before allowing them to fly.

Ricky was engrossed in what Roberta was showing him; explaining something about the beacons, that the aircraft's navigational systems would communicate with to help navigate the route plotted on the flight plan.

Leigh was mesmerised by the truly innocent, wide-eyed wonderment and excitement that he seemed to display, just by talking about or listening to this stuff.

She wondered if she'd been the same over the years whenever she thought about or heard of cabin crew exploits. In this moment, Ricky for all the world seemed like a child who'd been shown the flight-deck for the first time and knew he wanted to be a pilot.

This was so different from the usually flirtatious and suggestively promiscuous nature of how they normally saw each other. Leigh's head cocked to one side as she got lost in watching him.

She didn't notice the other of that morning's crews come in, all at once; hitting their call-time dead-on.

Carl was amongst them. He broke away from the rest of the crew and went to his locker in the corner with a spring in his step, slightly uncharacteristic of the new Carl they'd all got used to.

Lucas frowned as he absentmindedly watched Carl switch some things between his locker and his flight bag. "What are you all doing here?" he asked, to them all in general.

Deirdre, the number one, rolled her eyes. "Don't get me

started." She shrugged. She headed straight over to make herself a coffee. She checked back over her shoulder. "White two sugars captain?"

"Nice one" chirped Captain Bowen as he dumped his thick briefcase and his hat onto the sideboard that ran the length of the wall facing the large windows. He perched himself back against the worktop, being a little too short to actually sit on it without jumping, and being way past the stage of being young enough, or fit enough, to jump up and sit. He screwed his face up in disgust as he scrutinised the flight plan in his hand.

Captain Bowen looked up and caught Lucas looking at him questioningly.

"Bristol was closed last night; our aircraft is here apparently." The captain explained.

"Yeah, and they didn't bother telling us so we were all waiting in the bus stop out the front for the crew transport!" chimed in Deirdre as she brought the captain his coffee.

"Fog?"

The captain shrugged "Not according to this. Weather's been fine. Last night too, when we got in. Not tech either."

Lucas watched and waited for further explanation. *Tech* referred to an aircraft being technically unfit to fly.

But no explanation came. The captain simply shrugged

his shoulders and gestured to his first officer to follow
him over to a separate seating area nearer to the window
so they could go through their flight plans.

Deirdre offered nothing either. She simply raised her
eyebrows to Lucas as she took a sip of her drink. Then
she cockily waved for Carl and their third crew member;
a whispy looking, short redhead whom Lucas hadn't
seen before but assumed she was down from the
Glasgow base. They'd been a little short on numbers
this summer so far; despite the full class graduating; so
there had been quite a bit of shuffling around and
borrowing crews from other bases to cover flights.

Lucas looked back over his shoulder to check if Ricky
was ready for him. No; his line manager was still
looking over the paperwork to the sound of Roberta's
colourful step-by-step descriptions of the plan for their
flight as she discussed with her own First Officer,
Adrian, their route and suggested procedures.

Leigh was continuing to admire Ricky from afar and had
yet to be noticed by him. Lucas snorted to himself in
amusement as Mina appeared at the door.

"Updated weather" she said and handed a wad of paper
to Lucas, being the closest to the door.

"Who for?" he asked.

"Both."

"Why is Kilo Alpha here?" He said, absentmindedly
noting she'd scribbled the last two letters of each

aircraft's registration at the top of each weather report – both slightly different depending on the route.

He could tell enough from the mostly gobbledegook markings on the paper that 'KA' was going to Geneva – a flight that had supposedly been operating from Bristol Airport.

Mina shrugged. "Dunno. Marcus scribbled something on the handover about a security issue that shut down Bristol last night. Captain Edwards wasn't willing to hold so diverted here, and Megan had to road all the passengers back."

Lucas remembered those days. And Captain Edwards hadn't changed. Stubborn to the core, David Edwards was no-nonsense. Whatever the incident, he expected decisions to be made immediately; or else he made decisions himself. He didn't even like being put in a holding pattern. He hated flying around and around just waiting until Air Traffic Control told him it was clear to land. He wanted decisiveness & answers straight away.

They'd always wondered how he got away with making his own calls so much more than everyone else. Usually everyone deferred decisions to the airline's central operations department, who could weight up operational safety and security implications, with the flight and cabin crew's time limitations and how it would affect the next day's crewing; if any delays or ground transport ate into their required rest-periods; alongside the cost – both financial and reputational – to the airline in the eyes of its customers, passengers and in more extreme cases, the press.

There were rumours that he'd had an affair with the
CEO; or something along those lines. Either way; it was
only him that ever seemed to get away with making calls
without even a hint of input from Ops.

Then there were the delay and diversion nights that
Lucas had experienced more than once. Being left to
wait for one inbound flight, before being the one to lock
up the office at night; only to hear that the flight was
either extremely delayed; or else had diverted to
somewhere else; or even worse; as in this case; a flight
had diverted in from being supposed to land elsewhere.
This would mean having to call around all the local (and
not-so-local) coach companies at 11 o'clock at night
trying to find transport to get all of the diverted
passengers back to their original destination.

Bristol wasn't so bad, around an hour or so away, during
the night, with no traffic. He'd once had a diversion in
that had, for some reason, been supposed to go to Jersey!

He had no clue as to why the decision had been made to
send it his way. A series of events; which included some
closer airports to the south coast, like Exeter or
Bournemouth, had already closed for the night, saw him
single-handedly trying to arrange transport, overnight
accommodation, and consequent ferry services the next
day, on which there were no direct flights available, for
25 passengers.

"So is Bristol open now?" Lucas asked.

Mina nodded. "But they're bussing the passengers over here."

"Huh?"

"Well, it's cheaper apparently than positioning. And quicker." She shrugged; and with a small wave, turned on her heel and scurried off down the corridor.

Mina didn't usually leave her passenger services desk, but at this time of the morning, the regularly rostered members of staff were all assigned to check-ins, or preparing for dispatch of something-or-other, so if there were any deviations to the regular schedules, such as this extra flight to deal with, there was a little pitching in required.

Lucas watched her go. Much to his amazement at the cost of hiring a coach or two (he'd done it last year to bus everyone to Alton Towers for his birthday day out); he understood that the cost of fuel to take off, fly across the channel, land and pay landing charges at a second airport were probably higher. Not to mention the airline were probably going to be able to check in and have all the passengers here within enough time to limit their departure and subsequent arrival delay.

Interrupting his train of thought, Mina stuck her head back around the door frame.

"Captain Bowen!" She shouted, almost right into Lucas's ear. "Oops, sorry Luke…"

"Yes, my dear?" The Captain boomed.

"Bristol said they'd fax over the passenger details as soon as they've closed the check in so we can get on with the load sheet. Would you like a computerised one or a manual?"

"Oh, I'll do it myself if you like." He beamed at her and waved his hand dismissively.

Mina grinned back. Just as she'd hoped...one less job for her load controllers to worry about. She turned, and scurried away again.

Lucas turned to scan the room. The cabin crew for the diverted Geneva flight were already huddled around in the midst of their briefing. Captain Murphy and her first officer appeared to be gossiping about where the best place to eat whilst in Arizona when there doing their refresher training on the simulator; and the Geneva flight crew seemed to be speculating more on what exactly the security issue had been in Bristol last night for it to have completely shut for long enough to upset Captain Edwards to make a decision.

"Lucas!"

Lucas almost jumped out of his skin. He turned to find Ricky staring at him intently. Ricky raised his eyebrows questioningly .

"Oh!" Lucas realised what Ricky was waiting for when he saw Leigh looking at him equally as intently.

Lucas sauntered over and took his seat opposite Leigh on the other side of Ricky as the senior hostie flicked through the manuals choosing questions for them. While Ricky's head was bowed, Leigh glanced up and winked at Lucas.

This is actually going to be a fun flight, he told himself.

-15-

Within half an hour Lucas, Leigh and Ricky were boarding their aircraft. Leigh, at the top of the steps watched, although trying to look as though she wasn't, as Ricky effortlessly carried both his own bag and Captain Murphy's across the apron to the bottom of the yellow staircase that was pushed up to the side of the plane. They stopped at the steps for a little chat, from what Leigh could tell, before the Captain headed off to do her walk-around; sauntering, hands in pockets, around the aircraft checking that everything seemed to be in place.

Lucas reached the top of the steps and nudged Leigh from behind with a smirk.

"Come on!" he said with a wink.

Leigh rolled her eyes at him and went inside. The doors were already open; and their first instinct already was to check who had opened them. Leigh looked down the cabin and saw Gordon, one of the engineers, perched in the second row casually, filling out the tech log for the aircraft.

"Morning" she said brightly.

"Morning" he sullenly replied. She might have asked what was wrong, but this was his standard mood and expected response. He barely even looked up and continued scribbling. Leigh smiled to herself.

She busied herself checking the catering at the front of the aircraft, subconsciously out of habit checking the galley door, opposite where she had boarded, was closed properly.

At the back of the cabin, she could hear Lucas chatting with Pikey, who worked for *Omega*, the catering company. He'd reversed his lime-green truck to the side of the aircraft, and raised the rear platform on the truck's integrated hydraulic lift so that it was level with the cabin door.

Leigh was double checking the security ties on the catering trollies corresponded with the list she had; to ensure they hadn't been tampered with in any way. She didn't know how long she'd been at it before she became aware of being watched.

She turned round to see Ricky standing, looking down at her with a twinkle in his eye. She felt her cheeks burning a little; but kept her face neutral, or at least she tried to; not sure, still, if a smile of any kind would give the wrong impression.

Inside, however, she felt like she was grinning like a school-girl with a crush.

"Everything ok?" Ricky asked her.

"Yeah!" She said, possibly a little too quickly and enthusiastically.

"Great!" He said, raising his eyebrows, and after a further beat, added "I just wondered if you were waiting for something?"

Leigh suddenly cottoned on that the moments since she'd turned around, crouched on one knee in front of the catering trolley, to look up at him, had seemed like an age; and since her position was blocking the aisle and any chance he would have of accessing wither the cabin to stow his own bag, or the flight deck to put the Captain's bag in there ready for her; he had little choice but to wait for Leigh's next move.

"Oh!" she realised and stood up quickly, and turned away, attempting to hide her embarrassment and burning cheeks by trying to look busy.

Knowing full well he knew the location of everything in the galley and every procedure, she racked her brains quickly to come up with anything that might actually have made her busy.

"Coffee?" She mumbled, half to Ricky, half under her breath, as she pottered about with paper cups and a couple of sachets of instant-coffee granules.

"Yeah, thanks" Ricky answered as he hoisted his own bag into the first overhead locker above the front rows; which was already half-filled with emergency and first-aid equipment.

Leigh busied herself making the drinks as Ricky closed the locker, and turned to look in her direction, thoughtfully. After a few moments of her not noticing, or purposefully not looking up to meet his gaze, Ricky strode towards her and leaned on the edge of the galley wall lazily.

Whether or not Leigh was avoiding talking to him on purpose he couldn't tell. If she was, she was very good at hiding it, he thought, as he watched her delicate hands preparing the cups of basic instant coffee, and making it seem artful. The morning sun shone through the door and caught her dark hair. Her tightly-bound ponytail holding her dark hair in place glistened.

When she finally looked up with a contented smile and handed him his drink, the sun caught her blue eyes for a second so they glinted; brightening her smile even further. She appeared serene.

"Is everything ok?" Ricky blurted out, again. He'd hoped to have spoken to her this morning but had originally planned for them to have more time and a more private place to hold the conversation. He'd arrived early in case he could catch her before they had to do their briefing but she'd arrived dead on time and with Lucas in tow. Again.

"Hm?" Leigh murmured, looking a little confused, her brow furrowing. Now he felt bad for having delved into her thoughts and startled her.

"Um…I mean…" he faltered, "I just thought we should clear the air a little…"

Leigh's posture relaxed a little and half-smiled.

Ricky was relieved; maybe she'd only *seemed* startled by him bringing it up so suddenly.

"There's no air to clear, Rick" Leigh told him, with a shrug.

She glanced over his shoulder momentarily and caught a glimpse of Megan scurrying their way across the tarmac, no doubt coming to check on how long until they were ready for passengers.

Leigh glanced back at Ricky and gave him a confident smile. *As confident as she could muster.* She motioned for him to turn around or at least let her pass.

Leigh made her way slowly down the cabin, checking the open over-head lockers for anything suspicious; and that every seat had its seatbelts crossed and the relevant contents in the pockets. Ricky turned and followed her.

"Oh that's great. You know I wasn't sure…"

"Seriously?" She asked him "I mean all through training we were fine. We've been friends long enough to trust each other with…well…stuff. Right?" Leigh stopped and turned to look at him.

She didn't look as though she actually needed an answer. So he smiled, accepting her explanation. They held each other's gaze, maybe for a little longer than would have been comfortable for some.

Lucas managed to break any deadlock before it became uncomfortable for either of them, calling from the back, "Hey I'm missing a safety card from 28B".

Ricky grinned and looked down, answering without turning "No problem. I've got spares up here" and turned to head up to the front of the cabin.

Leigh attempted to move out of his way, but they both moved the same direction. They flustered, swaying the same directions for a couple of seconds, as though some unspoken dance, both giggling from amusement.

Eventually, Leigh stepped right into the foot well of the seats to her left, clearing the aisle completely to let Ricky past. She looked up in time to see Lucas making a childish motion of a fake French-kiss with his arms wrapped around himself in a faux-hug.

Leigh cocked her head to one side and made a sarcastic face at him, before grinning and turning around to follow Ricky up to the front of the cabin.

She reached the front door just a Megan, flustered, arrived at the top of the steps and handed her a passenger list.

"Morning!" Megan said brightly. "Nearly ready?"

"Of course!" Ricky cut in from his position, perched on the edge of seat 1C, reaching into the back of the overhead locker for a spare safety information card.

"Give us a few minutes" Leigh winked at Megan, gesturing with her hand towards Ricky. "Might not want passengers to see him standing on their seats!" she laughed and Megan smiled and nodded in return.

Captain Murphy made her way up the steps and coughed politely to let Megan know she was in the way.

"Oops, sorry boss!" said Megan, stepping aside. Captain Murphy nodded a thank you and sauntered past into the flight deck.

Ricky stepped down and nodded to Megan as he took up his position by the front door. Leigh passed him the passenger list, and he gave her the safety card he'd just found.

"Couldn't pass that to Lucas, could you?" He asked sweetly. Leigh grinned and nodded enthusiastically, before trotting off down the cabin to pass the card to Lucas. Megan raised her eyebrows and looked at Ricky.

"What?" He asked, not really expecting an answer, before changing his tone and telling her they were ready for passengers.

-16-

Half an hour later, with passengers in their seats and belted in; they were sat at the end of the runway waiting to take off. Through the window, Leigh could see the Bristol flight behind them on the taxiway, next in line.

She still couldn't get over how much of a different view this was, she thought, from being the one left on the ground at the gate; or on the apron on a day like today, waiting to confirm to the ops office that the plane had taken off so they could send the departure message.

Leigh closed her eyes and took deep calming breaths through her nose. Despite her love of flying and her job; which so far she had found was everything she had expected and more; she still got a little nervous on take-off and landing.

She felt a hand on her knee, opened her eyes and looked over at Ricky, in the crew seat next to her.

"You're doing great" he said; before looking at her and realising that might have been a little inappropriate. "Oh god I'm sorry!" he whispered.

"Don't worry about it!" Leigh reassured him, and smiled.

That was nice, she thought to herself as she settled back and closed her eyes again.

In her slightly meditative state, breathing deeply again, she attempted to stop her mind from spinning.

There was so much she did actually want to tell Ricky; not least that she was beginning to realise that she might be hiding her true feelings from herself as well as from him.

For whatever reason she had felt it easier to gloss over and return to the *'everything's fine'* ethos of their training course. At least, before the incident Lucas had told her about in the showers, and her subsequent night with him.

She wondered if it was time to say something, now that there was less chance of an outburst; with all of these people around.

Opening her eyes she looked towards Ricky, and around the cabin, at the passengers, all settled in their seats and facing her; and glanced quickly out through the window, as they banked around, over the airport terminal about to head out across the sea.

Something caught her eye as she was looking through the window, making her lose track of her own thoughts.

Just as the aircraft was about to level off, she could have

sworn she was watching a police car; high speed with flashing lights, heading down the airport approach road.

Leigh quickly turned her head to the other side, trying to make out the continuation of the scene as the aircraft levelled out a little; but she couldn't from her belted position.

She couldn't place why it disturbed her so much. The roads leading out to the airport were long and generally straight; and outside of busy airport periods, were pretty quiet. It wasn't unusual for local boy-racers to attract police attention and get scolded.

However that was during the nights, usually; and this one, she could have sworn, was headed straight towards the airport; and not in pursuit of any other vehicle, that she could see. Leigh's previous train of thought had been lost completely; and she was lost in thinking about the police car.

She hadn't noticed the ping of the seatbelt lights being turned off and Ricky getting up ready to start the cabin service until he tapped her on the shoulder.

"Oops…sorry!" she said, and snapped out of her own thoughts.

"Come on, let's smash our first flight together, eh?" Ricky grinned playfully as he picked up the cabin handset and buzzed the flight deck.

"Hey, Captain, tea or coffee?"

As Ricky waited for a response, Leigh got up and squeezed past him into the small galley area, and started preparing her refreshment trolley. Despite herself she did feel a little thrill as their bodies rubbed together briefly; but managed to channel the feeling into enhancing her customer-service smile for the passengers.

With her back turned, however, she didn't see Ricky's face fall into a slight frown. He nodded into the phone. "I understand, no problem." He said as he replaced the handset and scratched his head.

This, Leigh did see. "What's up?"

He shook his head lightly. "Hopefully nothing." And he picked up the handset again, pressing the tannoy button, setting it to talk to the passengers.

"Isn't Captain Murphy going to say anything first?" Leigh asked him.

From her limited experience, Roberta usually liked to do her ground welcome message, which she had done earlier, as they pushed back; and then another, slightly more technical, in some effort to alleviate any concerns of possible nervous passengers in the cabin, that she knew what she was doing.

Ricky looked at her, with an expression somewhere in between stern and worried, and shook his head slightly at her, with a silent "*shh*" mouthed at her before launching into his cabin announcement.

"Good morning Ladies and gentlemen; now that the

Captain Murphy has turned off the seatbelt signs please feel free to undo your seatbelts and move around the cabin. For your own safety we do however suggest that while you do remain in your seat please keep your seatbelts fastened.

My name is Ricardo and I am looking after you in the cabin today ably assisted by the lovely Leigh and the fabulous Lucas" he said, with a flourish of his hand and a grin as he mentioned Lucas.

Towards the back of the cabin, Lucas struck a playfully diva-like pose which raised a small laugh from a few passengers around him who saw.

Ricky continued. "We'll shortly be coming through the cabin with a selection of refreshments available. If there's anything you need during our flight please don't hesitate to push the call button above your heads. On behalf of Captain Murphy and the rest of the crew, I'd like to wish you a pleasant flight. "

Ricky replaced the handset, and looked at Leigh, who raised her eyebrows at him questioningly. "Don't worry about it," he told her, and rubbed her on the shoulder to reassure her. "You make a start, I'm just gonna check something" he told her, as he knocked on the flight-deck door and heard the door being unlocked from the inside.

The locks on flight deck doors had been introduced recently, to ensure that the flight deck couldn't be accessed without prior authorisation from the flight crew. Leigh smiled to herself that Ricky and Roberta had worked together so long that they had worked out a routine of their own. Whenever they were on a flight together, they would work out a single-flight 'special knock' between them; that only they knew.

Leigh watched him go, and decided to push any concerns to the back of her mind and get on with her job.

Turning to face the eager passengers with her biggest smile, she kicked off the break from the bottom of her trolley and moved it forward slightly, stopping it close enough to the front row to be able to talk to them and reach whatever it was they fancied.

"Good morning sir, can I get you anything today?" She grinned. The gentleman in 1c smiled back.

"Black coffee please. Didn't you used to work on check-in?" He asked. Leigh nodded enthusiastically; before recognising him as a regular traveller.

"Oh hello! Mr Andrews, isn't it?" She felt a wave of pride in herself for remembering his name. The man smiled and nodded in appreciation.

At the back of the cabin, Lucas watched her enjoying herself, and continued almost skipping his way down the cabin.

The back row was empty today and the row in front of that hadn't wanted anything; by the time he'd reached a family in the third row from the back, he felt like he was breezing through.

He caught sight of a young boy sat in three seats to his left on his own, looking up at him. Lucas glanced to the right and figured his parents and baby sister were seated in those seats; leaving the boy to sit across the aisle on his own.

The boy couldn't have been more than 5 years old and was staring at him intently.

"Are you the captain?" asked the boy, a concerned look on his face. He was clutching a picture book, resting it slightly on the drop-down tray table.

Lucas noted the book appeared to be about airplanes.

"Me? No! of course not!" Lucas told him with a wink.

"Where's the captain?" the boy asked.

"Sorry…" said the boy's mother, from behind him. Lucas turned and gave her a smile. She was sat in the aisle seat, cuddling a little girl, on her lap now from the middle seat, who sleepily yawned as she snuggled in to her mother.

"It's fine! Honestly!" Lucas reassured her. He took the opportunity to ask "Can I get you anything?"

"Oh, um…Bradley, do you want anything?" the mother asked, looking at the young boy.

Bradley shook his head, without taking his eyes off Lucas.

"OK, just a bottle of water please, for me. Do you want

anything Joe?" the mother asked her partner, who looked up briefly from his paper, in the window seat.

"No thanks." He replied nonchalantly before settling back into his read.

Lucas felt proud of his ability to read people. A dad, who flies all the time for work; taking the family, who don't usually travel by plane, on a short trip away.

Lucas reached down for a bottle of water, undoing the bottle for the mother who clearly had her hands full.

Bradley piped up again. "In my book the captain is a man and the waitress is a girl..." he pointed out, motioning to the pictures.

"Well, people can do any job they want to." Lucas told him.

Bradley nodded. "Daddy draws pictures."

Lucas raised his eyebrows at him. "Really?" he asked.

The mother giggled and explained "He's an architect" she told Lucas.

"Ah I see." Lucas said, nodding. "Well, I'm not really a waitress, Bradley."

"What are you?" the little boy asked.

"Um, well, I'm a lifeguard as well." Lucas said, making eye contact with the mother again, as though checking his explanation was sufficient. She grinned and nodded at her son as though to back Lucas up.

"Oh" said Bradley. "Well, that's ok then. I've seen them. They can be boys or girls."

Lucas smiled at him. "That's right."

Bradley, satisfied with their conversation, retuned without ceremony to his book. Lucas winked at the mother and moved his trolley further up the cabin.

Meanwhile, in the flight deck, Ricky was sat in the jumpseat; the fold-down third seat behind the Captain and First officer.

Adrian, the first officer, had control of the aircraft; while Captain Murphy finished explaining to Ricky what was going on. And if she was honest, she wasn't too sure herself.

"So, why aren't we being sent back?" Ricky frowned.

"I'm not too sure, to be honest. All they've said is to stay on course, and there's a slight possibility of a diversion."

"Diversion to where?"

Captain Murphy shrugged.

Ricky couldn't believe what he was hearing. Surely someone had to make a decision?

"So basically, something's up and no-one knows what it is?" Ricky tried to clarify.

"Pretty much." The Captain said. "Come on, Rick, ever since the World Trade Centre, everyone's been on edge and on alert. This probably is nothing and someone, somewhere is over-reacting."

"Well, let's hope so" Ricky said as he stood and brushed down his uniform before turning to leave.

"Ricky…" Roberta said "Just…try and play it down. For now, eh?"

Ricky nodded and left the flight deck. Roberta stood up and locked the door behind him.

By the time he came out of the flight deck, Leigh had returned to the galley and had begun putting away her refreshment trolley. This was only a 45 minute flight and they were already half an hour into it. Leigh frowned at him for his lack of presence for most of the flight.

"What's up?" she asked

"Look, don't react too…hey are you ok?" Ricky asked, suddenly side-tracked.

He looked at Leigh; she was beginning to feel a little woozy again. She pushed past him and into the toilet; before coming out again a couple of minutes later, looking as though the moment had passed.

"Is something up?" Ricky pressed as she tucked herself away in the corner of the galley, out of view of the passengers. She seemed to be avoiding his gaze.

"You can't say anything to anyone, not yet." She

murmured.

"What?" He asked. Ricky suddenly had an inkling as to what she was about to say.

Leigh took a deep breath and looked him directly in the eye. "I'm pregnant."

Ricky's head reeled a little. That's what he'd just suspected, but to hear her say it hit him harder than even he might have expected.

A million questions spun in his head.

"You knew this, this morning, before we flew?" he said, incredulously.

"I know. I'm sorry…"

They stood in silence for what seemed like an age. Of all the thoughts that were going around in Ricky's head, all he could muster was "Do you know what kind of position you have put me in?"

A dinging sound interrupted them, and Ricky glanced down the cabin. One of the passenger call lights was on further down the aisle. He glanced back at Leigh with a silent look of '*we'll deal with this later*' but by the time he had turned back to head down the aisle, Lucas had sprung into action and was buoyantly prancing towards the passenger from the back. He waved flippantly to Ricky, indicating he had it in hand.

Ricky nodded back and turned back to Leigh, who was biting her lip, sheepishly.

Questions, and concern, continued to spin around in his head. Ricky's initial shock must have come across as anger as he realised Leigh, despite her usual confident and bolshie self, suddenly looked quite vulnerable, and scared. She was showing the anxiety she usually hid so well from everyone.

Ricky stepped towards her and pulled her into a tight hug, which she gratefully reciprocated.

It seemed like the thing they both needed to calm them down, and after a few moments they separated & stood comfortably in each other's' presence again.

Leigh poured herself a drink of water, and as she fished around in her handbag, stowed in the corner for a breath mint, Ricky watched her intently. After a while, he decided to address the real question on his mind.

"Is it mine?"

"No." Leigh replied instantly. She sounded determined and answered instantly as though she'd anticipated that very question.

"Are you sure? Coz that night with Lucas we…"

Leigh cut him off again. "I had a period a week later. It wasn't that night." She told him confidently.

"Oh!" Ricky realised he felt a little disappointed at the finality of her answer. "Oh. I see."

He frowned at the floor. Did she really think so little of him that she casually slept around *that* often?

Had this been why she'd not seemed too upset when he insisted they act normal while they were training? Or had she been trying to get back at him?

Leigh suddenly realised his demeanour and realised what this must look like to him. She shook her head to clear it a little and whispered to him, "It's Lucas's."

Without looking at him, Leigh pushed past him and headed down the cabin to respond to another call button, just as the handset next to Ricky's head buzzed. He answered it, watching Leigh head down the cabin.

As he heard the Captain's voice on the other end of the line, he could see Lucas pottering about in the rear galley securing the remaining items from his trolley. His mind was elsewhere so much that he barely heard Captain Murphy telling him they were diverting to Antwerp.

Suddenly, the mention of the nearby city snapped his attention back to his job.

"Diversion? Have they confirmed why?" he asked quietly, turning away from the cabin.

"No," the Captain told him, "Just that an incident at Brussels has closed the airport."

"Okay. Let me tell the others." Ricky said and replaced the handset.

Midway down the cabin, Leigh was crouched, and chatting the Bradley.

"Oh he said that, did he?" She asked, amused, when

Bradley told her that Lucas had claimed they were lifeguards. "Well, yes, we are, in a way. We make drinks and stuff but if anything happens to the plane, we're here to look after you."

"What about mummy and daddy? They're right there!" Bradley argued.

His mother laughed. "See the problem is, Brad, I don't know anything about planes, do I?"

"Daddy does." Bradley reminded her.

His dad shrugged. "I go on them a lot; that's about it." He said.

Leigh smiled at the boy. "Don't worry, if anything happens, Lucas over there is really close to you, so he'll look after you, okay?" Bradley nodded to her and went back to his important book.

Leigh glanced back and saw Lucas holding and listening to the handset at the back of the plane; and looking towards the front could see Ricky on the other end. She excused herself from the family and joined Lucas in the rear galley.

"What's up?" she quizzed, as he replaced the handset.

Lucas turned his back to the cabin and spoke quietly. "We're diverting." He said, almost mouthing it.

Leigh frowned. "How come?"

"A 'security incident' at Brussels." He said, with a

shrug. "Captain's about to make an announcement so brace yourself…"

Leigh knew what he meant. Once the captain made an announcement about something like this, they had little doubt they'd be deluged with questions from anxious passengers about how they'd get to their destination; whether they'd get their luggage back from the hold, how long they'd be waiting…all kinds of things that no one…yet…knew the answer to.

Leigh was thankful though, having worked on the ground, both she and Lucas could give a little insight in to what kind of crazy organising was having to happen currently at Antwerp given that they, too, would have just been told to expect an extra few hundred passengers landing in the next 15 minutes.

Assuming, of course, that their colleagues on the repositioned flight from Bristol would also be having to divert away from Brussels; along with any number of other flights that were closer to their northern European destination than they were to where they originated from.

She wasn't wrong. Captain Murphy, with her limited knowledge of the situation, had made a calm and up-beat announcement, trying not to raise any more concern than she needed to with the little information she had. Given their close proximity to their new destination, the seatbelt signs were then turned back on and as Leigh made her way back up the cabin checking that belts were properly fastened in preparation for landing, she was stopped multiple times.

Lucas followed her up double checking overhead lockers and offering every now and again to place someone's bag up there.

By the time they both joined Ricky in the front galley, most questions had been answered, fears mostly alleviated, and passengers a little calmer.

"There's a couple of regular travellers anyway," Ricky said, "and if they appear accepting of the situation it tends to help en masse. Are you OK?" he asked, looking pointedly at Leigh, although masking the main point of the question a little by aiming it at both of them.

"I'm fine." Lucas said, distractedly, watching a passenger in the aisle seat in row 22. The woman, sat with her eyes closed, breathing deeply through her nose; had refused to give him her bag for the overhead locker and had told him she'd put it under the seat; but she had yet to do so. Nervous flier he thought; and had made a mental note to keep an eye on her.

Leigh cottoned on to the undertone of Ricky's question and just looked at him and shrugged, smiling. Ricky rubbed her comfortingly on the shoulder.

"Holding pattern for a bit I guess?" Lucas asked, turning to look at Ricky briefly.

"Yup." The cabin manager replied.

"Well, I'll head back down." Lucas said, taking his leave

239

from them. Without waiting for an acknowledgement, he flashed them a huge flamboyant grin before sashaying down the aisle and raising his arm at them in a limp-wristed wave.

Ricky frowned sarcastically and once Lucas was a little further down the cabin, he hoped out of earshot, he turned to Leigh.

"Seriously?" he stated, almost as though he didn't really expect an answer.

Leigh grinned to herself. She could see how implausible her earlier admission must seem to Ricky; especially when Lucas was so outwardly ostentatious. She looked up at Ricky and tried to put on the straightest of faces.

"Jealous?"

Ricky's mouth opened in surprise. "Of Lucas…?"

Leigh couldn't keep it up; and burst into giggles; a combination maybe of the ridiculousness of her personal situation combined with the suddenness of their course-change and the potential muck-up of their day's flying programme.

Ricky was caught in somewhere between total disbelief and wanting to join in her infectious laughter. "Does he know?"

She knew from experience that this simple diversion would work out to become a couple of days of tedious aircraft changes and empty positioning flights; not to

mention drawn-out explanations to the next weeks'
worth of passengers why the timetable was affected by
things that had happened days ago.

With that type of disruption, it was entirely possible she
couldn't bank on her next two days off being where
she'd originally planned for them to be; so where ten
minutes ago she'd been planning in her head to take
Ricky out for lunch in a pub beer-garden somewhere
along the coast and fill him in; she could very well be
having to explain herself over a bad coffee in a dingy
porta-cabin on some random stretch of tarmac
somewhere.

She bit her lip and looked Ricky in the eye. "No. And
don't you tell him anything! I'll explain everything
later."

He raised his eyebrows. "You better!" he said as he
picked up the intercom handset once again, in response
to the captain calling him.

Leigh figured they'd have a good couple of hours sat on
the ground waiting further instructions to come, so
plenty of time to talk; if they could find privacy.

He stood and listened for a second, and with a simple
"Yes Captain" he replaced the handset, looked at Leigh
and rubbed her on the shoulder again, with a tight-lipped
smile, and he turned away, entering the flight deck as the
flight crew unlocked and opened the door for him.

Leigh double checked the catches on the cabinets and
trolleys in the galley to make sure everything was secure

and flipped down her jump seat. She sat down and loosely did her seatbelt up around herself.

Mr Andrews, almost directly opposite her, gave her a weary smile.

"I don't suppose they're going to let us in on what the 'security incident' is?" he asked her. He was quite calm, and seemed unconcerned about their impending involuntary detour.

Leigh smiled and shrugged. "Do they ever?" she said. "Probably someone left a vibrator switched on in their luggage again..." she whispered to him.

As a regular passenger, she recalled having told him about the incident, as an anecdote during a quiet check-in session once. Mr Andrews smiled in amusement at the shared memory.

Leigh felt the heat rising in her cheeks in slight embarrassment when she realised the prissy looking woman in 1d across the aisle from Mr Andrews had heard their exchange and was glaring sternly between the two of them.

Leigh looked down at her shoes trying to hide her amusement.

Mr Andrews simply looked directly at the woman with an air of importance and raised his right hand in a casual salute, before settling back in his seat and picking up a work document he'd been previously flicking through, from the empty seat next to him.

-17-

Inside the flight deck, the mood was growing ever more sombre. Ricky was perched on the jump seat listening to the exchange between Roberta and the tower at Antwerp.

"You and the other *YouKayAir* will be the last ones in" the disembodied voice stated, in perfect English with a twinge of a Belgian accent.

Captain Murphy looked between Ricky and her FO before responding to the tower. "YouKay four-one-eight-two Antwerp Tower, you mean to tell me they're closing your airspace"

"YouKay four-one-eight-two, all Northern European airspace is being closed with immediate effect as a precaution." The voice came back. The three of them exchanged glances between them, before the voice added "...indefinitely."

Roberta pursed her lips and nodded to Ricky. He took that as his leave to exit the flight deck and leave them to it. He nodded a silent goodbye to them both and left. Roberta half-stood and reached up to lock the door behind him as he left.

Outside the flight deck door, Ricky took his seat
sombrely on the jump seat next to Leigh. She was still
in quite good spirits and smiled him a welcome as he sat
down. Then she saw his expression of seriousness and
her face dropped.

She had even more of an inkling that the situation was
more becoming serious than they'd first imagined when,
after doing his seatbelt up, he reached over and grabbed
her hand from her lap and held it, rubbing her fingers
tenderly with his thumb.

Mr Andrews watched them silently, accepting the same
knowledge that whatever information Ricky might have
learned from the flight deck indicated that their situation
was a little more serious than they had been joking
about.

The old man had enough experience of both people, and
traveling, to know that there would have been no benefit
to Ricky telling them anything, even if he had any solid
information.

Mr Andrews sighed to himself, and closed his document.
He decided whatever it was that was about to happened
would take precedence over his paperwork. He filed the
paper away in the briefcase next to him, locked it and
slid it under his feet. He looked up and exchanged an
understanding look with Ricky.

They were all sat in a metal tube floating in the air.

Any knowledge of useless details wouldn't help them
right now, at least not until they were safe on the ground;

and anything that gave his fellow passenger any reason
to feel that their situation was more serious would do
little else than cause, at very least, more concern; and
potentially over-reactions or worse, outright panic, on
board.

Mr Andrews silently commended Ricky for whatever
choice it was that he'd made.

In the rear galley, Lucas noticed Leigh and Ricky
holding hands, as he belted himself in. He couldn't
make out the nuances of their expressions; to him this
was a little flirtation that he had hoped for Leigh to
experience, and act upon. He was in these few moments,
quite excited; suddenly looking forward to the next time
he caught these two on a night out together.

While he had these thoughts running through his head,
he happened to glance through the window in the rear
door next to him to his left. They were descending. He
was trying to make out which direction they were
approaching Antwerp from. From the rate of their
descent he surmised, they were on approach and the next
ones in.

He almost didn't register the sudden bright light and the
ensuing plume of smoke that appeared on the horizon, at
the exact moment he was watching.

Lucas turned his face away and idly inspected his
fingernails for a few moments until his brain clicked in
to gear and he realised what he'd just seen.

Lucas closed his eyes tightly, as though trying to clear

his mind, in case his eyes had been playing tricks.

Within moments he was looking up and through the window again, and still in sight…they had yet to turn to line up with the runway…was an ever growing plume of dark, thick smoke, rising up, from what he imagined to be twenty, maybe twenty five miles away.

Lucas clenched his fist in frustration. He looked up the cabin towards Leigh and Ricky. No reaction. They were as before. They hadn't seen it.

His next split-second reaction was to check out the other side of the aircraft. He could clearly see, just outside the minimum separation distance, their fellow *YouKayAir* flight, the re-scheduled one from Bristol which had left just after them, was stacked, probably ready to be given landing clearance as soon as they were off the runway.

Good. The plume of smoke wasn't them. Carl and the others were ok.

Lucas's mind felt like it was in overdrive.

Realisations and decisions seemed to be going through his mind in perfect clarity over a period of time which in reality was a matter of seconds.

He reached down and unclipped his seat belt determinedly, stood with purpose, and strode up the cabin. He stopped at the aisle where Bradley and his family sat. He leaned over the little boy, sitting on his own on the left hand side and pulled down the window blind. Bradley paid little heed to him, and was idly flicking through a comic on his lap. Ricky saw Lucas and shot daggers at him with his look.

Lucas turned round to Bradley's mum. She looked at him, confused. "I thought they had to stay open." She said. Her husband, resting his eyes, opened them and looked past Lucas.

"I need a wee." Bradley interrupted. They both ignored him.

"Sh, keep it down…I don't want him to see…"

"Oh my god!" shouted a woman a few rows ahead, causing Ricky to look at her, follow her gaze and looked out of his window, and suddenly realised what she and Lucas had noticed. Ricky stayed where he was and waved at Lucas to sit.

Lucas nodded. On his way back to his jump seat, a man in 28c, who couldn't have been much older than himself, sitting as white as a sheet next to two traveling companions, wearing t-shirts matching his own, who seemed to be snoozing and oblivious to everything, grabbed his arm.

"Is that a plane, mate?" the lad asked him.

Lucas pursed his lips. "I don't know, sir. We won't know anything until we land. But we're almost there, so that out there is nowhere near where we're going. Just sit tight and I'm sure they'll tell us when we land."

Lucas threw himself into his seat just as he could see the

ground getting closer telling him touchdown was imminent.

As he clipped himself into his seat again, his intercom phone buzzed. He picked up the handset and Ricky hissed at him from the other end.

"What did you do that for?"

"Look, he's 5 years old. There's no one else in that row...what could him being able to see....whatever that was...possibly help us in any way."

"That's not the point." Ricky muttered.

Lucas looked up the cabin at him, and took a deep breath. "Is that...you know..." he asked, unable to let the words come out.

"It's Brussels Airport. That much I'm pretty sure of." Ricky said, quietly, confidently and sadly. His hand partially covered his mouth to avoid potential lip-readers.

Lucas hung up the handset without another word.

By the time the plane bumped down onto the runway, Leigh heaved a sigh of relief, for themselves, but her heart still pounding from what they'd possibly seen; murmurs were racing through the cabin, the chatter getting louder as word spread between passengers on the one side who'd seen the smoke, and swearing they'd seen flames.

Ricky watched out of the window as their aircraft taxied

off the runway. They passed a number of other aircraft, looking a little larger than this airfield would usually handle on an average day. They seemed to be passing by and turning away from the terminal building.

A remote stand, he noted. Not an unusual option given the overcrowding apron.

It could be hours before the limited staff here could get to them. He glanced down the cabin, and picked up the tannoy handset again. A few of the passengers were starting to move around, undoing seatbelts, readying themselves to get up. He was pretty confident this wasn't going to happen immediately, and maybe not for some time yet.

He took the initiative, unlatched his seatbelt and stood up. He lifted the handset again and turned on the tannoy.

"Ladies and gentlemen" he began, "I'm sure you're aware that the seatbelt signs are still lit; and that we normally request you stay in your seats until we have come to a complete standstill. I'd like to remind you all that we still do not know the full details of our diversion, and from the looks of things outside here in Antwerp they are a little overwhelmed with the sudden deluge of flights. Please take this into account and on behalf of *YouKayAir* and the rest of the crew I'd like to apologise for the further disruption. Please be aware, we could be waiting on board for some time."

He watched the passengers. This seemed to somehow calm them slightly. There was less fussing in general.

Bradley got up and danced awkwardly, holding his crotch. Ricky was about to say something when he saw Lucas step forward and take the boy by the hand and lead him to the toilet in the rear.

Leigh, still in her seat, craned her neck and watched through the small window in the forward cabin door, as Captain Bowen's plane landed just after them. She continued watching the runway, waiting for something else to come in as soon as the wake of the *YouKayAir* cleared. Nothing did.

She watched as Ricky didn't sit back down, but passed her, to look through the window. He shook his head and turned to look at her.

"What is it?" she asked him. "What happened?"

"They closed the airspace." He told her, quietly; keeping his back turned to any passenger view. Leigh frowned in confusion. Ricky crouched down in front of her, and looked her straight in the eye. "They don't do that if it's an accident…"

Leigh began to process what he was saying

He sat back down next to her. They were still moving across the tarmac, slowly turning.

Ricky imagined they were following a tug with a 'Follow me' sign on the back of it, to some out of the way parking stand to await a set of air-stairs, followed by a hurried, stressed dispatcher clinging to a clipboard to come out and explain what was going to happen next.

Until then, it would be a case of sitting and waiting.

"Listen," Ricky turned to her, "when we stop, I'll go speak to the Captain, see what she knows; you and Lucas, just, go through the cabin, yes? Check everyone's okay…"

"I don't think they will be…" Leigh cut in.

"I mean okay for now. Say we'll let them know as soon as we know anything; we just…have to sit tight. Offer what tea and coffee we have." Ricky said.

Leigh nodded. Ricky tapped her on the knee, comfortingly.

"No alcohol, though…" he added.

Leigh looked up at him with raised eyebrows. "I wouldn't…"

"Not you! The passengers!" he told her. She smiled apologetically. Ricky smiled too, allowing his mood to be lifted ever so slightly for a few moments.

Then they sat in silence and waited until the aircraft slowed to an almost complete stop.

-18-

It wasn't until they had actually stopped that Ricky noticed that one passenger seemed to be a little more nervous than the rest. The woman in 22c had caught Lucas's attention earlier.

He stood up and picked up his passenger list he'd folded and tucked behind the water heater in the galley. He ran his finger down the list of seat numbers. Seat 22c was supposed to be empty.

Ricky frowned to himself; but as Leigh pushed past him to start making her way down the cabin to pass the message on to Lucas about what Ricky had suggested; he pushed any initial doubt out of his mind and turned his attention back to his plan.

He tapped his coded knock on the flight deck door and heard it unlocking from the inside. Ricky opened the door, and Roberta turned around to wave him in. She was sat casually sideways across her seat, asking the ground operations office what was going on as he made his way in. Ricky closed the door behind him and locked it again, more out of habit than anything else.

At the back of the cabin, Lucas was loitering outside the toilet door for fear of Bradley getting stuck in there.

"Hey" Leigh muttered as she approached.

"What's going on?" Lucas asked, trying to control the panic in his voice. "Did you see the crash?"

"Ricky said they've closed airspace."

"What?" Lucas asked incredulously

"They were the last ones in." Leigh told him, indicating their fellow flight, which was just pulling onto the parking stand next to them on the left hand side of their aircraft, between them and the runway.

"Why…?" Lucas began before Leigh cut him off again.

"I don't know. We don't know anything else. We can guess all we like but we can't tell people what we don't know. Just….you start here, I'll start from the front, just go through, ask people if they're alright, okay? Tea, Coffee, whatever. No alcohol."

Leigh raised her eyebrows waiting for a response. Lucas looked at her, and eventually nodded submissively.

Leigh spun and started up the cabin. Lucas listened at the toilet door for a flush. Nothing.

"You ok buddy?" he called out.

"Yeah…" came a strained voice from inside. "I'm just doing a poo!" the five year old called, probably a little louder than was required.

Lucas laughed to himself. "OK dude!" he called back.

Satisfied the boy was ok in the cubicle, he made his way up the cabin. Passengers were a little sparse to begin with; the back row empty.

The first ones he came to were the lads with their matching t-shirts. He had guessed early on they were heading for a stag weekend, and if he'd been honest had been expecting more hassle from them from the off. They'd been pretty well-behaved, considering. Their matching t-shirts emblazoned with the embarrassing photo of the presumed groom with 'last flight of freedom' scrawled across it.

The two in the window and middle seats who'd been asleep before, were now staring at their companion in disbelief.

"I'm telling you, man, it's a plane crash!" he was telling them, quietly – maybe not wanting to be overheard and cause a panic. "They just won't tell us that, will they? Not if we're sitting on a plane!"

"Get out. It's probably a factory on fire or something…" said the man in the window seat.

Lucas crouched down next to them. "We haven't actually been told anything yet. But look, we're here, safe on the ground. This is quite a small airport though, and whatever it is that's happened, they're probably not set up for dealing with this many planes all of a sudden, so we just need to be patient for a bit, until they can get someone out to us."

"Did you see it?" The man in the middle asked Lucas.

"The smoke?" Lucas asked, clarifying "Yeah." He shrugged.

"Well, come on…you work on planes…you think it was one?"

Lucas shrugged lightly, "Just coz I work on them doesn't mean I know what it looks like when…" he trailed off.

It felt somewhat sacrilegious to speak of downed aircraft when they were on one. Or even anywhere in the vicinity of an airport. "Look, is there anything I can get you in the mean time? I mean we're a little low on food, this was just a short flight; but drinks?"

"Got any vodka?" 28c asked, hopefully. The other two grunted in approval.

"Non-alcoholic I'm afraid" Lucas told them.

"What?" asked the man in the middle. "If we ever needed a stiff drink it's now!" he stated, before sitting back and crossing his arms defiantly, as though not actually expecting an answer.

"Oh well in that case nah mate." Window-seat man scoffed at him and sat back in his seat, staring out of his window.

"Bit of water mate?" 28b asked. "All this got me a bit

dry-throated."

Lucas nodded in agreement and headed towards the back galley.

At the front, Mr Andrews had simply nodded at Leigh and rubbed her on the arm in a paternally caring way. They exchanged a look of understanding. He knew how stressful her job must be sometimes. And for this youngster to have this happen to her so soon after starting her new position must be worrying.

She had worked her way through about five or six rows before she noticed the woman in 22c standing up, in the middle of the aisle, not going anywhere.

Leigh looked up at her.

The woman looked spooked. She stood there staring blankly up the cabin, hands deep in her pockets.

Leigh might have said something, but her passenger in row 18 that she'd just been speaking to had asked for a sweet tea to calm her nerves, so she was about to get up and do that anyway.

Just as Leigh straightened up and faced the woman, just as Ricky let himself out of the flight deck and closed the door behind him, the plane next to them, on the closest parking stand to where they were, exploded.

-19-

At first it was hard to know what had happened. Ricky was on the floor in the galley. He reached up and touched his right temple. Liquid was pouring from it, checking his hand he realised it was blood.

His hand had pushed away something hard, something that had hit him and caused the injury maybe? He looked down as he sat up, the shard of metal fell to the ground covered in his blood. He looked up at the door and realised half of it was missing, mangled and bent in, exposing the horror scene outside. The other *YouKayAir* aircraft was ablaze and by the time he was coming to; two airport fire engines were already fighting the blaze.

Sirens and noise surrounded them on all sides. Ricky staggered up, putting his hand on the counter top in the galley to pull himself up and try to gauge what was going on.

Behind him, the Adrian, the FO, rushed out of the flight deck and almost pushed him over again. The young pilot hesitated as he stepped over Mister Andrews legs, protruding from the front row; and reached up for the first aid kit in the overhead locker.

Ricky squinted at him. "What about yours?" he asked, half motioning to the first aid kit in the flight deck

Adrian shook his head. "Already used up. Too much blood." He told the purser without stopping to explain further.

Ricky turned and saw Roberta slumped in her seat and blood soaked bandages strewn across the flight deck, the open and spent first aid kit lying on the floor.

Ricky's training kicked in to action. All he knew was he had to get these people off the aircraft; but his first thought was for Leigh and Lucas. He could see Lucas standing at the back. He seemed a little shocked but uninjured. He was already looking over the passengers in the area.

Where was Leigh? Ricky panicked slightly, before noticing her crouched next to an aisle seat a few rows in front of him, about where she was when he came out of the flight deck initially. She was holding the hand of an hysterical lady and sounded to be calming her with a soothing voice.

"We're going to be getting off, ok? Do your coat up, take your shoes off for me, I'm going to go and arm the escape shoot, ok? Rescue services will be outside waiting for us…" Leigh stood up and turned with purpose towards Ricky.

She looked as though she was about to say something to him, but the look on his face made her stop. He was seemingly looking straight through her.

Little did she know, he'd noticed, just as she was standing up, the standing woman, the woman from 22c, had barely moved from her earlier standing position; despite the explosion, despite the burning plane next to them; despite the blown in sections of their own fuselage that was letting in the intense heat from the jet-fuelled fire burning outside; which Ricky knew meant there was a risk of their still half-full fuel-tanks on the left wing catching at any given moment; the woman was still stood stock-still staring straight ahead, taking deep breaths, as though willing herself to do something. It must have been only a split-second that all of these realisations converged on him but in his head it was like slow motion.

She had pulled out her hand from her right pocket. In it was a handgun. She removed her hand from her left pocket and placed it over the right one as if to steady herself.

As Ricky watched Leigh stand, he also watched the gun being raised, and being aimed directly at Leigh's head.

Ricky lunged forward, his only aim was to pull Leigh down and out of the line of fire.

At the same moment, a panicked little boy fumbled with the lock of the toilet door at the back of the cabin. Lucas turned back towards the toilet, and fished in his pocket for the emergency key so he could open it from the outside. He turned to key in the small opening and released the door. As though a trapped animal realising his chance, Bradley pushed out the split-second the door was released and ran up the aisle.

"MUMMY!" he shouted.

Bradley's mother stood up in her seat and turned. She hurriedly passed her now crying younger daughter to her husband, who cuddled the little girl up in an airplane blanket he'd got hold of and shrunk down next to the window.

"Bradley! Come here!" his mother shouted; but Lucas saw the impending danger.

The woman with the gun, distracted by the shouts behind her, turned just as Ricky grabbed Leigh from behind and pulled her to the floor, throwing himself on top of her.

The woman with the gun fired without further warning; as though instinct was guiding her. The first bullet hit Bradley square in the chest. Almost before it hit its target, she had fired the second, which caught Lucas in the left shoulder, as he crouched forward ready to catch Bradley.

Bradley's small body flew backwards, crashed into Lucas and they both fell to the floor.

Bradley's mother screamed in terror, but her husband's free arm held her back.

Leigh struggled and pushed up against Ricky, who moved over and let her get up.

They watched helplessly as the woman took stock of her actions. She turned around, and kept turning in a full circle, shaking her head as she went. Leigh caught her eye briefly. Leigh was up on her knees by now but didn't want to startle the woman any further so stopped short of standing.

The haunted look on the woman's face told her that the intention hadn't been at that point to hurt a child. Maybe she'd been expecting to see the authorities? An adult passenger, storming to stop her? Either way, she was taking stock of a mistake. Having turned full circle, the woman appeared to have made a decision. She looked down at the gun again. She looked back at Leigh pointedly, and then turned to face the back of the plane again. She muttered something; but Leigh couldn't make it out.

She raised the gun once again. She fired two more shots, randomly, without aim, before turning the gun on herself, closing her eyes, muttering again and putting the gun into her mouth and pulling the trigger. Leigh closed her eyes and gagged in revulsion as she ducked; but still, the bullet passing through the woman's skull spread the contents of her head far and wide.

Some landed in Leigh's hair; but as her body slumped down, that was the least of Leigh's worries. She needed to get to Lucas.

Ricky at the same time sprang into action. They had fallen right next to row 12 when he had covered Leigh. He had gotten up and had instructed the single male passenger in 12a to open the emergency door over the wing. The man took the small lanyard from above the door and clipped it the small metal loop outside on the wing, and using it as a strap to hold himself in place sat there waiting to help others out through the door as he called them forward.

Ricky rushed back to the front galley, opened the door on the right side of the aircraft and activated the escape slide, as more and more sirens began sounding outside and vehicles headed for the aircraft side, along with a sea of yellow-vested ground staff seemingly flooding the areas like a swarm of ants to Ricky's blurred vision.

He helped the first couple of desperate passengers out through the door and reassured them as they threw themselves down the inflatable slide. He asked the next couple if they were ok and doubled back, confident there was now a ground-crew member at the bottom of the slide helping people off and away from the aircraft; he pushed past through the aisle to check on Mr Andrews, still slumped across the front seat.

The older gentleman was covering his head with his hands; Ricky carefully placed his hands on Mr Andrew's top arm. "Hey, are you ok?" he asked him.

Mr Andrews tentatively looked up at him. He nodded weakly.

"We're evacuating, can you move?" Ricky checked with him.

"Yes, yes, I can. Get this lady out first though." Mr Andrews, now realising it was safe to move, at least for now, seemed to recover his air of grace and calm, and helped Ricky assist the lady from 1a, the window seat in the corner, who had been cowering on the floor in front of her seat. Between them, Ricky and Mr Andrews led her to the slide and both she and Mr Andrews were the next ones down.

As Ricky continued helping passengers one by one through the cabin to the escape chute, and yet more were lining up to exit over the wing, Leigh was scampering over the body of the woman with the gun and had reached Bradley and Lucas. She instinctively put her hands over the gunshot wound on the small boy's chest. She knew there was little chance that he was still alive, purely from seeing him from a distance, but she couldn't help but check for a pulse and breath. But the blood, so much blood….she lifted her hand to her face, wiping loose hairs from her forehead and wiping blood all over her hair in the process.

She wasn't sure if there was more noise coming from her own cries or Bradley's mother behind her. The mother collapsed next to her, grabbing forward and pulling up the body of her child and holding it close to her.

Her husband behind her, clinging to their daughter, was calling her desperately.

"Stephanie…come on…please!" he called frantically, checking all around him, feeling the urgency of their situation.

"I can't leave him!" Stephanie cried.

Leigh put an arm around her and whispered "We have

to…" she sniffed, as she clung to Lucas's hand beneath Bradley's body with her other hand. She looked at Lucas's face, slumped almost out of view under the nearest seats. He was still there, looking back at her; but he looked down at his own blood soaked clothes and, with a trickle of blood appearing at the corner of his mouth and his breathing shallow, he looked at her sadly, and with what little remaining strength he had, slowly shook his head, then wrapped his arms around the little boy and pulled it back away from the mother.

Behind them, the stag lads from row 28 had been watching, in shocked silence.

"It's all fucked-up, man…" window-seat man whispered.

Leigh realised they were there. She looked up at them.

"Can you open the back door? The one on that side…" she indicated with her head, her left, the opposite side to the burning aircraft outside.

"Dunno…we can try…"

Leigh turned around and checked behind her. There were still passengers trying to clamber towards the over-wing exit. She sniffed and blinked back tears.

She gathered all her strength and stood, stepped over her dying friend and the body of the small boy he was clutching and pushed past the men, leading them to the back galley. She armed the emergency slide bar along the bottom of the door, opened the door and as the slide inflated she shouted "Get out! Get out!" and guided the three men down.

After them, a couple of solo travellers moved past her in a blur as more tears gathered in her eyes; followed by a middle-aged man holding tightly the hand of his highly emotional girlfriend. As they passed, Leigh gathered herself enough to look up and noticed a nasty looking gash on the woman's forehead. Putting her passengers first, she put her hand out and stopped them.

"Wait, let me look…" She inspected the girl's head. "Can you see?" Leigh asked the girl. The passenger nodded.

"Can they check her down there?" The boyfriend asked, hurriedly, desperate to get off.

Leigh held up three fingers in front of the girl. "How many?"

"Three?" the girl said.

Leigh nodded briefly to let them pass, but after a split-second thought, held the girl's arm again, and grabbed a pile of paper napkins from behind her in the galley and pressed them against the girl's head.

"Here, keep that pressed firmly against the wound until someone can look at you, OK?" Leigh told her, with an air of authority that she didn't believe she could have. If anyone had told her a year or so ago that she would cope with anything like this, she would have laughed them out of whatever pub they were drinking in.

She watched the last passengers get escorted off the bottom of her slide; and checked up the cabin. None more were coming towards her. She watched as one last person climbed through the over-wing exit by row 12, and held up a thumb when the passenger from row 12 who'd opened the door ducked his head back in to check if everyone was out. He waved back, and she saw him head off the wing himself.

No one was exiting the front any more now, either, and she could see Ricky and the first Officer struggling to get Roberta out of her seat in the flight deck.

Suddenly, Leigh was finally overcome. She burst into tears and shaking, rushed up the aisle and collapsed next to Lucas. He'd closed his eyes and both he and Bradley, despite the blood and obvious wounds, their faces looked calm and peaceful.

She put her hand over the little boy's. It was so tiny compared to hers, lying there on his tummy. Leigh closed her eyes and let the tears and sobs come.

-20-

Ricky , in the front galley, had seen the last of his passengers down the chute, checked and saw the last few heading for the other exits; and made a mental note to double check the cabin after; but first he turned and went into the flight deck. If there was any chance of getting Roberta out it had to be now.

"How's she doing?" he asked.

Adrian stood up and scratched his head. "I can't see where the blood's coming from. Hell of a lump on her head though."

Ricky felt the back of Roberta's head through her mop of dark hair. The FO was right.

Ricky looked over her torso. There was a wound on the left side of her chest. The window on her side had been blown in and there was glass everywhere, it appeared a wedge of glass had lodged into her chest; but Adrian had managed to bandage tightly around the glass, keeping it in place, and the bleeding from there had seemed to have slowed, or stopped. But there was still blood dripping down from under her seat.

He looked out at the burning aircraft next to them.

They'd have to move her. Ricky looked out to the left at the other aircraft. There were more fire engines, local ones appeared to have joined the airport ones.

"Come on." He said and motioned to the FO. They both moved forward and attempted to position themselves either side of the captain.

As they made an attempt to lift her, she groaned and her eyes flickered open.

"Ow." She managed. "What happened?" Her voice was slurred.

"Can we get to that later? We gotta get out." Ricky told her.

With Roberta being a little more alert, she managed to help them a little, they lifted and she at least managed to shuffle her feet. They managed to get her sideways, out through the flight deck door; and towards the open door leading onto the escape slide. The first officer looked at Ricky.

"Can you take her?" Ricky asked him. He definitely didn't want to leave until he knew he was the last one left on the aircraft.

Adrian looked her up and down. They finally realised that the wound dripping blood was at the top of her left thigh. They both looked at it, then back at each other.

"Hey!" came a shout from the bottom of the slide.

Ricky looked down. An ambulance, with its engine running, was stopped a little bit away from the slide, and two firemen had positioned themselves one either side of the slide; joining the airport ground crew who were already there.

Adrian looked at Ricky and nodded. Between them they manoeuvred Roberta to the top of the slide, and she and the FO slid down into the arms of the waiting emergency services.

Ricky heaved a sigh of relief as he watched Roberta be lifted onto a stretcher and carried immediately to the ambulance.

One of the firemen called up to Ricky as Ricky watched the man from row 12 be the final person to jump down off the wing and be hurried away by ground crew.

"Hey!" called the fireman. "Anyone else on board?"

"I'm going to check!"

The fireman waved a thumbs up sign at him. "Don't take too long!" he called but Ricky was already out of sight of the door.

Ricky was making his way through the cabin checking each row of seats either side as he went, but ultimately aiming for Leigh, hunched on the floor.

When he reached her, his heart ached at the sight of her distraught face, as he crouched down the other side of Lucas and Bradley.

"Hey," he said softly. She looked up at him and shook her head.

Ricky looked at the child and balked. He had thought Bradley had been hit but had pushed it to the back of his mind and had hoped against hope that they would both be ok.

Ricky grabbed Leigh's hand and pulled it away from Bradley's little one.

"We can't do anything now." He looked at her. He had tried his best, but he too was crying.

Suddenly there were shouts from outside and a huge crashing sound as the aircraft around them shuddered.

Ricky looked up. The wing to his right, the one next to the burning aircraft, had caught alight. In seconds they could be engulfed in aircraft fuel flames.

"Come on!" he grabbed Leigh and pulled her up. She was limp with emotion and lack of energy.

He found it really easy to shove her, turn her around and push her along the aisle towards the back of the cabin, and as they reached the top of the slide heading out of the rear galley, away from both of the *YouKayAir* aircraft, the only thing he could think of doing was holding her, so he threw his arms around her and jumped.

They half slid and half rolled down the chute; and when they reached the bottom the fireman from the front who had shouted to Ricky had seen them and run to the back, he grabbed Ricky by the arm and, with Ricky pulling Leigh by the hand behind him, led them away quickly to a waiting fire-service vehicle. Putting it in gear and driving away as fast as he could make it; they managed to get just far enough away from their aircraft as it, too, was engulfed in flames.

The fireman turned the vehicle side on as they sat at their safe distance and watched.

Leigh raised a hand and covered her mouth. Ricky put his arms around her and she turned and cried into his chest, as he watched their planes burn, and let his own tears flow.

*
.

-21-

The hours that followed, for Leigh and Ricky, were a blur.

They had initially been taken to a closed off gate boarding area, reserved for survivors, and walking wounded. They and the rest of the passengers acknowledged each other and comforted each other as much as they could.

Passenger Services agents assigned to this room provided them with pretty much anything they asked for. The girlfriend with the gash in her head, now treated and bandaged, snuggled against a wall with about twenty blankets and being held tightly by her boyfriend, had asked for haggis. She had muttered something about not even knowing why; she just suddenly had a craving for it; and bless them, the ground staff had somehow managed to figure out where to get a tinned haggis from and have it cooked up for her.

The smell of it turned Leigh's stomach and her one resounding memory of being in that survivors room was lurching over a small metal bowl she'd been passed to throw up into; and the resoundingly comforting feeling of Ricky's strong hand rubbing her back rhythmically, and holding her hair back for her. Her damp hair that was no longer tied up in her cabin crew style, as she'd been allowed to rinse it in a sink, to try get the blood out.

The thought of the blood that was no longer in her hair had made her look up and search the room for Bradley's family. They weren't here. She'd made Ricky ask. They were told that they'd been found a small side-room to grieve in. Leigh nodded. They needed that.

Leigh's tears had stopped a while ago. All she felt like doing now was staring. Staring at her own hands. Staring at the straggly ends of her hair hanging down around her face that was drying naturally, with no dryer and no brush. Staring out through the windows of the gate area they were being held in; which was looking out over a quiet, countrified area. There was no sign at this side of the airport that anything amiss had ever happened. They were looking out over a field of spring meadow flowers. The only thing that seemed amiss was the stench. Stuck in the air and their noses, the smell of burning, or fuel, and dried blood.

She didn't feel like crying, she didn't feel anything but emptiness. Except that all she knew was that Ricky was right next to her with his arms around her the whole time.

And she didn't want to ever be anywhere else.

Ricky answered any questions that were put to him. There were, within an hour, investigators around. They were tactful. They had compassion training. They were accompanied by psychologists and counsellors who had been trained for this kind of thing.

He knew all of this.

He knew the facts and the figures and the training.

He told them everything he had made mental notes of during the whole event.

He watched as Leigh did the same; rattling off facts and figures and step-by-step recounts of what procedures they'd followed, and what they'd not been able to, and why things that had been missed had been missed.

But with all the training and recreations and simulations in the world that they'd gone through to teach them procedures and actions, nothing could teach them how to feel.

And nothing had prepared them for watching their friend and colleague die.

And nothing had prepared them for hearing that someone they had thought of as a close friend and valued colleague was mainly responsible for the events of the day.

On the other side of the airport, a friends and family room had been set up, and as the hours went by, one by one, survivors were taken and 'matched up' with people who had been supposed to meet them or collect them.

For those who were local, who were heading home or to

work in Brussels, their greeters arrived a lot sooner.

For those who were heading out away from home, it wasn't so easy.

Especially as airspace was still closed; and even when it opened, whenever that might be, very few airlines had all of their aircraft in the right place across northern Europe – everyone's flight schedules were going to be all over the place for many days, even weeks, to come.

A number of the passengers were still here as the sun was setting.

As their numbers dwindled, Ricky, Leigh and Adrian, were eventually moved to a small side room.

It didn't take long for them to realise why.

Leigh looked around, morbidly amused that this was the same room Bradley's family had been put in to grieve. They were gone now.

One of the investigators was kind enough to let them know that the family had been given a private vehicle and driver to take them all the way back home by road, via the channel tunnel.

Bradley and Lucas, and the female with the gun, were the only lives lost from their aircraft, they were told.

Leigh and Ricky should feel proud of themselves, they were told.

They managed to get everyone else away to safety.

Leigh asked about the other aircraft. She was met with silence, pursed lips, and dropped eye contact.

There were no survivors, they were told.

It was soon clear to them why they'd been moved away from the remaining passengers.

The questions of the investigators started taking a darker turn.

They had begun asking questions about Carl.

"Carl?" Leigh looked up, shocked. "Why Carl?"

"How well did you know him?" asked a Dutch-accented investigator; a stern looking woman with a tight bun who barely looked up from her clipboard, and had an annoying habit of continually clicking her ball point pen with her long nails.

"He started as a part-time check-in agent the same time as me. I've known him for years."

"He, um...well, he didn't always hang out with everyone but he was just....well, the same, really." Ricky looked at Leigh, and shrugged.

"He didn't "hang out"?" The investigator asked.

Ricky frowned. "You know, we have...work nights out and stuff. He tended to stay home, family man kind of stuff..."

The investigator fell silent and added notes. Ricky and

Leigh exchanged glances. Adrian sat silently. He was a relatively new transfer from another base and didn't really know any of them well.

"Who was the woman with the gun?" the FO asked.

The investigator looked up and pushed her glasses up her nose.

"We are still trying to track her. The name on the passenger list…"

"Brenda" Ricky suddenly remembered.

Leigh looked at him.

"Brenda Hicks. She never was in 22c. There was a Brenda Hicks in 22a, she must have just decided to sit in the aisle instead." He said, randomly.

The investigator put down her clipboard and pen on the table, with a sigh.

"The passport that the scanner logged before departure was reported as stolen, after the incident." She said.

Ricky hung his head.

Leigh yawned and broke into tears again.

"She's…we're exhausted…" Ricky said. He looked up at the counsellor who was stood behind the investigator. A small woman, older, with a kind face and an oversized handbag; she looked like his grandmother.

The counsellor looked at the investigator.

"Let's get them somewhere to rest." She said.

The investigator nodded.

"Come on," the counsellor said, as she stood up and held the door open for them.

Ricky stood and helped Leigh up, and they and the FO followed the counsellor.

-22-

An airport hotel.

At any other time, Leigh could have laughed.

Her room was overlooking the still-smouldering remains of two burned-out aircraft.

She had had a proper hot shower, rewashed her hair and dried it this time.

She was wearing a snuggly warm hotel robe and slippers, had pulled the pure white quilt off the bed, wrapped it around herself and was curled up on the sofa by the window, just overlooking the runway.

Unlike other airport hotels she'd stayed in, in years past, watching aircraft coming and going constantly; all through the night; this one was silent of any air traffic.

There weren't even any lights in the sky.

On the tarmac that she could see, there were still plenty of emergency vehicles; but there were no flashing lights. What looked even more odd, was that there weren't even that many flashing orange lights.

Usually, on an active apron, with planes coming and going, any vehicle driving around, had to have its orange lights flashing – including visiting vehicles, who would have their hazards on. The fact that there were no aircraft coming and going meant there weren't even as many orange lights as usual.

Leigh felt like the end of the world was happening in front of her eyes.

Even when your world is collapsing, life usually goes on as normal for everyone else outside the window.

This felt like life had stopped for everyone, everywhere.

There was a knock at her door.

She pushed the quilt off her and padded over to the door.

She knew who it was.

It was the only person she wanted it to be.

She opened the door without checking the spy-hole and Ricky stood there looking down at her, leaning his hand on the door frame; also wearing a hotel robe and slippers. His hair was damp now too. The deep gash on the side of his forehead cleaned up he almost looked like his old self again.

Leigh stood aside to let him in. He wandered in, as though he didn't need an invitation, but stopped short of going further into the room.

"Hey, you ok?" he asked. He stayed where he was in the

doorway.

"Are you coming in?" she asked, quietly.

"Is that alright?" he checked.

"Why would it not be alright?" She challenged, almost on the verge of tears again purely from having what would otherwise have been a normal conversation.

"I just…I don't know if I can sleep tonight and I don't want to keep you up…" he attempted, with some mumbling, as though he was waiting for her to cut him off.

Which she did. "I can't sleep. And I don't want to be on my own" she told him pointedly.

He walked past her and she closed the door behind him. Ricky walked towards the window where her quilt lay on the sofa, and looked out. Leigh walked back into the room after putting the safety chain on the door.

She stopped.

In the middle of the room and suddenly, just let herself cry.

Silently to begin with, but eventually a sob escaped her lips and made Ricky turn.

His heart melted just looking at her.

He rushed forwards and caught her, hugging her tightly as she let herself cry properly.

He moved her over to the bed, sat her proper up against some pillows and went over the grab the quilt from the sofa. He sat next to her on the bed, pulled the quilt over them and put his arms around her.

Leigh turned her face round, then her body sideways, and buried herself against his chest as his arms wrapped around her. Once comfortable, Ricky finally let himself start crying too.

And that's how they stayed, as the night carried on outside the window; until dawn broke over the runway the next morning.

-23-

"*Tea?*" Leigh stood in her kitchen and raised an eyebrow.

"What's wrong with tea?" Sasha asked her, flopping down on the sofa and dropping her slouchy boho handbag at her feet.

Leigh was looking at her as though she'd just announced she didn't like her job anymore.

Leigh shook her head and flicked on the kettle.

"I do drink tea, you know…" Sasha added, a little defensively.

"I know!" Leigh shrugged, still a little taken aback.

"Sorry." Sasha suddenly realised that with her curt responses she might be coming across as insensitive.

She'd been feeling like this for weeks, if she was honest with herself. Walking on eggshells any time she heard from Leigh; and she'd been putting off visiting for as long as possible.

Of course she'd been there when Leigh first got home.

They hadn't talked.

Sasha had met her at Central train station; and just hugged her. They'd stood on the platform hugging for so long that when they separated the platform was almost deserted. All the other passengers on the train from London had dissipated.

Leigh had refused a flight home. She never thought she'd be affected by anything enough to stop her getting on a plane but she had, this time.

She and Ricky had slept, purely from exhaustion rather than anything else, in each other's arms.

The following morning, the curtains still open, the sunrise flooded in and woke them. They'd barely spoken. Ricky had woken her with a gentle kiss on the lips.

 Then they'd simply exchanged knowing looks and sad smiles. Ricky had excused himself to go back to his room to get dressed. As well as he could. They'd been given some clothing raided from the airport's baggage departments lost property, and an overnight kit with a disposable toothbrush and a t-shirt; with the promise that 'something would be sorted' tomorrow.

It had been. By the next morning a vociferous yet mousy girl from head office called Nyree had appeared, having travelled over on the last ferry, with a seemingly unlimited credit in HQ's name. She, having completed a basic course in counselling, she told them, offered a caring but constant voice to them, suggesting ways to get home, suggesting they go to get some clothes; would they like something to eat? Would they like to go somewhere or have it brought to them?

Leigh barely heard anything the girl was saying. She had tuned pretty much any conversation out; and Nyree seemed quite happy to just ramble on. Until she sat, waiting, expectantly, for an answer as she sat in front of a computer terminal in the business centre of the hotel. She was staring at Leigh.

Leigh didn't know for how long; but became aware that she was supposed to give an answer to something. She shook her head a little, and looked at the screen next to Nyree. She was trying to book flights.

"No!" Leigh had snapped. "Sorry." She added, sheepishly as the girl jumped. "Sorry, can I go on the Eurostar or something?" Leigh asked, quietly, feeling numb all of a sudden.

Nyree's face fell. "Of course! I'm SO sorry! Can't believe I could be so insensitive. I mean they sent me on that course for a reason and everything. I suppose Ricardo would want that too…lemme see what the times are from here, if we can get a connection…"

"I think Ricky wants to go home…I mean Spain, for a bit?" Leigh suggested. He'd mumbled something about seeing home last night.

Nyree stopped and looked at her, blankly; before a look

of recognition spread across her soft unpronounced features a few moments later. "Oh! Yeah! 'Course. I'll talk to him later." She mumbled, busying herself looking at train timetables and tickets for one on various browser windows.

Leigh stifled a yawn and sat staring at her feet, letting the girl get on with her job, yet continuing to chatter inanely in the background; as though somehow believing that silence of any kind would be the worst kind of offence she could commit.

Within minutes, Leigh held in her hands printouts of her booking from Antwerp, via Brussels, on the Eurostar to London St Pancras, and a detailed instruction page on how to easily get to Paddington for a train to Cardiff.

By the same afternoon, Leigh was stood in the foyer, a small bag of what meagre items she'd gathered over the past 24 hours; hardly worth keeping, except her passport, which had been in her uniform pocket, out of habit; and her dirty uniform. But it seemed weird to her to travel anywhere without a bag. Nyree was checking her out at the counter. Ricky joined Leigh, and simply stood next to her. For a few moments they just stared out through the foyer doors at the well-manicured flower beds.

"You gonna be ok?" Ricky asked, quietly. No small talk left.

Leigh looked up at him. She forced a tight-lipped smile. "Yeah."

Nyree joined them, chattering before she was even in

earshot. She held out a hire-car envelope to Ricky.

"Here. It's parked out front and the tank is full. Don't worry about it being full handing it back. You sure you're ok to drive? Because there are other options you know. I've been told by the Office to not let you go if you're going to be any kind of risk…"

"I'm fine." Ricky cut over her, taking the envelope from her and fishing the car keys out.

He took a deep breath and started towards the door.

Leigh felt a lump in her throat. A sudden fear that he'd walk out the door and not look back.

He stopped, dropped his bag, turned and in a single step, reached her, and without looking her in the eye at all he put his arms around her in a massive bear hug. Leigh reciprocated her face down, and her face screwed up in an attempt to hold back tears.

Still without any eye contact, he turned away again, picked up his bag and sauntered, in his casual, confident way, out through the door.

Within minutes he was gone; and Leigh continued staring at the space outside the window.

She didn't know how long it was before she realised that Nyree was stood watching her; silently waiting for her to be ready. The girl was simply blinking at her; a sympathetic and patient look on her face.

When Nyree saw Leigh looking at her she shrugged and

simply asked "Are you ready? I'll drop you at the train station before I drop my hire car off."

Leigh sniffed, and nodded. They drove in silence the whole way there.

Stopped outside the train station on Pelikaanstraat, they sat in silence for a few minutes, people watching. Not that there were many about. Leigh's mind wandered to how many millions of people around the world were today staying at home; hugging their families.

"Want me to come in with you?" Nyree offered, compassionately.

"Nah. I'm fine." Leigh answered quietly and grabbed her bag, ready to let herself out.

"I'm not sure you are." Nyree said, looking at her intently. She looked down and fished around in her handbag, and pulled out a crumpled piece of paper, an old receipt it looked like to Leigh; and a pen, then scribbled something on it. "I'm on the staff intranet, but just in case, here's my number. Any time, ok?"

Leigh took it and smiled. She doubted she'd use it; but she appreciated the sentiment. She stepped out onto the grey pavement, and turned to watch Nyree in her little hire car pull away from the row of taxis parked along the narrow street.

Leigh had scurried into the terminal, ignoring the urge to grab a coffee from the Starbucks near the entrance. She didn't really have any interest in appreciating the architecture and simply wanted to get on with her journey. Any moments taken to stop and breathe and relax in any way might let in emotions she didn't really want to deal with right now.

She did, on and off, while she was on the train. She'd had little choice. She had little else to do but sit and watch through the window as the Belgian countryside passed by for 40 minutes.

She meandered around the station at Brussels after figuring out her connecting platform. She rubbed her tummy as she contemplated outside Sam's coffee shop...did she really want to, or was caffeine just a risk she didn't need? She had decided against it and wandered off to find a seat.

Caught up in her own mind she had even less interest in the shiny modernist architecture of this station than the one in Antwerp.

The only thing that struck her, that she couldn't ignore, was the heavy presence of armed security, everywhere. She'd had to show her passport along with her ticket as she ambled to the platform. Her airport pass had fallen out of her passport holder and the policeman who bent down to pick it up smiled sadly at her as he handed it back.

By the time she'd boarded the Eurostar to London, exhaustion overcame her again. She didn't know if it was the early pregnancy stages that were catching up with her; or the huge toll of the events. She didn't even feel emotional.

Overall she still felt quite numb, and her mind blank.
Like she couldn't think, or feel anything. It was
beginning to seem like she'd never feel anything else
again.

It wasn't like she could even put it down to shock by this
point. She'd slept, and spoken, and listened, and
showered, and continued breathing...

Leigh simply continued to function. She even smiled at
people who came and went through the train carriage,
looking for empty seats; or squeezing past from having
visited the buffet. They were just empty smiles,
followed by looking away and staring blankly through
the window once more. Even when the train entered the
channel tunnel and there was nothing at all to look at,
she continued staring at the window.

All she could do was think about how to get rid of the
lingering smell from her nostrils. Wherever she went, it
was there. She began to wonder if it stayed with her to
give her something to concentrate on, so she could
continue feeling numb about everything else.

When she reached St Pancras and the familiar London
surroundings she easily blended in on the
Hammersmith&City line with the emotionless faces,
trying their best in the British way, to look at anything
other than their fellow passengers for fear of making
polite conversation.

Paddington greeted her, with even more familiarity. She

needed even less concentration to find her way around here and, despite again the presence of more visible security, armed police officers patrolling; extra checks at the gates onto each platform, she sat on the *Intercity 125* out of the station bound for Cardiff barely even being aware of how she'd got there. She knew, of course she did; but recalling the experience was seemingly impossible.

The relief of seeing Sasha stood there on the platform waiting for her as it pulled in to Cardiff Central, it was as though this was the first moment she could finally allow herself to feel.

Leigh's breathing had deepened, and as she stepped off the train, the tears had already welled up.

Sasha stepped forward and grabbed the meagre bag from Leigh's hand; then looked at her friend; and reading her expression instantly, simply threw her arms around her. And for the first time since the hotel room with Ricky, Leigh cried. And Sasha held her; as long as she felt was necessary.

From the empty platform, out onto the city street, and walking down to the carpark on Westgate Street, Sasha'd linked arms with her, to keep her close and ensure she stayed upright.

Sasha had kept silence at bay with inane chatter about banal stuff, completely avoiding any talk of what had happened or anything airport-related. Leigh knew what she was doing was on purpose. She knew that airport life for the past 48 hours would have been crazy; and scary; and manic; and emotional; but Sasha didn't even touch on that. She filled the walk with how Jason at Landing Lights had managed to slice his hand on that dodgy old bottle opener that Elise had refused to replace so now she was having to rethink that; and how there were suspicions that Philippa and Will were having issues…

They got to the car and Sasha changed the subject to how her old banger was on its last legs and could she hear that rattling noise, and really she was going to have to do a load of overtime before even thinking about booking it in for a service…Leigh watched the South Wales countryside going past with an extra sadness.

Home suddenly didn't seem like home anymore; despite it being the only thing she'd thought she wanted since this had all happened.

She watched the road speeding past and wondered how Ricky was getting on.

Was he going to just drive? Would he keep going through the night? Would he get home to a relative's home cooking and feel a comfort he hadn't for years and just fall apart there? Or would he stop along the way, at some seedy bar and get drunk and do himself some damage?

Sasha stopped outside Leigh's apartment block and without even asking if she should come up, got out and carried Leigh's bag for her, up the stairs, still talking;

this time about how Olga had forgotten to feed the goldfish in the baggage office tank apparently and they'd all come in to find them floating on the top of the tank yesterday morning.

They got to the door of Leigh's apartment and Leigh suddenly realised she didn't even have her keys.

Sasha looked at her, smiled, and held up her spare key.

Leigh's relief showed itself in another burst of tears; and Sasha wasn't quite sure what to do with herself. She opened the door quickly and shuffled her friend in.

Sasha had fussed around for a good hour or so, checking the heating was working and sorting the mail; not that there was much there; making Leigh a cup of tea and running her a bath; then preparing her a meal from the paltry contents of the freezer, but managed to make the best of it and had a plate of hot food ready for her friend after she'd had a soak.

Sasha had offered to stay on the sofa that first night but Leigh had managed to relax enough to tell her no, that she'd be fine, and that she'd call if she needed anything.

Sasha had left, and Leigh had noticed a flashing light on her answer machine in the corner.

She pressed play, and after a few seconds of silence, apart from the sound of traffic in the background, she heard Ricky's voice.

"Uh...I'm not sure what to say. I hate messages." He

laughed uncomfortably. "*I hope you got home OK. I'm fine. I just wanted to say that. I'm at a payphone. And I made it to a place called Poitiers. Reminds me of that actor. I'm gonna sleep here. Don't worry about me driving with no rest, eh? I'll...uh...I don't know how long I'm gonna stay. But I'll be back, soon. Ok? So, don't worry.*"

There was silence again. Leigh expected the click of the phone hanging up but there was a shuffle as the phone went back up to Ricky's ear. "*I miss you.*" He said, tentatively. "*So, anyway, I just wanted to say, you know. That. Bye.*" And then there was the click.

Leigh felt comforted to hear his voice, and had slept well. Finally.

And then spent what seemed like months, but actually turned out to be a couple of weeks, pretty much on her own.

She'd watched the news, intermittently. Tried to, at least.

A highly organised, deadly terrorist attack on multiple airports in Northern Europe, primarily around Brussels, possibly targeting the seat of the European Union's Parliament...various groups had claimed responsibility...police and security services working together to discount some...could have been worse as security services started acting on tip offs and started making arrests before the attacks took place...were too late in a number of instances.

Leigh cast her mind back and saw in her mind's eye, that

police car with lights flashing heading for the airport as they had taken off and banked around…

Arrests had been made across the continent at airports as potential perpetrators attempted to board…or operate…flights.

Leigh closed her eyes to re-centre her brain as mug-shot type images of the suspects plastered across the screen. Some weren't even mug-shots. They were holiday snaps. Or work-ID smart & smiley poses. These weren't people with records, or known to the police…

There, right in the centre, was Carl.

They were using his photo from his airport pass.

"Aviation across the world is on critical alert and is likely to be for some time to come. A lot of the perpetrators, including suspects who died in the attacks, were employees of airlines and aviation in general, with clean records, no previous tenable links to any organised crime or terrorist organisations…" the correspondent, stood outside some random airport they happened to be near, was droning on about.

Leigh had been alone, watching as each day a little more information was reported.

She couldn't bring herself to call anyone at work just yet; but dreaded to think what it was like at the airport. They would be snowed under. Days of airspace closures combined with reroutes because of damage done to Brussels and Antwerp's runways and apron would mean displaced crews....if they weren't suspects...and aircraft...and continuing delays and diversions and every flight that did manage to go anywhere would be packed as those from cancelled flights were trying to all squash on to those that were going.

It had been getting too much to think about. Within a couple of years of the attacks on the World Trade Centre in New York, the world was being subjected to this aftermath all over again.

But Sasha had turned up at exactly the right moment; just when Leigh really didn't believe she could take any more.

And now Leigh was stood in the kitchen, about to automatically spoon some instant coffee into a mug for her friend as the kettle boiled, and Sasha was asking for tea.

The world really had gone mad.

-24-

Leigh walked around the breakfast bar counter and put the two steaming mugs down on the little glass coffee table. Sasha picked hers up straight away, with tentative fingers, and began to blow it to cool it.

Leigh walked over to the French doors and opened them wide, letting in the streams of sunlight over the small Juliette balcony; and paused a moment watching the sunbeams dancing in the water in the old harbour they overlooked.

"How are you doing?" Sasha asked her as Leigh turned around to join her, perching in the arm chair facing the window.

"Do you know what, I don't really know." Leigh confided. "Every now and again I wake up and think everything's normal; and then, I remember. It's not...and..." she trailed off as she sipped her tea.

"Have you spoken to work? Do you think going back will help?"

"Well...about that..." Leigh started. But Sasha cut in,

as she put her mug down.

"I guess they've got a minimum amount of personal time you have to take though? I mean I haven't seen Ricky, or anyone else, back yet. I mean there's not that many flights operating, still. And I heard that Captain Murphy's still in hospital. Lucky escape they said…" Sasha continued, until she noticed Leigh looking at her pointedly. "Sorry…"

"I know." Leigh said. "It's kind of hard to know WHAT to say, isn't it?"

"I'm pregnant." Sasha said, as though she couldn't think of any other way of changing the subject.

Leigh took a moment to take in what Sasha had just said. Given that the phrase had been going and over in her own head and she'd been trying to figure out how…and when…to tell Sasha.

"What?" Leigh managed to force out.

"Yeah. I know. We hadn't been planning it…not yet, anyway, that's why I'm on tea. Decaf mainly. But…well…" Sasha trailed off, and then looked up at Leigh. "I know…you're going through stuff. And I didn't come here to tell you that. I was going to keep it to myself for a bit…but…"

"Me too." Leigh said quietly.

"Yeah, I guess they've got councillors and stuff calling you and talking you through stuff. I think that's why

I've stayed away for so long really, and why I'm talking ten to the dozen and not allowing you a word in edgeways coz I don't want you thinking I'm hanging around for the gossip…and I feel so guilty about the sandwiches even though they said I was not a suspect and they cleared me and everything. Well, there was a caution…" Sasha paused and took a sip of her tea.

"I mean, I'm pregnant too." Leigh corrected her.

Sasha's tea sprayed out of her mouth across the glass table. She immediately sprang into action, rushing to the kitchen and grabbing a tea towel off a hook in the corner and wiping her own face with the back of her hand as she returned with it to wipe the table.

Sasha, kneeling at the table, wiping, looked up at leigh in surprise and lowered her voice. "What? With who? I mean…Is there someone here?" She asked, glancing towards the bedroom.

"What? No!" Leigh exclaimed. "It's been two weeks…you think I've moved someone in and impregnated myself in response to being on a plane being shot up by terrorists?"

"No." Sasha shrugged. "No, now you put it like that…" She said as she finished wiping and sat back on the sofa, trying to make sense of Leigh's news. "Ricky?"

"You wouldn't believe me if I told you." Leigh mumbled and sipped her drink. After a moment, she frowned. "What makes you think it was Ricky?"

"Oh, COME ON!" Sasha snorted. She flashed Leigh a look. "Did you think I was blind?" she raised her eyebrows. She leaned forward and picked up her mug again. "Speaking of Ricky..." Sasha began again "Have you heard from him?"

Leigh nodded lightly. "He left me a message on his way to Spain."

"That's it?" Sasha pushed.

"A nice message." Leigh shrugged, "He needs time, I think."

"I suppose." Sasha agreed. "He was close to Lucas."

Leigh looked at her then looked down.

"I'm sorry," Sasha realised what she'd said. "I know you were too. I can't imagine what it was like on there. Look, I know you would have got him out, if you could."

"There was no point. He was already dead..." Leigh reminisced.

"How?" Sasha asked, softly.

"She shot him."

Sasha was silent. In shock, not really knowing what to say.

Leigh looked at her, and continued. "I don't even know if I'm supposed to say anything. I mean they took our statements. They asked about Carl. They said they'd be looking into our backgrounds. VERY deeply. I just shrugged when they said that. I think. I mean, Carl, of all people, right?"

Sasha nodded. "I know. I mean, apart from you, going through it and all, that's the hardest part to understand. We've all racked our brains about that. You know, the why and all that."

"There was a woman, on our flight, with a gun."

"I know."

Leigh nodded. "I mean, she didn't get it out until the end but it must've been there the whole time. And all I can think of is this time when Carl had left his lunch under a seat and I found it and he got all defensive about it…and now I'm wondering if it wasn't actually his lunch at all…What do you mean you know?"

Sasha's face fell and her cheeks reddened.

"That's why I was cautioned." She admitted.

"Cautioned about what?" Leigh gasped.

Sasha leaned forwards and put her cup down. "There was a thing that happened. An incident, I mean…It was days before…well, Sally was by the fence. They scoured the CCTV. She said she'd had a text from Carl saying he'd left his sandwiches on the side and she'd rushed it down to give it to him. So she passed it through the fence and said it was for him."

A look of horror spread across Leigh's face. She stared at her friend incredulously.

"The package? I found it on the plane...that was weeks..."

Sasha looked down, sheepishly. "They think he kept it in his locker until...well, you know."

"SASHA!" Leigh was mortified.

"Don't you think I've been over and over it in my head? After everything I went through with Col too. He won't let me forget it. We argued a bit." Sasha shrugged.

Leigh stared at her for a long while. "How do you still have a job?"

"I almost didn't."

"You brought a gun past security!"

"I didn't! I was filling out paperwork. I saw Sally over there and she was waving. And I just...just like that time Sandra passed me the keys, right? Sally's there with this little foil package in a bag and I think "sandwiches" and Megan was stood there, waiting to call passengers. So I sent her over..."

"What?!" Leigh exclaimed.

"She took the package from Sally and took it to Carl, and came back and said it was his lunch and that was that. I didn't think about it again. And then they started interviewing us and combing through everything..."

Sasha's voice trailed off.

"Megan?" Leigh asked, quietly.

Sasha shook her head. She shrugged and picked up her tea again. "She said they were thinking of moving away, anyway."

"Oh no!" Leigh exclaimed. "She didn't know what it was though?"

"They said it didn't matter. They have her on the CCTV tape receiving something from outside the airport perimeter and handing it off to Carl on the plane. After that there was no way she was going to hold on to her airside pass."

Leigh sat back, trying to process the story. "She's been there for years!"

Sasha nodded sadly.

A realisation hit Leigh, one that she hadn't considered before. "Oh my god, Sally! How is she?"

Sasha shrugged again. "Still in custody. We don't know much. I think they're still, you know, investigating and all that."

"Custody? She's not involved? Carl is bad enough but Sally?"

"I honestly don't know!" Sasha said. "I hope not. Megan said, when she came back to the gate, Sally just said she'd had a text from Carl saying could she drop his lunch off at the staff car park. I hope that's as far as she was involved."

"Does anyone know why? I mean... All of them. But Carl...It's just...it's not right is it?" Leigh sighed heavily.

Sasha shook her head again. "Nobody knows anything. Or at least they're not saying. I suppose they won't tell us anyway. Even when they do finish investigating. There's been nothing more on the news about any of those terrorist groups that claimed responsibility, you know? It's like they've been warned off..." Sasha stopped to gulp some more of her tea, as though trying to calm herself. She looked up at Leigh, sheepishly, unsure whether to ask for details of that day. "Did the woman on the plane say anything?" she asked, quietly.

"I don't know. I don't think she did. I tried to remember everything when they interviewed us. But she shot Lucas. And a little boy." Leigh continued. She found herself recounting matter-of-factly as though filing in some kind of report; as though her emotions were entirely separate.

Sasha sat back on the sofa, enthralled, in a macabre sort of way; wanting to know everything but not having had the confidence to ask before now.

When Leigh finished recounting as much as she could remember; they both sat in silence, contemplating the events.

"You can't say anything though." Leigh reminded

Sasha.

"I know. I can't anyway, can I?" Sasha reassured her.

"I mean, they're still investigating. It'll probably take them ..." Leigh was interrupted by a buzzing sound, from the intercom by the front door.

Leigh frowned. The only person she'd expect an unannounced visit from was already here.

She got up and padded to the intercom and picked up the handset.

"Hello?"

"Hi. It's...er...it's me." A voice crackled through. Leigh's heart skipped a beat. She could have sworn it sounded like the only other person she'd want to see.

"Who's me?" she pressed.

"Ricky!" He answered.

Leigh's face broke out in a smile as she pressed the button to release the communal door at the entrance to the block of flats.

Ignoring Sasha still sat in the living room, Leigh opened her door and rushed to the top of the stairs to see Ricky bounding up two at a time.

When he reached the top he just stopped and looked at her.

"You look good!" She grinned at him.

"You don't." He chided, and winked at her. She screwed her face up and rushed towards him and threw her arms around him. He hugged her back. As they separated he cupped her face in his hands and looked her straight in the eye.

"Are you ok?" He asked, full of concern.

"Me? I'm fine! You're the one who went AWOL." Leigh play-punched him in the shoulder and led him by the hand into her apartment.

-25-

Sasha, initially confused by Leigh's sudden departure, realised who had arrived and leapt up. She too, ran towards Ricky and hugged him.

"Oh my God are you ok? You've been missed." Sasha gushed.

"Of course I am." Ricky grinned.

"How long have you been back?" Sasha asked him.

Leigh skulked nervously in the kitchenette area. She wished suddenly that Sasha wasn't here. She'd have liked to have had Ricky to herself at first. They had so much to talk about, after all. *And that's the only reason*, she told herself.

"Not long, I came straight here…" he trailed off, looking around for Leigh, and looking relieved when he found her not far away. He winked at Leigh before turning back to Sasha. "I might not have come for another week or so, but my landlord over here was getting antsy…"

"Why?" Sasha gasped. "Doesn't he know what you've been through?"

"Yeah, that's exactly why. He wanted this month's rent and a little reassurance I think...ya know, he actually said, 'How do I know you're not one of the undercover worker terrorists?'" Ricky scoffed.

Sasha's eyes widened in shock. "He ACTUALLY said that?!" She gasped.

"I know, right?" Ricky said.

Suddenly, there was an uncomfortable silence. Sasha narrowed her eyes and looked at Leigh, who looked back at her and raised her eyes expectantly. Sasha got the impression Leigh wanted her to leave.

Ricky broke the deadlock with a sudden, "Uh, I just have to use the bathroom," he began, and turned to Leigh "ok?" Leigh nodded and he skipped out to the hall.

Leigh looked at Sasha apologetically. "We have a lot to talk about, you know?"

"I know, I know." Sasha smiled. She turned around to the living room area and picked up her mug and brought it to the kitchen. She placed it in the sink and turned around to hug Leigh again. "Well, anyway, I'm glad I came over. I was scared of what state I'd find you in, to be honest. But hey, we're going to have to get together and talk about baby stuff soon!" She said excitedly.

"You told her already?" Ricky butted in, appearing behind them from the small corridor.

Leigh winced.

"He knows?" Sasha gaped at Leigh.

Leigh shrugged. "It… came up… during the flight. Before… everything… you know…" she trailed off.

"OK. Well, I should leave you to it…I guess..." Sasha mumbled, pulling her handbag's long strap up over her shoulder.

"Hey," Leigh stopped her with a hand on her arm. "Can I tell him?"

"What?" Ricky asked.

Sasha grinned and squared up to Ricky. "I'm pregnant too."

"Wow!" He said. "Congratulations!"

"Thanks! Yeah, well," Sasha continued, "I'm going to leave you to it."

Sasha turned and winked at Leigh and headed for the door.

Ricky watched them go and headed over to the sofa, and sat down. Leigh returned from the door having seen Sasha out.

"Well! Make yourself comfortable!" She chided.

"I am!" Ricky teased her.

Leigh sat back down in the chair she'd been in before. "Did your landlord really say that?"

Ricky gave a brief shrug. "I guess he's adding anyone who works at the airport to his growing list of people he doesn't trust to rent his properties."

"That's awful!" Leigh shook her head.

They both sat in silence for a little while, looking out at the bright sunshine.

Someone on a bright red jetski had launched themselves into the basin and was throwing up spray all around the old dock. Life outside the window seemed to be continuing as normal. As long as Leigh didn't turn on the TV.

She glanced at the blank TV screen. It had been pretty much her only company for days; but it had simply kept her mind on the whole sorry affair that there had been occasions, sometimes hours at a time, where she'd totally forgotten about Lucas's baby growing inside her.

Now that Sasha knew, and Ricky was around again…it was seemingly something that she'd have to face.

Suddenly, Leigh felt the silence she had been embracing for weeks was uncomfortable. She got up and pulled a Tracy Chapman CD out of the rack on her sideboard and put it on a low volume in the CD player.

"I've been really worried about you, you know?" Ricky cut into her thoughts.

"I was worried about you too." She smiled slightly without looking at him. "I'm glad you left that message."

"I didn't just come back for the landlord thing."

"What are you going to do about him, anyway?" Leigh cut back, hardly giving him a chance to finish.

"Oh, he's ok. I guess I'm a hero so he's overlooking it for now."

"Ha ha yeh. My hero." Leigh teased him.

Ricky's face stayed straight. "Leigh, I've been thinking about you, a lot…"

"Oh, Ricky, don't…" Leigh tried to stop him.

"Don't what? I mean, we're close. We always have been, right? And you're in a …predicament…" He offered, seemingly struggling to find words.

"A predicament?" Leigh suddenly felt offended and turned to face him, defiantly. "Is that how you see this? Women have babies all the time! Women have babies *on their own*, all the time."

"I know!" Flustered, Ricky stood up and put a hand on her arms in some kind of attempt to calm her down. "I know. I didn't mean…"

She stopped feeling defensive, but mainly because she was surprised at his position. "I don't need help."

"I know full well that you, of all people, don't *need* help!" He reassured her, looking her over in awe and admiration. "But what if I *want* to help?"

"Why? Because you feel guilty somehow?" Leigh shook her head slightly, a little confused. "Lucas not being here isn't your fault! It's no one's fault. And besides, even if he was...what do you think? He and I would get married and play happy families?!" Leigh scoffed. "Even the thought of that is just...!" she trailed off, unable to think of a suitable word.

Ricky laughed, in spite of himself, at the thought of Lucas being a stand-up dad with a happy wife...Leigh caught on and smiled to herself too.

Ricky tried to make a decision on his next move. Should he sit back down, or stay where he was?

He looked down, moved his hands down and took her hands in his. "I care about you, Leigh," he said, without looking up. "Maybe more than a friend, I don't know." Ricky felt like he was opening up a little too much, "But best friends is fine;" he added quickly. "And, ok you might not think you need friends but it wouldn't harm to let me help you. And the baby."

A thought suddenly struck him and he looked up at her. "Are you keeping the baby?"

Leigh stared at him, her lips slightly parted.

"I...I hadn't really thought about it." She murmured.

Which, she realised, was true.

Suddenly, all kinds of new thoughts entered her head.

She pulled her hand from Ricky's grasp and stood up, wringing her hands as she paced around the room.

"Oh my god! I'd spent all those weeks before, letting it sink in, and then since…well…all this…I've not really thought at all." She leaned against the open French door, watching the water for a moment, then turned to look at Ricky, who had sat back on the sofa. He was calm, open, waiting for her to tell him anything and support her.

Leigh came to a realisation. "I'm not going to be able to fly with a baby, am I? Not on my own. I mean even paying for childcare, what about delays? Nightstops? Other bases…My mum's not going to be able to cope…Sasha's going to have her hands full…"

Ricky stood up and approached her, wrapping his arms around her again. Leigh suddenly fell apart again and started sobbing into his chest.

He let her cry for a bit, before holding her by the shoulders and looking into her face. "This is what I was thinking. You couldn't, not on your own; but what if I…"

"No!" she cut over him. "I can't do that to you."

"You're not doing anything to me!" Ricky protested.

"It's not your problem!" Leigh argued back.

"A baby isn't a problem!" Ricky scoffed. He looked down at his feet and took a breath. "OK, look…can you see yourself getting rid of it?"

Leigh shrugged, then looked at him, then sniffed back the end of her tears. She shook her head weakly. "No." she whispered.

"Then we deal with it." Ricky said, confidently.

"Why we, though? I'm pregnant. This isn't your baby…!" Leigh said quietly.

"But it so easily could have been, right?" Ricky reminded her.

Leigh looked at him, blankly. Ricky rolled his head. Was he going to have to spell it out to her?

"We're the same, you and me; aren't we?" he said, lifting his hand to stroke her hair gently. "We have led…promiscuous lives. Never having a second thought about some of our actions. If I were a girl who's to say I wouldn't have had some random person's baby by now, eh?" he laughed.

Leigh scoffed at his ridiculous analogy. "Random person!"

Ricky looked at her, vulnerable and in need and somehow knew he had to bare his soul now or he'd never do it.

"Remember that night, after Landing lights and Kev's house and we all ended up back here…" Ricky began.

Leigh looked at him. "Not hard to forget!" she sniffed again.

"It was...fun...right?" Ricky asked, hopefully.

Leigh nodded. And thought for a moment. "More than..."

"Exactly..." Ricky cut over her. "More than fun. I mean, I've been thinking ever since..." he stopped.

Leigh was looking at him with furrowed brow.

"Yes," he continued, "ever since... if Lucas hadn't been there... if it were just you and me...I might have...stayed...you know?" Ricky took a breath.

Leigh moved away from him and sat on the sofa, thoughtful.

Ricky followed her over and sat next to her. Side by side, without looking at each other. Ricky talked and Leigh listened.

"And then...training happened. And it would have been wrong, you know? So, I kept away from you. As much as I could. To give you the best chance of passing. Because that's what you always wanted. And you did! And besides if there was a thing going on between you and Lucas maybe it's..."

"There was no 'thing'..." Leigh cut in.

"I'm sorry," Ricky said quietly. "I just assumed it happened during training..."

"It did." Leigh looked at him.

Ricky didn't say anything, he just cocked his head to one side, questioningly.

Leigh took a deep breath and began again. "Lucas came to my room, one night. Well, we all were there at a study group. Anyway, we left and went to my room. And he started telling me about…" Leigh paused, searching for words to use. "…about a thing that happened that day. In the showers…"

Ricky quickly drew in a breath.

"Oh." He said, recognising what she was referring to.

"He was… describing a lot… and it got me excited… and… well…I…" Leigh trailed off. She wasn't sure how to continue without making it sound like she'd forced herself on the poor boy.

Ricky picked up on one word. "Excited?"

Leigh looked at him. "You get me excited. Ok? There. I said it. Like you didn't know that already…"

"Actually I didn't…" Ricky shrugged. "I thought it was just me." He looked at Leigh. She didn't understand. "I thought it was just one sided. When I think about you."

Leigh bit her bottom lip, unsure where to go from here.

"So, he told you…and?" Ricky pushed.

"And… I don't know what was going through my head. But, I kind of made a move; while he was talking about… describing… you. And he didn't push me away. And…well…it just felt…good. Normal, you know?"

Ricky watched her intently. Leigh was beginning to feel a little exposed. And there were stirrings deep inside her that she knew she shouldn't act on. Not right now.

"Anyway," she continued, "afterwards we just giggled and talked, just like we always had. We drank hot chocolate, and went to bed. Together. And I dreamed of you. And the next morning…everything was normal again."

"Wow!" was all Ricky could say.

They sat in silence, looking at the wall opposite.

After a while, Leigh rubbed her arms and felt a chill. Looking up at the French doors she noticed the sun had gone in. She got up and headed over to close them.

Ricky by this time had managed to get his head around what she'd told him. "So," he began, slowly. "I am kinda the reason this baby exists…"

Leigh let out a laugh. "Well, if you want to look at it that way…" she giggled as she sat down again; this time on the arm chair facing Ricky. She looked directly at him, studying every inch of his features.

Ricky shook his head, as though trying to break out of a trance.

"So, here's one scenario I'd been thinking about…and, just let me get it out, ok?" Ricky looked at her questioningly.

Leigh nodded. "Go on."

"So, I'm not suggesting anything. Not for us. OK. Let's leave that," he gave her a long drawn out, almost smouldering, look. "... for now. But, well, I guess they call it co-parenting, right? I mean the whole of society is set up for a mother figure and a father figure in a child's life; even when it comes to working parents. Right? So, we could do that. I mean, you can work, and I can work, and we take it in turns. And I...I dunno...take the kid playing football after school and you take it swimming..." Ricky trailed off.

Leigh's brain ticked over. "I'm not saying it's yours."

"What do you mean?" Ricky asked.

"I mean, I'm not going to pretend, ever, that this baby isn't Lucas's. If anything, if it's all anyone has left of him...I want to tell his parents, and everything." Leigh said quietly.

"Of course! I'm not suggesting, ever, that we play happy families and pretend anything..." Ricky trailed off.

"So, what? You adopt it?" Leigh shrugged.

"I don't know. For now, let's just say, we're going to do this together..."

Leigh rubbed her eyes with her hand. Boy, was she feeling worn out.

She looked up at Ricky, then leaned forwards and took his hands in hers. "OK. Step-dad, adopted dad, favourite uncle." She smiled. "But once you're signed on, you're signed on!" she warned him.

"You count on it!" He grinned.

They stood up at the same time and hugged. Leigh felt herself going a little weak in the knees again. She lifted her face and looked into Ricky's, who had looked down at almost the same instant.

Leigh's heart skipped a beat. It would be so easy to lean up a little and suggest a kiss; but she knew now that that might be a sure fire way to ruin this new-found arrangement.

"I'm going to lie down. I think. This thing's taking it out of me, a lot!" she pushed away gently.

Ricky took her cue. "Of course!" He said. "I gotta go see this landlord, remember?" he reminded her, and headed for the door.

Leigh followed him, he turned and hugged her at the door and gave her a chaste kiss on the cheek before trotting towards the stairs with a spring in his step that made her smile.

Leigh closed the door and breathed deeply. She double locked the door, checked the French doors were locked, and overcome with fatigue, stumbled into her bedroom and collapsed onto the bed. She sat herself up enough to unclip her bra underneath her t-shirt; and pulled the straps down her arms under her sleeves before slipping it out from underneath. She pushed down her knickers and the slouchy jogging bottoms she was wearing, and left them where they fell onto the floor next to the bed, and shuffled herself down under the oversized quilt. She lay there in just her t-shirt, the cotton quilt-cover felt smooth and cooling on her legs.

And now, she couldn't sleep. She tried closing her eyes but images of Ricky kneeling in front of her constantly came to mind. And then they'd meld with the images she'd had when Lucas was describing the shower incident to her. And then more and more thoughts of her sexual encounters filled her head; each and every one seemingly taking on Ricky's face. And then she remembered him being in this bed. With her and Lucas.

Leigh had no idea if masturbation during pregnancy was a good or a bad thing. She made a mental note to get one of those 'guide to pregnancy' books the next day. If they were going to do this, they'd need to do this properly.

Right now, though, she could feel throbbing sensations around her vulva with just the thought of Ricky. Her hand found its way down to her clitoris and she found a familiar wetness.

Leigh brought herself to a satisfying orgasm, and she finally fell asleep; not from exhaustion and the basic biological need that had driven her sleeping patterns through the stress and aftermath of the attacks; but from the comforting thoughts of Ricky, and what the future might bring.

-26-

In the weeks and months that followed, Sasha and Leigh found themselves buddying up, and attending appointments at the same time; they signed up for the same ante-natal classes and where they used to go clothes shopping they now spent hours browsing baby stores and avoiding caffeine in the cafes.

Ricky came round to Leigh's almost every day, to 'check on her', he told her. They usually veged out, watching TV; or laughing their way through 'baby names' books; or the pregnancy guide books that Leigh had splurged on.

After a couple of months, they'd made a joint decision to replace her sofa with a pull-out sofa-bed. Leigh's small one-bedroom flat was fine for now, she turned a corner of her bedroom into a baby corner, with a crib and changing mat and mobile; and she'd been adamant it would be suitable, at least for the first year; while they got themselves sorted. But it made sense to have a second bed available; while they were working out timetables.

Ricky went back to work. He had gone for a series of

meetings and interviews at Head Office and been deemed fit to fly again. He'd put a lot of his recovery down to having something else to concentrate on.

Leigh's pregnancy had been announced the week after she and Ricky had reached their decision to co-parent. They'd gone together to see Gaynor as the senior base cabin crew first; who'd been surprised, but happy for Leigh; and a little dubious at first at the timing, until they'd assured her that Ricky was not the biological father and nothing untoward had happened between them at training.

Operations had taken Leigh off flying duties and given her some admin work around the airport; and given her experience on check-in, allowed her to work with *Air2Ground* as well; which pleased Sasha no end.

Mina had trouble on occasion though, and had taken to separating the 'mothers meeting' as she called them, from spending too much time gossiping on check-in.

Leigh stuck to her word and went to see Lucas's parents, quite soon after she'd told Ricky that's what she wanted to do; and before she saw them at his funeral.

The admission was an emotional one. They didn't quite believe her at first; they were fully aware of his preference; but they knew how close the two were, and when she explained the circumstances surrounding the act were more of a comfort to each of them, an experiment in friendship, than any kind of sordid arrangement; they came around to seeing the presence of a biological grandchild they never thought they'd see as a blessing, from the ashes of their shattered lives.

There were very few remains ever identified of Lucas's body; after intricate forensic analysis of the wreckage; but what they could identify, was carefully gathered and solemnly returned to his family so that a funeral service, and cremation, could take place.

Leigh and Ricky stood with Lucas's parents as next of kin; prepared to answer a barrage of questions at the wake following the service; which never came.

Not as a barrage, in any case. More of a trickle, which then spread itself out across the airport family and with a basic explanation, no one seemed to bat an eyelid.

Lucas's funeral did more than allow everyone to say goodbye to the well-liked boy. It helped everyone in the airport family to draw a veil over another difficult period in global aviation.

In the backs of their minds, they feared for the future of certain companies and airlines and agencies with another blow like this hitting passenger confidence; but for now, life was slowly getting back to normal.

And so, by the time Leigh was nearing the end of her pregnancy, a new order seemed to have settled over their lives.

Sasha's due date was a couple of weeks before Leigh's; and she had passed 41 weeks pregnant just as Leigh reached week 38.

Leigh had spent most of the last week sitting on the sofa. She had a daily call from Sasha, who would moan constantly about being overdue; which made her feel a little better, given that her actual due date was a couple of weeks away; but still, at the end of the call, she would hang up and continue feeling sorry for herself.

On a particularly cold Saturday afternoon, with nothing to look at through the window across the bay but grey skies; Leigh had been on the phone with Sasha for over an hour by the time Ricky let himself in.

The wafting smell of chips from the takeaway filled the apartment and Leigh looked at him longingly. He grinned, holding up the bags, and dumped them on the kitchen counter, before heading over and kissing her on the cheek.

"Sasha again?" He asked quietly.

Leigh nodded enthusiastically. "This is it!" She murmured to him.

"What?" Asked Sasha, on the other end of the line. "Owwwwwww!" she moaned.

Leigh waved at Ricky to sit down and spoke into the phone. "Another one? Blimey Sash…" Leigh looked at her mobile phone on the coffee table which was set to 'stopwatch' mode, and pressed a button to pause it. "That's six minutes! Aren't you supposed to call the midwife now?"

There was a long silence on the other end of the line,

followed by some heavy breathing as Sasha let long breaths out of her mouth. "Col did, don't worry." Sasha managed to force out. "He's just putting the bags in the car."

"Well you should go!" Leigh gasped excitedly.

"I don't want to…I want to keep talking!" Sasha said, before letting out another loud moan and then "Oh, god…yes…I think we have to go…that was my waters breaking!"

"Go!" Leigh shouted. "I'm fine. Ricky's here with dinner."

"OK. I'll get Col to call from the hospital" Sasha breathed and hung up.

Leigh shook her head with a smile and hung up the phone. She looked at Ricky.

"You look really fed up." He told her.

"I feel like a whale. What did you get?" She asked, looking longingly at the bags on the kitchen counter.

"I thought you weren't eating takeaways?" Ricky challenged her.

"Well of course that was an issue earlier on…and if you got the chicken you can eat that…" she blathered, still eyeing up the bags. "But if those are chips from *Reenie's*, just try keeping me away."

Ricky winked and leaped up to go and serve the food.

Leigh rubbed her hands together with glee.

"Hope you got spicy curry sauce coz at this point I'm willing to try anything!" Leigh called over.

Ricky served up the food and brought it over to her. Leigh smiled up at him sweetly, grateful.

"Have you been drinking that tea?" Ricky asked her.

"Three cups so far today. Don't think I'm supposed to have more than that." Leigh sighed.

Pilar had mentioned Raspberry leaf tea, and then Leigh had read about it in her pregnancy book, and had started drinking it as soon as she passed 37 weeks.

Ricky had been worried about her attempts to bring on labour too early.

"It's not bringing it on; it's encouraging. Besides, most of these are old wives tales; and the most they're going to do is prepare the cervix for birth. Apparently." Leigh had scoffed back at him every time he tried to warn her.

"Isn't the safest place for the baby inside, exactly where he is?"

"*SHE* is perfectly well cooked and can't wait to meet us so *SHE* will come out when she's good and ready. I'm just giving her a helping hand." She said, stuffing a huge forkful of chips, dripping with curry sauce, into her mouth, and screwing her face up to him in defiance.

"Really attractive, dear." Ricky chided her as he sat

down in the arm chair next to her with his plate of food.

Leigh rolled her eyes. "At this moment in time, I don't feel the least bit attractive to anyone so it doesn't make any difference!" she laughed.

Ricky looked at her intently. "You're always attractive to me." He said.

Leigh looked at him. His face told her he was being deadly serious. She blushed. And he felt a little awkward.

"I'm sorry." Ricky offered.

"Don't be!" Leigh told him. Now she felt bad. "Really, it's nice, being told I'm attractive."

"Well, you know you are. To me." Ricky pressed again.

Leigh pulled a cushion out from behind her and threw it at him. He laughed, and picked up the remote control to turn on the TV.

They settled in to watch as Ricky flicked through channels trying to decide on something.

Leigh shuffled in her seat and looked around for the cushion she'd thrown.

"Gah!" she screeched, frustrated.

"What?" Ricky sat up, worried.

"Just trying to get comfortable. It's so bloody

annoying!" Leigh moaned.

She stood up and took her plate to the kitchen, before pacing around the room with her hands on her lower back. Ricky watched her as he stopped flicking channels and stopped on a soap opera; and continued eating his food, thoughtfully.

"Come, sit down." He said, getting up himself to take his plate to the kitchen.

Leigh wrung her hands and turned to follow him. She leaned on the other side of the breakfast bar as he rinsed the plates in the sink.

"I tried that, remember? I've tried EVERYTHING! Except sex. But that's not likely to happen is it?!" Leigh said, turning and heading back to the sofa, picking up the cushion on the way, and shoving it behind her back.

Ricky put the plates on the draining board and turned to head back to the living area. "Sex?" He asked, confused.

"Yeah, remember? We laughed about it but there was the bit in the back of the book that said something about semen softening the cervix …" Leigh laughed, half out of embarrassment at suddenly having to discuss sex with Ricky.

"I don't think you told me about this one." Ricky frowned. "I'm sure I'd have remembered…"

Leigh frowned back. "Really?"

"Really what? That I wouldn't have remembered that

you want to have sex?" Ricky raised his eyebrows.

"Hmm." Leigh said. "Maybe it was Sasha I was talking to." She muttered quickly, trying to cover her discomfort.

"Hmm." Ricky mumbled, and turned his attention to the TV.

Leigh looked at him, a little sheepishly, and turned to look at the TV as well.

They sat in silence for a while, vaguely watching the end of the soap; but each lost in their own thoughts.

The end credits rolled. Leigh looked down absentmindedly at her fingernails.

"Would it be too weird?" She asked, without looking up.

"I don't know." Ricky answered.

Clearly, he was still thinking about the same thing she was.

"Too weird in what way?" Ricky piped up again, "Like, having sex with a pregnant woman?"

"No. I mean, I'm sure we can figure out the logistics." Leigh looked up at him. Her face was a little flushed. She'd spent the past twenty minutes feeling quite horny thinking about how she'd pretty much just suggested to Ricky that they sleep together. "I mean, after."

"Well, if it does what it's supposed to, won't we be a

little distracted after?" Ricky offered.

Leigh laughed, a little out of awkwardness.

It seemed ludicrous that she fancied him so much and yet the suggestion of having sex with him came down to being purely a means to bring on labour.

"I mean *after*-after…you know…our relationship, going forward…" Leigh managed.

Ricky thought for a moment and sat forward. "OK. What do you want?" Ricky asked her, pointedly.

Leigh shook her head, confused.

Ricky continued to look at her stoically. "Because, I wasn't going to broach this now, again. Not until much later. But I want you."

Leigh bit her lip, held up a finger to his mouth to quieten him.

"OK, let's not do this now." She whispered.

Ricky raised his eyebrows. "The sex?"

"No, the talking." Leigh said, and she leaned forward from her sofa position over him in the chair, and kissed him, lightly, on the lips. Then she sank back to the sofa again.

"I'm pregnant, and I don't want to be for more than I need to be. And I'm horny. Maybe because I'm pregnant or maybe…for other reasons…but can we just, tonight, forget about the reasons? Because…well, we did it before, and we moved on. And this time…well…we can have a specific reason why we can tell ourselves we made love to each other tonight, to help us move on. If we need to. Right?"

He stared at her pointedly for a few moments.

"If we're calling it '*making love*'…I think the reasons why we're doing it are changing." Ricky mumbled, as he crawled forward from his chair to the sofa that Leigh had sunk back in to.

He kneeled on the floor next to her, and gently began to explore her mouth with his tongue. Leigh reciprocated and draped her arms loosely around his neck.

They must have stayed there, kissing passionately for some time, until the TV in the background suddenly started playing some loud energetic music as a celebrity chat-show started.

Ricky pulled away and grimaced at the sound.

Leigh took a moment to catch her breath as he picked up the remote and pressed the standby button.

He stood up and held out his hand for her. Leigh lifted her head lazily.

"You'll have to pull, I'm having trouble moving these days" she murmured.

"Such a turn on" Ricky teased.

"Ha ha." Leigh feigned as she grabbed his hand and tugged herself up to a standing position.

She was ready to move into the bedroom but Ricky stayed where he was, chest heaving, looking down at her.

"You're always a turn on." He whispered to her; this time without a hint of sarcasm or mocking.

Leigh's breath caught.

For once, she was speechless.

She could usually see through pillow-talk and chat-up lines. Why was she now feeling weak at the knees?

Hormones. She told herself. Yes, that was it, hormones...

Ricky leaned in and drew her into another deep kiss which she willingly succumbed to, until they both realised they'd accomplish more lying down.

Ricky glanced sideways, drawing away from the kiss and mumbled "uhm...your bed or mine?" he asked, looking at the sofa.

Leigh was getting impatient by this point. Her eyes glistened with excitement.

"I don't think I can wait for that one to be made up." She said, following his gaze to the sofa.

"Yours it is then." Ricky said.

Leigh took his hand, gently, and began leading him to the bedroom.

"Ours." She said, quietly, but defiantly.

Ricky stopped moving and stared at her.

She turned to look at him. "I think it should be ours." She confirmed, before turning and continuing to lead him through the small corridor.

In the bedroom, Leigh lifted the loose maternity skater-dress she'd been wearing over her head, unclipped her bra, and wriggled out of her panties before clambering under the quilt; suddenly slightly nervous.

She looked over to Ricky, still standing on the other side of the bed. He'd watched her undress, intently.

"Well?" she asked, as provocatively as she could.

Ricky rubbed his hand across his mouth, as though wiping away something he wanted to say. He paused a little longer, before undoing his jeans and letting them drop to the floor and swiping off his t-shirt effortlessly. Leigh raised her eyebrows in anticipation, looking at his underpants.

Ricky bit his bottom lip, climbed into the bed next to her and pressed himself up against her.

"I think," he said, thoughtfully, "We go back to the 'whose bed this is' discussion in the morning." He looked at her intently. "Agreed?"

"If I agree, will you take your pants off?" Leigh asked, playfully.

"If I take my pants off, will you agree?" Ricky retorted.

Leigh winked. "If you take your pants off, I'm going to be too busy to say anything!" she murmured, grabbing his crotch. She delighted to find that he was already rock hard and throbbing, begging to be released.

At least she wasn't the only one whose body had been betraying her one-track thoughts.

Ricky gasped in surprise, but recovered himself, and raised his eyebrows to her with a stern look.

"OK!" Leigh breathed. "We talk tomorrow."

Ricky broke into a smile, and raised himself up onto his knees. Leaning forward to start kissing her again, he simultaneously pushed his underwear down with his hands as far as he could.

He lay down closer to her and wriggled his legs, kicking off his underpants while his arms snaked around her as far as they could, exploring her heavily pregnant form for the first; and probably the last, time.

Leigh pushed her arms down and started caressing Ricky's taut bottom, before bringing her right hand back around to grasp his penis.

Ricky, still engrossed in deep kisses, let out a guttural groan into her mouth as she grabbed; and responded by searching for her vulva with his free arm.

He moaned again at the revelation that she was as wet already as he was hard.

They both realised this wasn't likely to be a long encounter.

As much as they had both been waiting for it for a very long time; it was almost like a first time for both of them; a fast, furious coupling they both felt a primal need to get over with, before they could move on to enjoying each other properly.

Ricky pulled his head back and looked her in the eye.

"How do we do this, exactly?" He asked, indicating her swollen belly with a nod of his head. "I don't want to squash you…"

Leigh kissed him quickly and grinned, before turning over on all fours and rearranging her pillows under her chest.

Ricky, kneeling, sat back on his heels for a moment, admiring the view she was presenting. Leigh looked back over her shoulder at him with a seductive smile and Ricky seized the moment.

He positioned himself behind her, but before entering her, leaned forward and traced the line of her spine with soft licks and kisses. Leigh moaned in pleasure, a feeling in her groin that she was dripping all over the bed in desperation.

Leigh reached down with one hand and started gently

stroking her clitoris, as Ricky repositioned himself and entered her in one movement. That millisecond was like a sudden release in itself for both of them. An emotional climax they'd both been holding off allowing themselves for many, many months.

As Ricky began rhythmically moving in and out of her, he took one hand and pushed hers aside, gathering up some of her juices in his hand and taking it round to her bottom.

Her position meant that her anus was on full display to him, and it was just too tempting to him to not play. He took his wet hand and began kneading around her behind, moistening around her anus with his wet fingers. His massaging fell into rhythm with the movement of his penis, and as he felt his climax approaching, the rhythm of both increased.

Leigh began to moan in pleasure as her hand returned to her clitoris, rubbing in time with his hand on her arse.

"I'm going to come." She moaned into her pillow.

"Go on." Ricky whispered, as though giving her permission to let go. Just as he knew he was going to shoot his semen into her, he pushed two fingers into her anus, taking her by pleasant surprise and giving them both a cue to reach their orgasms at exactly the same time.

Leigh cried out as her orgasm rocked her body to exhaustion.

Ricky grunted as he pushed as much of his semen shooting from his member as far into her as he could before collapsing forward onto her back, supporting his weight with one arm holding him up from the bed.

Slowly, in the afterglow, Leigh let her knees slip down and rolled slightly onto her side to allow her belly room to rest to the side; Ricky allowed his body to move with her and, still inside her, lay behind her, spooning her. He let his penis slip out of her, and as it did so, it slipped up and rubbed against her anus as it passed; giving her a secondary shiver which caused her to let out a tiny moan of delight.

"You ok?" He whispered in her ear.

"Uh-huh" she managed to respond. Leigh closed her eyes.

"Do you think that's going to do the trick?" Ricky murmured into her ear, his arms snaking around her chest from behind.

"I hope not." Leigh murmured, sleepily.

"Eh?" Ricky questioned.

"Because then we get to do it again." She answered, before drifting off to sleep.

Ricky smiled and tightened his arms around her. His Leigh.

He glanced around the room, not quite dark, his eyes accustomed to the moonlit darkness.

He heard her breathing change to that of someone in a deep and comfortable sleep; he felt, in this moment, that this was, indeed, their room; and this is where he wanted to stay, forever; before closing his eyes and joining her slumber.

The End

Landing Lights is a series of tales linked by a place – a regional airport in the UK. The characters who work there and their lives are intertwined and yet individual; romantic; adventurous; tragic; ultimately giving a place, a series of tin sheds and boarding gates, a life of its own, a living, breathing, ever changing, community.
Coming soon...
"Landing Lights"
The origins of the airport social club

About the Author

R.A.Watson-Wood lives in Wales but has lived a varied life since being born in Cornwall to Scottish and Welsh parents, from growing up at sea on cargo ships, to living in pubs, to traveling the USA and Brazil alone, to working in Travel and Aviation for many years. Writing from a very young age, Dreamboat is the first in a series of fictional tales set around a regional airport and its' workers.

Facebook.com/landinglightsbooks

Cover photo © R.A.Watson-Wood 2012 "Bahama Blue"

Also by R.A.Watson-Wood:

"DREAMBOAT"
(Landing Lights Book 2)
ISBN: 9781980653929

Manufactured by Amazon.ca
Bolton, ON

19470451R00199